MISTAKEN IDENTITY

by Stephanie R. Caffrey

© COPYRIGHT 2024 by Stephanie R. Caffrey

Warning: Not intended for persons under the age of 18. May contain coarse language and mature content that may disturb some readers. Reader discretion advised.

Cover Art Design by: Kelly Moran/Rowan Prose Publishing
Photo Credit: Adobe Images
First Edition
ISBN: 978-1-961967-27-4
Rowan Prose Publishing, LLC
www.RowanProsePublishing.com

Published in the United States of America

For Dawn.
Thank you for believing in me.

Acknowledgements

This book was born of a lot of hard work, and many drafts. And a lot of support from many, many people.

First, I would like to thank the amazing Dawn Dowdle. My first agent, and someone who read the first three chapters of this book, and immediately saw the potential in it. Thank you so much for believing in me and my writing. Thank you for being a great agent and friend, and I hope you're somewhere watching as this little book you believed in finally makes its way into the world. I miss you.

To Kelly, Shelly, and everyone at Rowan Prose Publishing, thank you for everything you've done to help *Mistaken Identity* make its way into the world. Everything from your support to the amazing covers, you all have been amazing, and I can't thank you enough.

Sydney, we've been friends for over a decade, and you have read and critiqued everything I've ever written. I appreciate your friendship so much, especially your enthusiasm for my books. I never could have gotten here without you, and I'm so thankful for fandom bringing us together all those years ago.

Louise, my wonderful Brit-Picker, thank you for being so patient with this American and not making fun of me too much when I gave Patrick and James baseball bats at one point. This book would be a whole lot less British without your help.

Sharon, Jamie, and Sarah, I never would have had the courage to put this book out in the world if it hadn't been for you three. Your friendship and encouragement mean more to me than you'll ever know. You're not only my best friends, you're family. And I love you ladies.

Alex, thank you for listening to all my woes while getting this out in the world.

To The Super Awesome Book Club for letting me bounce ideas off you. When you read this book, please be gentle.

To my parents, for always encouraging me to reach for my dreams. Your belief in me kept me going even if others said it could never happen.

My sisters, thank you for being the best, and inspiring a few characters in this book. I'm sure you can figure out who.

Arthur and Beatrice, this book started before you were in this world, but you both have been so patient with Mom while she worked on endless edits. And I thank you for the times you've let me work while I could have been playing with you.

And finally, to Matthew. Thanks for everything. For taking kid duty while I wrote, encouraging me to have this thing of my own outside of being a mom. For being my romantic lead in this life we share together. Hopefully you can see yourself in my heroes, because the best parts of you are there in the best parts of them. I love you.

CHAPTER 1

EVELYN

Evelyn Stevenson briskly walked through the jetway into the terminal, and almost stopped. Heathrow was no Des Moines airport. The gray walls were all bare, and there was a distinct lack of signs directing her where to go. Crowds of people were bustling here and there, everyone trying to catch their flights, like her. She had never seen so many people in one place before. Toto, she wasn't in Iowa anymore.

Glancing around, she noticed most of the crowd was heading in one direction, so it was probably a safe bet to follow them. They probably knew better than she did. Besides, there should be signs that said where her connecting flight to Athens would be. Right?

Picking up her speed again, she began weaving in and out of the crowd. When Evelyn had booked the flight, with the help of the Iowa State University study abroad office, they had assured her the layover would be plenty long enough. However, they obviously didn't take circling the city for half an hour before landing into account. Nor the fact walking in the airport was akin to salmon swimming upstream.

She hitched her duffel bag up higher on her shoulder. The weight of it dragged her shoulder down, acting as an anchor, slowing her pace through the airport. It was almost enough to make her regret filling it so full of her research for her thesis. Maybe she should have kept some books in her checked bag. Did she honestly think there would be an opportunity to work on her paper before arriving to the dig site in Epidaurus?

As she got closer to her destination, at least Evelyn hoped it was, the denser the crowd became. Despite having to dodge people coming directly at her, she seemed to be making great time, and might actually make her connecting flight. As the optimism of not being stranded in London went through her mind, someone collided headlong into her, causing them both to crash to the hard tile.

"Oi, watch where yer going, mate!"

Evelyn looked up, trying to catch her breath after having the wind knocked out of her, and took in the woman she'd crashed into. Like herself, she had chin-length brown hair and brown eyes that were glaring at her.

Evelyn opened her mouth to apologize, but the woman quickly stood, grabbed her duffel bag, and began running in the direction she'd been heading.

Evelyn shook her head as the woman ran off and shrugged her shoulders before slowly pulling herself up from the ground.

She picked up her bag and began walking toward the transfer station. Shifting the bag on her shoulder, she frowned. That was odd. The bag didn't feel the same as it had before. It was lighter. Significantly lighter. Looking at it, her frown deepened. This wasn't her bag. It was the same brand and model, but Evelyn's was black with purple trim. The one currently in her hand was black with blue trim.

"Fuck," she muttered under her breath. Looking in the direction where she *should* go, and then in the direction the girl had rushed off with her bag, she began weighing her options. Thoughts of all those books and research currently in her bag, she hadn't checked it onto the plane for a reason. Evelyn needed what all was in there, and if that woman realized she had the wrong bag, she'd probably turn it in to this terminal.

She glanced at her watch. No matter how hard she tried, she would miss her connecting flight, so she might as well visit the ticketing counter in this terminal after she dealt with this bag-switch situation.

Frustrated, she headed in the opposite direction.

"Excuse me," she asked a random person. "Do you know if there's an information desk or a lost and found anywhere close by?"

"Yes. Keep heading in this direction, and the terminal will open up into an atrium. You'll find a security desk there. They'll be able to help you."

"Thank you." Evelyn smiled and began going to where the Good Samaritan had pointed.

Once reaching the atrium, the density of the crowds almost paralyzed her. It was so busy. She moved to a railing, bracing herself against it, and glanced down. From what she could determine, everything she needed was a level below her. Bustling with people, various types of restaurants and shops lined the perimeter of the lower level. In the center, there was a circular counter area marked 'Information.' That must be where she needed to go. The only downside was it was on the other side of the security line.

She looked out toward the line for customs and bit her lip. Was it worth going through customs to get her bag back? On one hand, she really didn't want to wait in the really long line. On the other, she really needed her bag.

Sighing, she figured she needed to re-book her flight, anyway. It didn't matter if she was stuck on the other side of security. Besides, it would be fun to have an extra stamp in her passport. Optimism!

After waiting through what had to be the slowest line she had ever been in, Evelyn descended on the escalator and began weaving her way through the crowds of people toward the kiosk at a brisk pace. Once the counter came into view, she began slowing down, but not before she slammed into someone coming the opposite direction.

She gasped and held tight to the duffel bag, cursing herself for getting into the same situation *twice* in one trip. Maybe she should just re-book and go home. Was this all an omen?

"Sorry," the man she'd crashed into said with a thick British accent as he steadied her.

She looked up and was taken aback. He had to be one of the most handsome men she had ever seen. His features were very sharp, and his blue eyes stood out against his dark eyelashes. Dark hair was cut close to his scalp. He was lean, muscular, and looked like he spent his free time in the gym. She was struck speechless and couldn't help but stare. Handsome and British. Evelyn had one weakness, and he'd slammed into her.

She opened her mouth to respond to him, but he didn't give her a chance. He was pushing past her and moving through the airport. She watched him disappear into the crowd with slight regret. If only she had said something to him.

Evelyn continued to make her way through the crowd toward her destination, and just as the kiosk was within striking distance, a hand tightly gripped her upper arm, stopping her.

"Excuse me, Miss, but I think I can help you." The man's accent was thick. "If you'll just come with me."

She turned to look at the man. He was tall and, with her five-foot, three height, she had to look up to view his face as he stood at least a foot taller than her. She gasped. It was the man she had just run into. Mr. Handsome and British. Who she had immediately regretted not speaking to. Here he was, holding onto her arm, preventing her from moving.

She involuntarily took a step back. "What the—"

She was cut off by his large hand tightening its grip around her upper arm. She began to panic as he dragged her in the opposite direction of the kiosk.

Evelyn tried to get away, but he overpowered her. When she tried to drag her heels to stop them, he moved his arm so it wrapped around her upper body and brought his other hand up, holding onto her mouth so she couldn't scream. She tried harder to plant her feet to slow down her abductor, but it didn't matter. He was too strong.

Her gaze darted around, hoping someone would notice her abduction and put a stop to it, but everyone around them seemed so engrossed in their travels, no one even glanced their way. She brought her hands up in a feeble attempt to pry his away, but it, too, was fruitless.

Just as visions of being sent into the sex slave trade began to fly through her head, they stopped moving. She narrowed her eyes in confusion before they moved again, entering a room. Her abductor closed the door behind them, trapping her.

Her mind played different scenarios of things being done to her as full panic set in.

CHAPTER 2

PATRICK

The room was dark, smelled of antiseptics and other cleaning items. Patrick held back a sigh when he realized, in his haste to remove the girl from the airport atrium, he had put them in a cupboard full of janitorial supplies. In addition to the potent smell of chemicals wafting through the air, the room was dank and overly cooled. The girl shivered against him. Although, he wasn't sure if it was because she was cold or if she was terrified. His decision to force her into the closet probably wasn't the best idea he could have come up with. In fact, feeling her body close to his, and how small it was comparatively, really made him believe he hadn't thought his actions through enough.

The room was silent, save for the sound of their breathing—his even, hers rapid. Her chest rose and fell under his arm, increasing in speed with each breath. Patrick swallowed and decided to break the silence, put her at ease.

"You can relax." He cringed. *Smooth.* "I'm not here to hurt you. I'm here to take you to safety. The solicitor's office sent me after you called and said you were skipping town with everything you collected. I'm honestly surprised I even found you. I only had a grainy photograph to go on. And then, *boom*! You ran right into me. How about that?"

He frowned. Megan didn't seem to relax, even though he'd told her who he was. Then it dawned on him. Of course, she wouldn't be relaxed. She was being held against his body with his hand over her mouth.

"If I remove my hand, do you promise to not scream, to remain calm?"

She nodded vigorously. He removed it, and as soon as he loosened his grip, she hurried away from him. Probably about as far as she could get from him in the cramped space of the room.

"I don't know who you think I am, but I'm pretty sure you have the wrong girl."

He frowned. The voice coming through the dark room was wrong. It was all wrong.

"You're American."

"That's right, I am."

"Fuck," he muttered under his breath, storming across the space with surprising ease, despite the dark. Brushing against the woman as he made his way toward the door, he groped along the smooth wall until he finally found what he needed. With a flip of his finger, the switch on the wall moved, filling the room with a fluorescent light. He squinted at the sudden brightness, but soon his eyes adjusted and he could take in the sight of the woman he'd dragged, believing she was Megan.

Now that he'd had a full look at her, Patrick realized his mistake.

"You're not Megan."

"No, I'm not. Can I go now?"

"It's uncanny. You look almost exactly like her. Same height, same hair color and length, same eye color, same build, even the same bag."

The woman straightened. "Wait, you're looking for a girl who looks like me and was carrying the same bag as me?"

He narrowed his eyes. "Yes, I am."

"I saw her."

He took a step forward, forcing her to take a step back, causing her to bump into a mop bucket. "Where?"

"On my way to switch terminals. She was running in the opposite direction, and we crashed into each other."

"Which way did she go?"

"I'm actually not quite sure. The opposite way I was heading after I got off the plane. I tried to follow her, but I lost her in the crowd. When we collided, we accidentally switched bags. Before you grabbed me, I was about to turn this one in to security with the hope she had done the same with mine."

He glared at the woman before moving his gaze to the bag. "That's Megan's bag?"

She shrugged. "If it was indeed Megan I crashed into a little while ago, then yes, it is."

Patrick stared at the bag. "Bloody hell. What are the odds? I mean they have to be miniscule. I wonder if Colin will be satisfied with *only* the bag, but no Megan?" he muttered to himself. He looked up and caught the eye of the woman. She had drawn her bottom lip between her teeth as she shifted from foot to foot.

"Um, since we can agree we have a case of mistaken identity, can I continue on my way? I really need to get going. I've already missed my connecting flight and really should re-book, so I can try to leave today."

Patrick looked up as the woman shouldered the bag and made her way to the door of the cupboard.

He moved to block the exit. "You're not leaving with that bag."

"What do you mean? I have to take it up to the information kiosk so I can try to get mine back."

"Yeah, I can't let that happen. I need that bag." He lunged at her, trying to grab it.

She jerked back. "I don't think so. I need my bag, and I think the only way this Megan girl will give me mine is if I give her this. So, forgive me if I don't give some random guy in a storage closet in the airport her property."

He glared at her. He thought this would be easy. Instead, this annoyingly attractive woman was giving him a headache as he tried to do his job.

He frowned and shook his head. This was no time to notice the woman in front of him was beautiful, especially with her eyes lit with the fire of annoyance as they were. He was on a job. And he needed to complete this job without losing his patience on a stranger in a broom cupboard. "I'll get your bag back when I find Megan. Right now, you can give me her bag and you can be on your way. You can even leave me your address and I'll post your bag back to you. How does that sound?"

The woman returned his glare. "How do I know you're really going to send me my bag? I have some important things in there. I need it."

Patrick couldn't help it. He laughed. "Important things? What could possibly be in there that's so important? Your extra makeup? Your hair dryer? Don't be so overly dramatic."

She narrowed her eyes into slits. "You know nothing about me, so I'd appreciate it if you'd withhold your judgment."

She was right. He didn't know her, but he would like to. In several different ways. But now wasn't the time.

"C'mon. Just give me the bag and write down your address, and I'll send you your beauty products." He held out his hand, smirking.

The American growled in frustration. "I'll give you this damn bag and the address of the Institute I'll be staying at in Greece, and you *will* send me my *research* materials. How does that sound?"

Fuck. Not only was she attractive, she was bloody smart as well? He was regretting the fact she was the wrong person. "Sure. That works."

The woman rolled her eyes and dropped the duffel on the ground. Shrugging out of her backpack, she pulled out a notebook. After scribbling some information on a piece of paper, she replaced the notebook and backpack to their rightful places. She pushed the bag toward him with her foot and shoved the piece of paper into his hand. He smiled as he opened the paper and took in what she'd written.

"Alright, Miss Evelyn Stevenson. I'll make sure you get your bag. Thank you for your cooperation. You may be on your way."

Evelyn raised her eyebrows, but said nothing. Instead, she moved around him and opened the door to the cupboard. The second she took one step out, it occurred to him that maybe letting her leave was a bad idea. Perhaps the worst idea he'd had all day. Moving quicker than he thought he could, he reached out and grabbed onto her backpack, dragging her back into the cupboard before slamming the door in her face.

CHAPTER 3

EVELYN

"What the hell?" Evelyn whipped around to face her abductor.

"Change of plans, sweetheart. You're going to have to stick with me. I'll take you to the solicitor's office, and we'll find a way for you to go on your merry way after that."

"Excuse me? I'm not going anywhere with you. I will not leave an airport with a stranger! Especially not to some 'solicitor's office.' You said I could leave if I gave you the bag. I gave you the bag. Now let me go."

The man sighed. "Look, I'd *love* to send you on your way right now and have you out of my hands. The last thing I want right now is to babysit some American bird. However, outside that door, somewhere in this airport, are members of the Fitzgerald family, looking for Megan, and now you. I can't, in good faith, let you walk out there and get taken by those men because they certainly won't be as nice as I am."

"Wait, I'm confused. Who is the Fitzgerald family, and why would they want me?"

"The Fitzgerald family is a notorious firm—" He pinched his lips together, stopping himself. He took a deep breath before continuing. "Look, you just need to know they're the bad guys, and they're outside the door."

"Firm?" she asked.

The man sighed. "Gang is what you'd call it in America. The mob, essentially."

She shook her head. "Wait. The mob wants *Megan*? I really don't understand what's going on here."

"Look, I don't have time to explain. I'm a private investigator, and the solicitor I work for sent me here to collect Megan. Instead, I found you. Now, I'm guessing, the firm thinks you know what Megan knows. The only solution is for me to take you to my connection at the solicitor's office, and we'll figure out where to go from there."

"No."

"No? What do you mean, no?" He threw his hands up before clenching them into fists, bringing one up to his mouth as if stopping himself from saying more.

"I mean no. I'm not going with you. I'm going to walk out of this room and go to ticketing to get on my flight to Athens. I have no intention of staying here any longer than necessary."

"Didn't you hear anything I've said? Those men are no good. They're not going to let you waltz on by."

"How do you even know they're here for me? You just said you're an investigator hired to pick up Megan. Maybe they're here for you?"

She didn't give the investigator any chance to respond. She turned on her heel, flung the door open, and walked out into the busy airport.

She looked around and found signs showing the counters for ticketing. She started walking toward them.

Hands grabbed both of her arms, squeezing tight, halting her right where she stood. She slowly turned her head, expecting it to be the investigator stopping her from continuing on her journey, but instead, two men glared at her.

The men were tall and wore black slacks, black shirts, and leather jackets. They were both bald, and their faces were expressionless. What made them look even more intimidating was the fact they wore sunglasses inside of the airport.

"Miss, we need you to come with us," one man stated.

"Well, I was just on my way to make my connecting flight…"

"We've been looking for you, sunshine, and you're going to come with us now."

The men tightened their grips on her arms and tried to drag her, but she planted her feet, attempting to stay put.

"Listen, guys, you both seem pretty reasonable. I'm not who you're looking for. Seriously. Look, I'm not even British. So, can you just let me go on my way?"

The man on her right let go of her arm and reached under his leather jacket with his right hand. His left hand carefully pulled the jacket back from his chest, revealing his hand holding a gun.

"We can do this the easy way or the hard way. And the hard way can get really messy," the man not holding the gun replied. "Where's the bag?"

She couldn't take her gaze off the gun pointed discretely at her. Her heart was pounding. "Wh-what bag?"

"Stop being cheeky. You know exactly what bag we're talking about. Where is it?"

"I-I-I lost it." She didn't know what to say. No way to know how to act in this situation. She was regretting leaving the safety of the janitorial closet and the investigator. At least *he* didn't have a gun. At least she didn't think he did. If he did, he hadn't pointed it at her.

"You're being cheeky again. It looks like we're going to have to do this the hard way."

The man holding the gun let go of his jacket and formed his left hand into a fist.

She tried to move away, but the other man still had an extremely tight grip on her arm. She watched in slow motion as the man's fist came toward her. She closed her eyes, braced herself, and waited for the hit.

However, it never made impact. She opened her eyes in time to watch him go crashing to the ground. What apparently was a trashcan fell to the floor beside him. She looked to where the man had been previously standing and there stood the PI. He'd come after her. She tried, and failed, to not swoon at the fact he was rescuing her from the bad guys.

The man holding her arm loosened his grip and made to take a step toward the investigator. However, a fist made contact with his face instead. The force of the blow caused him to let go of Evelyn's arm completely. She moved herself out of the way as the PI landed another blow to the gang member's face, causing him to fall to the ground next to his partner.

The man didn't waste any time. He closed the distance between himself and Evelyn, taking hold of her hand. He had the duffel bag slung across his chest.

"Alright, time to make our great escape." The PI tightened his grip on her hand and dragged her through the busy terminal.

He seemed to know where he was going. Glancing up, her gaze caught on a sign pointing toward baggage claim and the exit. She opened her mouth to protest, to tell him she had absolutely no intention of leaving this airport, especially with a strange man whom she'd just met, but she never had a chance. They ran right through the doorway and then, before she could even process what was going on, they were outside, the sun blinding her momentarily.

The investigator didn't slow down. She tried to keep up as he pulled her through the parking lot, his grip tight on her hand. He led her to a No Parking zone, where a blue MINI Cooper was parked. He stopped in front of the car, opened a door, and shoved her unceremoniously inside, backpack still on her back, closing the door behind her. Before she processed what was going on, he climbed in the opposite side, threw the bag into the backseat, started the car, and peeled away from the curb.

All Evelyn could do was stare at the man sitting beside her, as Heathrow Airport faded into the distance.

The scenery outside the window quickly turned from various businesses and hotels to rolling hills and trees as they sped away from the airport. Her mind raced, trying to process the encounter at the airport, while also trying to reassure herself they were *not* driving on the wrong side of the road.

"I would at least put your seatbelt on," he spoke up from beside her, without taking his gaze off the road.

She said nothing. Instead, she slipped her backpack off, settling it by her feet, and pulled the seatbelt around her. "Where are you taking me?"

"To my contact at the solicitor's office. I figure we need to let him know what's going on. He'll probably know what we should do next."

She was quiet for a second. "I'm going to die," she muttered, mostly to herself.

"What are you on about?"

"I'm going to die! My mother with her endless viewings of *Unsolved Mysteries* and all of her worries about me getting sold into sex slavery are coming true. And I've made the gravest error of all. I'm in a car with a stranger, heading to a second location. You're never supposed to go to a second location. And regardless of whether you're going to murder me or sell me, what about my luggage? Did my luggage go to Greece without me, or did it stay here? What—"

"Oh, bloody hell. Will you shut your trap for one bloody minute?" He growled. "You're not going to die. I have no intention of killing you. Well, if you keep prattling on like you are, you may drive me to contemplate it, albeit briefly. But I'm not a killer. If you had let those other men take you to a second location, well, that would be another kettle of fish entirely. The solicitor is a lawyer. He's not going to sell you. Everything else you don't need to worry about at this moment, so can we just drive for a few minutes in peace?"

"Well, excuse me for being concerned about my situation. I'm not exactly used to fleeing from airports in foreign countries with strange men."

The man barked out a laugh before quickly stifling it. He glanced over at her, his eyes bulging as he held in his mirth.

She shook her head. "Oh, fuck off. It's not that funny."

"I mean, it is a bit. 'Fleeing airports with strange men.' You make it sound very Hollywood."

"It doesn't feel very Hollywood to the person who it is affecting."

"I imagine you do little fleeing in your real life. More like sitting with your nose in a book, shirking from sunlight like a vampire."

"Fuck off. You don't even know me. For all you know, I could run half marathons."

He laughed. "I'm an investigator. I'm pretty good at telling someone's character from a glance."

"Oh, really? And what have you deduced about my character in the five minutes you've known me, Sherlock?"

The investigator glanced at her quickly before returning his gaze to the road. "Well, you're in your early twenties, and a student at University. You prefer books to sports. You care a great deal about your appearance, judging that you've just flown across an ocean and you don't look like you spent eight hours on an airplane. You carry yourself with an air of confidence, are very intelligent, and yet you can't defend yourself or think logically when you're presented with a crisis."

Her cheeks heated before she glanced at her loose-fitting jeans and the plain blue tunic she was wearing. She quickly took in her appearance in the side mirror. She looked like hell. "In what world does my current appearance give off that I haven't been traveling for eight hours on a plane?"

"It just does."

She took a deep breath, her face warming at the implication of his statement. "Well, you want to know what impression I get from you?"

"Not particularly."

She ignored him. "You're a pretentious ass who thinks he's better than everyone else. You think you're so important because you're this private investigator. And I'm guessing by the way you look, your name is Nigel."

The PI's hands gripped and re-gripped the steering wheel as his gaze grew stormy. "Patrick. My name is Patrick. Nigel? What the fuck is that?"

"Not so great being on the other side of the judgment, is it?" She laughed and turned her attention back to the changing scenery as they approached what she deduced to be the Thames River, with the London Eye looming in the distance.

CHAPTER 4

PATRICK

Patrick said nothing for the rest of the drive. He kept his gaze on the road as he maneuvered the narrow streets of the neighborhood. He couldn't believe how completely fucked up this case was, and one day into it. One job. He had one job. Get the girl, get the bag, bring them to the solicitor, and get paid. That was it.

Oh, if only it were that easy. Instead, he'd grabbed the wrong woman but the right bag, and now he was stuck with an American who wouldn't stop shooting him dirty looks as he drove. When she wasn't looking out the window, that was. He was usually pretty good at his job, considered one of the top private investigators in the city. So, it was pretty damn frustrating when he did something wrong.

He glanced over at the woman, relieved she was looking out the window. He didn't want her to catch him looking. She seemed like a nice enough person, and his stomach turned when he thought about what he was putting her through. He ran his gaze down her body for the first time since they left the airport before moving his gaze back to the road. Fuck, she was fit. Very fit. He wouldn't mind taking her back to the flat and—

He shook his head. He couldn't afford to be having thoughts like that. She was a client, sort of. Plus, she probably hated him right now. Any ideas of wooing her he'd held when he first ran into her at the airport were now irrelevant.

He groaned as he pulled in front of the posh building. He sat behind the wheel for a second, gathering his patience before he needed to enter the building.

He never enjoyed visiting here on a good day. Now he was expected to go upstairs and tell his contact, his *father,* Colin, he'd failed at the first assignment he was given in the case. He could just hear the derision in his voice now.

"Where are we?" Evelyn spoke from beside him, interrupting his thoughts. "I thought you said we were going to the solicitor's office?"

Patrick rolled his eyes as he turned the car off and opened the door. "It's Sunday." He stepped out of the car, carrying the duffel bag.

He didn't even pause to see if she was following. He took the stairs to the entrance two at a time. When he heard her footsteps behind him, he opened the door to the building.

"It's Sunday? I don't even know what that means." She was practically jogging in order to match his steps as he walked to his destination.

"You're a smart woman. What do you think it means?" He stopped in front of a door, raising his hand to knock.

"Has anyone ever told you how much of an ass you are?"

"Several."

The door to the flat opened before either one could say anything more.

Colin was middle-aged with hair that was grayer than brown, and stood in the doorway. "Patrick."

"Colin."

"Your...errand took much longer than I had expected. I expected you here thirty minutes ago."

"I ran into some complications."

Colin looked toward Evelyn. "Who's that?"

"The complication."

"I see. Why don't the two of you come inside? We shouldn't be discussing business in the hallway." He stood aside, letting Patrick and Evelyn enter the flat.

The flat was still as sparsely decorated as it had been the last time he'd visited. The living area housed only a leather couch and a coffee table. Off to the side, where one would normally keep a dining room table, sat a large wooden desk, piled high with paperwork, the screen of a computer monitor, barely visible. There was a small kitchen that was rarely used and then a full-sized bed against a wall. He wasn't surprised.

Patrick moved immediately in the couch's direction, setting the duffel bag on the coffee table before plopping himself down. Evelyn stood near the entrance, arms folded across her chest, her gaze shifting between Colin and Patrick.

"Don't be shy, love. Have a seat." Patrick patted the spot next to him.

She walked over to the couch and perched as far away as she could from him.

"This isn't Megan." Colin pointed at Evelyn. "I specifically told you to go to the airport and stop Megan from fleeing the country."

"Well, if you'd provided me with an actual picture of Megan, rather than one that was so blurry I could only make out vague features, I may have been able to get her. The picture showed she was short, had brown hair to her shoulders, and was carrying this duffel. Evelyn here fit that description, so I stopped her."

Colin sighed, pinching the bridge of his nose, closing his eyes. "And why didn't you let her go on her way once you realized your mistake?"

"Two Fitzgerald goons were waiting for her. They apparently realized she had the bag. I couldn't let them take her."

"I still don't understand *why* she's here. Why did you bring her *here*? Why is she not at Heathrow, waiting to go wherever it is she is planning on traveling?"

It was Patrick's turn to sigh and pinch his nose in frustration. He gestured to the duffel bag on the coffee table. "She was carrying that bag. The Fitzgerald arseholes were about to fucking shoot her. What was I supposed to do? Grab the bag and let them kill her?"

"You keep gesturing to her bag. Mentioning her bag. What's so special about her bag? We were after *Megan's* bag."

"That's Megan's bag!" Patrick shouted. "That bag right there. They somehow swapped them at the airport, and now she has it. I was going to keep the bag and let her on her way, but the Fitzgerald goons grabbed her not five seconds after I let her leave. And I'm not in the business of letting innocent girls get murdered, so here she is. Do you understand now, you senile old man?"

"That's Megan's bag?" He gestured to the bag in question.

She sighed. "Yes, that's Megan's bag. She and I crashed into each other and switched bags accidentally. I wanted to turn the bag into security, hoping Megan had done the same with mine. However, this jackass grabbed and stopped me before I could. I'm pretty sure he's the reason I was put on the radar of those goons in the first place. Now, can we please figure out what to do about getting me where I need to go? I really want to go to Greece."

"What on earth is she talking about?"

"He dragged me out of the airport! I'm not supposed to be here. I need to have this figured out so I can get back into the airport and continue on to my program. Patrick said you'd be able to take care of everything."

Colin closed his eyes and massaged his temples. "You've made a right mess of this whole situation. When I suggested to my office we hire outside help to gather evidence against the Fitzgeralds, I assured them you and James were the right way to go. I said you were mature and professional and would get the job done. And now, one step into the endeavor, and you've made a bloody mess of the whole damn thing."

"This isn't my fault! If you had just—"

"I don't want to hear it. This is spiraling out of control. Maybe you aren't the right person to be on this job."

"You know I'm the right person for this job. You know why I need to do this. I didn't fuck anything up. If anything, I did a damn good job with the information you gave me. We have the duffel bag, and that's the most important piece, right? We'll find Megan. I fail to see where I've fouled this up." Patrick's face was burning with rage.

"You've upset this poor girl, for one thing. You've literally kidnapped her. You've let Megan slip away to God knows where. And you're letting your emotions get the best of you. You've created quite the mess for me to clean up already. I can't imagine what will happen if I let you continue to work on this case."

Patrick opened his mouth to retort, but was cut off.

"You need to go cool down. When you're ready to act your age, we'll continue this conversation."

Patrick cursed and stormed out of the living area, kicking the desk chair on his way to the farthest corner of the flat. He was far enough away to be alone, but close enough to still hear and see what was going on.

Colin turned toward Evelyn. "Now, dear, why don't you tell me about what is going on and where you need to go. I'll make some calls tomorrow, and we'll get you on your way."

"Well, you see, sir—"

The doorbell rang, interrupting her.

"Hold that thought." Colin excused himself to go answer the door.

Patrick took a few more deep calming breaths before he walked back into the living area and took a seat next to Evelyn. "I'm sorry about that."

She looked at him. "It's alright. I would have been frustrated, too. I mean, how many ways did you really need to explain the bag isn't mine?"

He smiled. "I know, right? I swear, the older that man gets, the denser he is. Bloody annoying, that."

She gave him a tight smile. "Do you work with him a lot? You guys seem close."

He shrugged. "This is the first time we're working together professionally. But he's my dad. Even though I would never describe my father and me as being 'close.'"

She stared at him. "Your father? But you referred to him by his first name."

He shrugged again. "Like I said, close isn't a word I'd use to describe my relationship with him."

She looked like she wanted to ask more questions, but was interrupted by Colin walking back into the room.

He was carrying a plain cardboard box. He didn't speak as he carried the box over to his dining room table to set it down.

Patrick followed him to the table, gesturing for Evelyn to follow him. They joined him around the box. The three stood there staring at it until Colin pulled out his pocketknife and sliced open the top, his hand shaking. He peeled open the lid and peeked in. Then he slammed the top of the box closed and moved away, covering his mouth.

Curious, Patrick and Evelyn looked at each other before she nodded at Patrick.

He moved forward and opened the box. She peeked over his shoulder. She covered her mouth and stifled a scream.

"Jesus Christ," Patrick breathed at the sight.

Inside the box, nestled next to Evelyn's duffel bag, Megan's head sat staring up at him.

CHAPTER 5

PATRICK

"Shit, shit, shit." Patrick ran his hand through his hair. He couldn't tear his gaze away from the box on his dad's table. He'd never seen a dead body before. It wasn't as cool as he'd imagined. In fact, it was downright terrifying.

He stole a glance at Evelyn. She didn't look well. She was also still staring at the box, but she looked a little green around the gills and was swaying. Before he could react, Colin came up behind her, wrapping an arm around her shoulders.

"Come on, my dear. Let's walk away and take a seat, shall we?"

He led her to the couch and sat her down. As soon as she made contact with the sofa, it was like flipping a switch, and she began to sob. Colin tried to comfort her, but she shrugged him away, laying down on her side, curling into herself.

Colin walked back over to where Patrick stood at the table. "That's it. You're officially off the case."

"Fuck off! You can't sack me without giving me a compelling and reasonable reason why."

Colin pointed at the box. "That's why. This is no laughing matter. And there's no way I'm letting you continue on this case when I'm getting heads delivered to my place of residence. This has grown too dangerous. I'm not willing to risk your life for this. I'll talk to my partners tomorrow, and we'll figure something else out."

Patrick shook his head. "No way, Colin. No way am I letting you take me off this case now. If anything, you need me to stay. We have leverage. We have the bag. We have the evidence we need against the group. All I need to do is find someone willing to place Mickey Fitzgerald under arrest, and we're good. Can't you see we have the advantage here?"

Colin shook his head. "And what about her?" He pointed at Evelyn. "We've already put her in too much danger as it is. I refuse to put her in anymore."

"She's not in any danger. They just want the bloody bag. They don't even know who she is. I'll take her back to the airport tomorrow morning and get her on a plane to wherever it is she is going, and then she'll be as far out of harm's way as possible."

Colin ignored his outburst. Instead, he reached inside the box.

"What are you doing?"

Colin pulled out the bag that had been nestled next to the severed head and placed it on the table.

"Evelyn, dear, will you please come over here? I want to determine if there's anything missing from your bag."

She got up from the couch and wiped her eyes. She inched toward the table, avoiding looking at the box.

"Should we even be touching any of this? Isn't it evidence?" she asked, hesitating.

"Technically, yes. In any other case, we wouldn't be touching it, but it really doesn't matter. Any investigation is going to be just for show. Nothing ever happens to The Fitzgeralds. We'll call the police, and within twenty-four hours, all the evidence will disappear. You might as well have your things before I call it in," Colin explained. "Go ahead and open the bag."

She carefully unzipped the bag and reached inside.

Patrick looked on. Instead of what he considered typical items he thought a girl would have in her bag, Evelyn was pulling out book after book. He shifted closer and looked at some titles. They were all regarding Ancient Greek history, and some city named Epidaurus. There were about seven books on the table, along with several composition notebooks, before the bag was empty.

He let out a long, slow whistle. "Blimey, that's a lot of books. It's like you're a grad student or something." He brought his gaze up to meet hers and smirked, giving a wink.

She narrowed her eyes. "Hmm, imagine that. I was telling the truth."

"Is there anything missing?" Colin asked, bringing everyone back to the situation in the room.

She nodded. "The first draft of my thesis."

Patrick frowned. "Why would they want to keep a copy of your thesis? I can't imagine they're interested in," he picked up a book off the table, "*Sleeping Rituals at the Temple of Asclepius.*"

She shook her head. "Well, inside that draft, I had slipped my itinerary for this trip. It has my name, the location of the dig, the address of my accommodations, and every single excursion planned for my stay."

"Well, there you have it." Colin slammed his hand on the table, causing everyone to jump. "There's no way you can take her to the airport now and put her on a plane."

"I'm still not following. Why not?" Patrick asked.

"They know who she is. They know what she looks like, her name, and where she's going. It's not safe for her any longer. She's no longer anonymous."

She frowned. "I don't understand why they have an interest in me. I didn't even know who they were until today."

"You have the duffel bag, my dear. They probably feel you know too much."

"But I don't even know what's inside the bag. I know nothing. At this point, I want to go home. I don't even want to go to Greece anymore. I just want to go home." Tears welled in her eyes.

Colin looked at Patrick and gestured at him.

Patrick looked at the crying woman beside him and panicked. He knew nothing about comforting women. He knew nothing about women. There was a reason he was still single at nearly thirty.

"Look, Evelyn, you heard Colin. You're going to be stuck in London for a while, so you should get used to the idea." The minute the words were out, he knew he'd said the wrong thing.

Her mouth dropped open. She sputtered for a moment before words finally formed. "How is this helpful? Have you ever comforted anyone? It's like you've never interacted with humans. Are you a robot?"

"I'm not a robot! I'm not saying anything that isn't true. You're stuck here. You should just get over it. There's no point in crying," Patrick shouted.

"Patrick!" Colin chastised. "That's quite enough. I didn't bring you up to be so rude to women."

"You didn't bring me up at all, old man," Patrick spit out.

"That's enough. I won't sit here and listen to you be so insensitive to this poor woman or take your anger out on me. You're nearly thirty, and I expect you to have a little more respect."

"Fuck you, Colin. You don't have any right to—"

"I said, that's enough! If you wish to continue on this case, you're going to have to set aside your personal feelings and grudges, and act like the professional you are."

Patrick let out a growl. "Fine."

"Apologize," Colin demanded.

Patrick turned toward Evelyn, who was standing with her arms crossed, staring at the floor. "I'm sorry I've been such an arse to you. I don't know why I'm being a tosser, and I'll endeavor to try to be more civilized from this point forward."

She looked up from the floor and met his gaze. She narrowed her eyes at him. "I accept your weak apology and I hope I get to see this more civilized version of yourself."

He opened his mouth to retort, but Colin spoke instead.

"Great. Now that that's settled, let's move on, yes?"

Evelyn and Patrick reluctantly nodded.

"Now, Evelyn, as much as you want to go home right now, you have to accept you're where you're safest. If we let you go now, we'll most likely be receiving your head in a box next. Patrick, you need to let go of any personal feelings tying you to this case. Emotions cloud your judgment. If you want to remain involved, you need to become neutral. It's too dangerous to lose focus. The second your focus shifts, it's over. This isn't a cheating spouse case, son. This is a different kettle of fish altogether."

Patrick nodded. "I understand. I'll be better, I promise. No more emotions until Fitzgerald and his compatriots are locked behind bars."

"Excellent." Colin sounded weary. "Now, there's not much we can accomplish this afternoon, as it's Sunday, and I'm sure Evelyn is feeling the effects of traveling. I'll call you tomorrow once I meet with my partners. You take the bag. It'll be safer with you, and you'll be able to use whatever's in it to move the case along."

"Yeah, that works." Patrick moved around the table and into the living room, grabbing the bag and moving toward the door.

"Ahem." Colin cleared his throat. "Aren't you forgetting something?"

Patrick looked around the flat and shrugged. "I didn't come in with anything else. Just the duffel. I've got everything I need."

"The girl, Patrick. You're forgetting the girl." Colin appeared to be running out of patience for him.

"Wait, what?" She sputtered. "You expect me to go with him? I thought I'd be staying here with you."

Colin shook his head. "You're not safe here. The Fitzgeralds obviously know where I live, and they probably already expect you'll be here, as evidenced by your bag being delivered with the head. You'll be much safer going with Patrick. His residence isn't as well-known as mine, and he and his partner, James, are better equipped to protect you than I am."

Patrick sighed and moved back into the room. He went over to the table and threw all the books and notebooks back into Evelyn's bag, and slung it over his shoulder. He walked to the couch and picked up her backpack, where she'd left it. He then moved to the entryway before stopping and turning around to glance at Evelyn, who was still standing by the table.

"Well, are you coming or not?"

Behind him, she huffed, and her hurried footsteps tapped behind him. His stride was longer than hers, and it would be with their height difference. It was petty of him to not slow down. He was frustrated with his dad, not with her, per se.

He opened the driver's side of his car, throwing the bags and backpack into the backseat before climbing in.

Seconds after he shut the door, the passenger door opened, and she climbed in. She'd barely closed the door before he peeled away from the curb.

CHAPTER 6

EVELYN

They drove the twenty minutes to his flat in complete silence. Evelyn spent the entire drive staring out the window, trying to take in what little she could see of the city. Which were mostly tall, stone buildings that surrounded either side of the narrow road they were driving down.

They pulled up to a building, and Patrick turned to her after shutting off the engine.

"As my dad told you, I live with my best mate, James. He's also my business partner. I don't want you to panic if you run into him in our modest flat. Good news. Unlike Colin's, the flat is a two bedroom, so I'll bunk you in mine. Follow me."

Before waiting for a response, he reached into the backseat, grabbed all the bags, and exited the vehicle.

She sighed and opened her door. She had to run to catch up to Patrick as he unlocked the door to the building. She followed him up a flight of stairs and then down a hallway to the first door on the left. Once the door was open, he entered and began flipping on lights as he moved through the flat.

She followed him inside and into a small, crowded living room. There was a worn couch along one wall and desks piled high with papers lining the other two.

Patrick moved to a door on the left, throwing it open. The sparsely decorated room housed a full-sized bed whose rumpled solid green bedding made it obvious it was rarely, if not ever, made. He dropped her duffel and backpack on the floor at the foot of the bed. She wrinkled her nose at the thought of sleeping in the clearly unwashed bed.

"This is my room. You can use it for the duration of your stay. I'll take the couch." He turned, left the room, and headed toward the desk under the window. He placed Megan's duffel on the floor beside the chair and booted up his computer. His desk was a mess, covered in papers and empty energy drink cans. In fact, the entire flat was a mess. It truly held up to the stereotypical 'bachelor pad' environment.

Evelyn looked around at the empty cans and beer bottles that lined the surface of most of the furniture and the counters in the kitchen, which was open to the living room. She counted at least three pairs of socks strewn about the floor. She looked down the hallway, which she assumed led to the bathroom and the second bedroom. There was a wet towel lying in the middle of the floor, as if the two feet into the bedroom were just too much to handle to travel. The floor of Patrick's bedroom was littered with clothing. Whether they were clean or dirty, she wasn't sure.

"You can have a seat." Patrick didn't look up from his computer screen.

She looked toward the couch and wrinkled her nose in disgust. The couch looked like something they'd found on the side of the street. The brown upholstery was worn and stained and the cushions sagging.

"I'm actually kind of hungry. I haven't eaten since this morning on the airplane," she said.

Patrick, still glued to his computer, gestured toward the kitchen. "Help yourself to anything you want."

She glared at the back of his head and moved into the kitchen. She opened the refrigerator and narrowed her eyes. The only things inside were beer, energy drinks, and half-eaten takeaway containers. She closed the fridge and began opening cupboards.

Empty. Empty. Empty.

"Um, Patrick?" She was trying to control her temper.

"Yeah?"

"You are aware you have absolutely nothing edible in your kitchen, right?"

"Not true. I'm fairly certain we have some takeaway in there. You're more than welcome to it. And I know for certain we have tea. We always have tea. We would be terrible British men if we didn't. In fact, I'll make some in a minute, since you Americans are rubbish at making tea. Care for a cuppa?"

"Hate to break it to you, but I couldn't find any tea. Your cupboards are literally bare. Also, how old is that takeaway?"

"Honestly, I have no idea. I can't actually remember the last time we've eaten a meal here. Which would also explain the lack of tea in the flat. Been picking that up from the corner shop lately."

She couldn't control herself any longer. She picked up an empty beer can from the counter and chucked it at him, nailing him in the head.

"Oi! What was that for?" He rubbed his head.

"I'm hungry. I'm supposed to stay here with you for who knows how long, and you and your roommate live like pigs. Oh, and did I mention I'm *hungry?*"

"Order takeaway, then. Bloody hell, are you useless."

"How? From where? Patrick, I'm not *from* here. You need to help me with these things."

"There's a curry place three doors down. Just walk down there and get something."

"Fine." She started for the door, patting her pockets to make sure she still had her money. It was a good thing she'd had the mind to get money in the right currency before leaving on her trip. She had just placed her hand on the doorknob to leave when a hand on her arm stopped her.

"Never mind," Patrick said. "I don't know what I was thinking. It's Sunday, the curry place is closed on Sunday."

"What about a grocery store? I can walk to a grocery store and get *something.*"

He shook his head. "I can't just let you go out there alone. Have you already forgotten? You're wanted by an infamous crime syndicate. I think the jet lag is getting to you. You should go have a lie down. We can get you food later. Perhaps I can text James to bring something home with him."

"When will he be home?"

"Who knows? It depends if he's doing something for a case or if he's just out."

"Argh!" She growled in frustration. "You know, I think I've solved the mystery."

"What mystery?"

"Why you're so rude. There's no food here. You're hangry."

"Hangry?!" Patrick laughed. "I am not hangry. I am just concerned about your safety. Once the shops and restaurants are open, I will feed you. It is Sunday, remember?"

"Oh, that's right. It's Sunday. How could I have possibly forgotten?" she threw back at him, her words positively dripping with sarcasm.

"Who's the hangry one now?" he asked, not quite under his breath.

She let out a screech in frustration before grabbing her backpack and storming into Patrick's room, slamming the door behind her.

CHAPTER 7

EVELYN

Evelyn gasped, sitting straight upright in the bed. The room was dark and unfamiliar. She threw the covers off and jumped out of bed before remembering where she was.

She glanced around, taking in the dirty clothes on the floor and the bare walls. "That's right," she muttered, "I'm in Patrick's room, somewhere in London." She sat back down on the bed, placing her head in her hands, breathing slowly. Oddly, the familiar rich, woodsy smell of his cologne that permeated the air calmed her. As she exhaled, her heart rate slowed to a normal level. A few more deep breaths in and out, and she became calm.

She removed her hands and laid back on the bed. A strange dream had awoken her. In it she was back at the airport, and she was running. Only this time, Patrick wasn't with her. She was alone. And this time, she didn't get away from those men. They'd caught her and dragged her out of the airport, kicking and screaming. The next thing she knew, she was in some nondescript room, tied to a chair. A man with a scarred face came in and, with a thick New Jersey accent, began telling her all the things he was going to do to her now he had her. He pulled out a hammer and began slapping it against his hand and walking slowly toward her, laughing maniacally. She'd started screaming, and that was when she woke up.

Evelyn let out a small, quiet laugh. "No more gangster movies when I get out of this mess."

She was about to settle herself back in the bed to get more sleep when her bladder chose that moment to remind her it needed attention. She sighed and thought about the location of the bathroom in relation to the room she was currently sleeping in and of all the crap on the floor between here and there and let out a groan. After getting off the bed, she went to where Patrick had dropped her backpack. It only took her a second to find the tiny flashlight she'd packed with her for emergencies, and finding her way to the bathroom without sticking her bare foot in an old slice of pizza was definitely an emergency.

Not sure of the time, she quietly opened the door and peeked her head out into the main living space. The room was lit with the glow of a computer screen. She glanced toward where she knew Patrick's desk was located. He was slumped over with his head on his desk, obviously asleep. In his sleep, he looked relaxed and peaceful. More handsome than he had appeared all day without the stress tightening up his features. He didn't look very comfortable, but Evelyn didn't want to be the one to wake him. She wasn't sure which Patrick would appear. Joking, sarcastic Patrick, or snarky, rude and hangry Patrick, and she wasn't in the mood to deal with either if she was being honest. Besides, sleep might actually make him more pleasant to deal with later. She clicked on her flashlight, taking care to make sure she pointed it at the floor, and started her journey to the bathroom. As she made her way down the hallway, she noted the towel that had been in the middle of the floor earlier had made its way out of the hallway.

She turned into the bathroom, closed the door, flipped the light on, and had to stifle a groan of disgust. The sink was covered in whiskers and dried toothpaste. The toilet lid was up and looked as if it had been a while since someone last scrubbed it. She closed her eyes and counted to ten before opening them and walking over and flipping the seat down and lining it with toilet paper. After doing her business, and trying her hardest to wash her hands, even though the action made her feel dirtier for the effort, she decided that if she were going to be stuck in this apartment for an indefinite amount of time, when it came time to purchase food for the apartment, she'd demand cleaning supplies too, and she would clean the damn apartment herself.

The thought of buying food reminded her it had been a very long time since she'd last eaten, and she was starving. Which, of course, reminded her that these men kept no food in the apartment, and she was going to be hungry until the morning when they could venture out in search of food. She flung open the door and stepped into the hallway. She began walking toward the bedroom, only to run into a solid wall of man.

She looked up, expecting it to be Patrick, but instead was greeted by someone who she had never seen before. He had longish, dark, rusty-red hair and green eyes. He was wearing a Pink Floyd shirt and jeans, and was barefoot. And he was smiling at her with a big wide grin that showed off white, slightly crooked teeth.

"Oi." He laughed. "Is it my birthday? To what do I owe the pleasure of having a gorgeous bird run into me after exiting my bathroom?"

Her cheeks heated. "I'm sorry. I wasn't watching where I was going."

The man tilted his head to the side, still smiling. "An American bird. How odd. When I came home, I noticed Patrick asleep at his desk, but no one else. Did he bring you home and shag you and then leave you alone in bed so he could work? *Tsk tsk*. What bad manners he has. You'll find I have much better manners than he has."

She shook her head. "No, no shagging. He brought me home, but we didn't do anything, believe me."

"Oh? Then what are you doing in our home?"

"It's a long story. A very long story. One that I would probably be better at telling you in the morning, after I've had something to eat. I think the hunger has moved on from eating my stomach lining to eating my brain cells. I'm having a hard time focusing on things. Like who are you?"

The man let out a laugh, taking a step back from her. "I'm James, Patrick's flat mate and fellow investigator." He stuck out his hand.

She grasped his hand and shook it. "I'm Evelyn, Patrick's client, or hostage. I haven't quite figured out what I am exactly."

James threw his head back and laughed. "You're funny. I like you. Now, what was this you were saying about hunger? Didn't Patrick feed you?"

She shook her head. "I have had nothing to eat since breakfast on the airplane. What, yesterday morning now?"

He clicked his tongue, shaking his head. "Remind me to take Patrick to task for not properly entertaining a lady." He reached into his pocket, pulled out a chocolate bar, and handed it over to her. "It may be a bit melted, but it's something, right?"

She took the chocolate bar and smiled. "It is. Thank you very much."

"You're very welcome, milady. Now, if you'll excuse me, I'm knackered and was about to head to bed. But we'll have a chance to chat more in the morning, yeah?"

She smiled and nodded. "Yeah."

"Brilliant. Goodnight, Evelyn. It was a pleasure meeting you." And before she could respond, he walked the few feet into his bedroom and closed the door.

She stood in the hallway for a few minutes and tried to figure out what had just happened. Was he flirting with her? He'd thought she was there with Patrick, but that didn't stop him from flirting and trying to pick her up. Did the two of them share women? She shook her head, trying not to think about the sex lives of the men she was staying with, and began walking to Patrick's room.

She took a quick peek at Patrick as she walked past. Still slumped over, sleeping on his desk. He hadn't moved a muscle. Unbelievable. She wondered if he was always such a heavy sleeper or if he was faking it so he wouldn't have to talk to her. She shrugged and moved to open the door to his room.

When she got back into the room and closed the door, she looked at the candy bar. It was a Flake Bar. She had never had one of these before. She ripped off the wrapper and took a big bite and moaned. The thin chocolate flakes melted the second they hit her tongue. It was probably because she was starving, but she was pretty sure it was the best chocolate she had ever tasted. She ate the rest in two bites before climbing back into bed. She pulled the covers up and was asleep as soon as her head hit the pillow.

CHAPTER 8

PATRICK

The sun came in the window, causing Patrick to flinch as it reached his eyes. Odd. He had blackout curtains on his window. The sun shouldn't be shining in his face. He moved to sit up and then immediately regretted that decision. His neck had a crick in it, and his back was stiff. He opened his eyes and was greeted by his computer screen.

"Fuuuck," he groaned, stretching his back.

"You fell asleep at your computer again."

He turned. James was leaning against the kitchen island, holding a steaming cup of coffee.

"Where the hell did you get coffee? I thought we ran out last week." Patrick's voice was still rough from sleep.

"Well, Sleeping Beauty, while you were snoring away on your keyboard, I ran up the road to the shop and picked up a few things to get us through breakfast. It's come to my attention we have no food in this flat, and if you're going to be entertaining gorgeous birds, you're going to have to feed them." James smirked.

Patrick ran his hands through his hair and down his face. "I'm not enter—wait, how do you know about Evelyn? You didn't come in until late, and she's been in bed for ages."

"I ran into her in the hallway in the middle of the night. Chatted her up and gave her my Flake Bar. What were you doing sleeping at your computer when you had *that* waiting for you in your bed?"

"It's not like that. It's a long story."

"That's what she said, too. I think it's time you fill me in on this so-called long story. Because, now, I've gone beyond curious and am moving slightly into dead-cat territory."

Patrick rolled his eyes, standing. "I think I need some of that coffee first, and then I'll start filling you in."

James reached behind him and produced an already filled cup of coffee. "I'm one step ahead of you. Start talking."

Patrick sighed, taking the coffee from James. "Fine. You know the Fitzgerald case we're working for Colin?"

James nodded. "Yeah, you were supposed to be at Heathrow to stop Fitzgerald's ex from fleeing the country with a bunch of evidence."

"Yeah, I was there, at Heathrow, and Colin didn't tell me much, just that I was supposed to be meeting a girl with brown hair carrying a certain duffel bag. So, I'm at Heathrow, and I grab the girl with the bag that looked like the one he described. Only, it's not the one I was supposed to nab. It's this American, and she somehow has the bag we need. I keep the bag and I let her go. Only Fitzgerald's lackeys have already honed in on her and are waiting. I'm not about to let her get hurt, so I help her, and I may have technically kidnapped her."

James took a sip of his coffee. "Did you ever find the girl you were supposed to find?"

"Yeah, they delivered her head to Colin's yesterday."

"Fuck!" James almost dropped his coffee mug. "Her head was delivered to your father's home?"

Patrick nodded. "In a cardboard box. Colin wanted me to drop the case, but I refused. He sent me home with the bag and Evelyn, and when Evelyn went to bed, I went through the bag and shit got worse."

"How can things get worse than your contact's severed head being sent to your father like some kind of fucking message?"

Patrick walked over to the duffel bag and opened it. He reached in and pulled out one picture and handed it to James.

"Is that Superintendent McGovern and Mickey Fitzgerald?" James asked.

"Yep."

"And Fitzgerald's handing him loads of pounds?"

"Yep."

"Fucking shit."

"Yep."

"What the fuck are we going to do?" James asked. "I thought the plan was to get the bag and the girl and get her to testify against Fitzgerald. And then *turn everything over* to the police so they could actually arrest the fuckers."

"Yeah, that was the plan. I wasn't expecting to find out the plan was doomed to fail from the start. We can't get anyone to arrest the arsehole. He's virtually untouchable. I can't even think of one officer in Tower Hamlets who probably is *not* being paid off by the Fitzgeralds."

"C'mon, there has to be one. I seem to remember not everyone was willing to become a corrupt arse while we were there."

Patrick shook his head. "We're going to have to do some digging. There are hundreds of officers in the borough. We're going to have to be thorough, but we might be able to come up with at least one. But don't get your hopes up."

"That's the spirit! Now, what are you doing about Evelyn? Is she stuck here?"

He shrugged. "Colin seems to think the Fitzgeralds are gunning for her because they assume she knows what's in the bag. Which she doesn't, by the way. She can't know what's in the bag. She can't know anything, really. If she knows nothing, she'll be able to leave and not have to stay for the trial. Also, if she were to get captured, she'll have plausible deniability."

"But we'll not let it come to that, yeah? We're going to make sure the Fitzgeralds don't get to her."

Patrick said nothing.

"We're going to protect her, right? That's our job. That's why Colin sent her here rather than keeping her at his fortress, where they sent a fucking head, right?"

"Well, we need to lure the Fitzgeralds out into the open and become vulnerable so we can get our loyal officer to arrest them, yeah? And they want the bag and the girl, yeah? So..." Patrick motioned with his hands, as if the rest of the sentence was obvious.

James swung his arm around to gesture toward the door which Evelyn was behind, forgetting he was holding a mug of coffee as it sloshed out and onto the floor. "We're not using that girl as bait, Patrick! Jesus Christ. What's going on with you? I know this case is personal, but my best mate would never suggest using an innocent girl to lure crazed criminals into the open."

"Oi! There's nothing wrong with me. And I said nothing about using the *girl* as bait, did I?" Patrick shouted.

"The words never came out of your mouth, but you heavily implied them. Look, I'm upset about what happened to your mum, too, but that doesn't mean we need to sacrifice an innocent woman to get your vengeance. Think about what you're saying, mate!" James' expression softened with the mention of Patrick's mum, but neither wanted to ruminate on the subject.

"I know what I'm saying, and I am not saying we sacrifice that part of our bounty. I'm talking about the other part. Because when it all comes down to it, does it matter what we sacrifice if Mickey Fitzgerald is sitting behind bars, paying for all the crimes he's committed? The only person who would be upset at the loss would be my dad. What's wrong with a little collateral damage?" Patrick gestured at the floor next to his computer.

James opened his mouth to respond, but the slamming of a door interrupted him. The two men whipped around to see Evelyn, disheveled from sleep, standing in the room, tears in her eyes.

"Collateral damage?" she whispered through tears.

"Evelyn, I—" Guilt ate away at Patrick.

She shook her head. "Don't. I was able to hear everything. These walls aren't exactly soundproof, just so you know." She closed her eyes as tears made their way down her cheeks. "I need some air." She ran to the apartment door, opened it, and ran into the hallway, leaving two shocked men staring after her.

CHAPTER 9

EVELYN

Evelyn burst through the doorway to the street. She stopped and stared at the road for a minute before choosing a direction. She didn't know where she was going, but she knew she had to get away from that apartment and, more importantly, Patrick.

She wiped tears off her face, but they kept coming. After doing really well holding herself together over the last twenty-four hours, she'd found the proverbial straw that broke the camel's back.

Patrick was an ass. A handsome ass, but still an ass. They'd been at odds ever since they met, but sacrificing her to the Fitzgeralds? Not caring if she lived or died as long as he got what he needed in the end? That was low. And she didn't want to spend a second longer in the same room as him. She wanted to get as far away from him as possible.

She had absolutely no idea where she was or where she was going, but that was an insignificant detail she could eventually deal with. Everyone here spoke English, and she'd watched enough movies and documentaries to know London was all connected to a subway system, so she was bound to find an entry to get on eventually. Right?

"Evelyn! Wait!"

She paused and looked over her shoulder. "Fuck."

Patrick was running up the sidewalk toward her.

She turned back around and continued. "Go away, Patrick." She didn't pause.

It didn't take long until Patrick had caught up and was matching her strides. Even though he had basically sprinted to catch up with her, he wasn't even remotely out of breath. That made her resent him even more.

"Where are you going?" he asked.

"I don't know. Away from you. But apparently, that's not going to work."

He sighed. "Look, I'm sorry. I didn't mean for you to hear anything I said back there."

She scoffed. "Yeah, I gathered that. Most people who want to sacrifice their hostage for the 'greater good' rarely tell their grand scheme to said hostage before offering them up to the bad guy."

"I'm not..." He paused. "I'm not going to sacrifice you to the greater good. I never even said I wanted to sacrifice you."

"No, but you did say I would be collateral damage."

He sighed. "No, I didn't. You heard wrong, or interpreted it wrong, or whatever. I was telling James we would sacrifice the *bag*, not you. I'm not a monster."

She stopped walking and turned to look at him. "The bag? You were talking about the bag?"

He shrugged. "I was. I don't know why you and James jumped to the conclusion I was willing to sacrifice you to Fitzgerald. I wasn't that bad yesterday, was I?"

"You were rude. You yelled at me. You starved me," Evelyn enumerated on her fingers. "I'm pretty sure you may actually hate me."

He had the decency to look embarrassed. "Okay, so yesterday may not have been my finest moment. But I don't hate you. Am I annoyed by you? Yes, very much so, but I don't hate you. I don't think I hate anyone, other than, you know, the Fitzgeralds. I'm sorry I came across that way, but I have a one-track mind, and when something doesn't go the way I want it to, I overreact."

"And put women in your room to slowly starve to death?"

"Bloody hell, you were not going to starve to death, but you're right, I've been an utter bastard."

"Well, I wouldn't classify you as an *utter* bastard. Just bastard will do."

Patrick looked at her like he was seeing her for the first time before he started laughing. Really laughing. She had barely seen the man smile in the last twenty-four hours, let alone laugh.

She looked at him like he'd grown three heads. "What's so funny?"

"You. In fact, this entire fucking situation we're in."

She grew more confused. "Situation we're in? How is our situation at all funny?"

"I can't explain it. It's just that I admit, I *have* been a complete arse to you the last twenty-four hours, and you *still* stopped and talked to me after running out of my flat after you had thought I'd said I'd gladly sacrifice you for my cause. You're an anomaly, Evelyn... I'm sorry, but I don't really recall your last name."

"Stevenson," she answered automatically, still trying to process what the hell was going on in front of her.

"Let's start over a bit, eh? Patrick Miller." He offered his hand.

She looked at the hand in front of her suspiciously. This was a complete one eighty from the day before. He barely gave his name before dragging her all over London. And he wasn't exactly warm toward her the entire day. What was his game? Was he trying to gain her trust so he could turn around and betray her later by giving her up to the Fitzgeralds, despite saying she had misheard him? Should she even trust this man?

On the one hand, her gut was screaming at her *hell no*, telling her she should run in the opposite direction, and keep running until she found her way out of the country and onto the first plane to Greece. On the other, her head was telling her she did not know where she was or how to navigate London. For all she knew, she was being watched by the Fitzgeralds right this very second, the man in front of her could very well be telling the truth, and be the only person able to protect her. Besides, even through all the times he was being an ass to her, Patrick had some moments where he seemed like a decent enough guy. There was potential for something, she didn't know what yet, but something.

"It's not going to bite you, is it?" Patrick gestured to his hand.

Making a split-second decision, she grabbed his hand, shaking it. "Evelyn Stevenson."

He broke out into a wide grin. "Nice to meet you, Evelyn. Now, James is back at the flat doing his best Mr. Muscle impression and making it much more hospitable for guests. How about we continue down this road to the small café and get a bite to eat, and we can try to be honest with each other for a change, yeah?"

She nodded and began following him down the road, hoping with every step she took she hadn't made the world's biggest mistake and just signed her own death sentence.

CHAPTER 10

PATRICK

Silverware scraped against plates, and soft music filled in the background of Little Rock Café. Patrick looked on as Evelyn sipped her cup of coffee while they awaited their food. She kept looking at him over the rim of her coffee mug and narrowing her eyes. He hid his smile behind his own mug. It wouldn't do to have her see his amusement at her suspicion.

Since their confrontation in the middle of the sidewalk, she hadn't said a word to him. She quietly followed him to the café and then only spoke to give the waitress her order before falling silent again and observing him. She didn't trust him. And he didn't blame her. He hadn't been very kind to her in the last twenty-four hours. He wouldn't trust him either.

What had happened to him in the last year? When did he become this utter bastard who Evelyn met yesterday? There was a time when he would have seen a girl like Evelyn and turned on the charm, flirting with her. Gaining her trust and getting her to think her actions were her own idea rather than his.

He looked back at the girl, who sat across from him, and again had to admit she was very attractive, even for being in the same clothes she'd obviously been wearing for two days and not having had a shower in just as many. Her brown hair was mussed, and she had bags under her chocolate eyes, but there was something about her simplicity that was attractive.

He shook his head. He couldn't risk seeing her as anything more than a client. That was what she was. His client and his responsibility. She was in trouble, and he needed to do everything in his power to protect her. Even if it was forgetting about how well her T-shirt accentuated her curves. Patrick closed his eyes and counted to ten. If James wanted to shag her, he could shag her. Patrick was going to keep things completely one-hundred percent professional between them. He neither wanted nor needed the complications of a woman right now. He needed to focus on protecting her and getting that fucker Fitzgerald behind bars.

"Are you okay?" Evelyn asked.

He opened his eyes and looked at her. She'd gone from eying him suspiciously to looking over at him with concern.

"Yeah, yeah. I'm good. Sorry. I didn't sleep well last night."

She smiled. "Yeah, I saw you asleep in front of your computer. It didn't look very comfortable."

"It wasn't. I've got a wicked cramp in my neck that won't let up, and there's a pain between my shoulders. It's quite the reminder I'm not as young as I used to be."

"Your dad said you were almost thirty. That's not old."

He smiled. "Thirty is ancient. Thirty is the new fifty, don't you know? It's quite a bit older than you. You're in Uni, yeah? So, you're what, nineteen, twenty?"

She laughed. "Yeah, I'm attending university, but I'm a grad student, not an undergrad. I'm actually twenty-three. But thanks for thinking I was nineteen. That made me feel good."

"Well, I'm not much older than you. I'm the ripe old age of twenty-seven."

"Have you always been a private investigator? How does one even go about getting a job like that?"

He shook his head, swallowing the bite of his newly arrived eggs. "No. Actually, after I completed my A-levels, I joined the Metropolitan Police Service, and I was an officer for about seven years. I've only been a private investigator for the last two years."

"Why did you stop being a police officer?" She cut through her Spanish omelet.

She was obviously starved as he took in the several plates of food surrounding her. He smiled. It seemed pretty on brand she wasn't coy or timid when it came to food. He dated too many women who were afraid to eat around him. She closed her eyes as she took a bite of omelet and smiled. She was beautiful when she smiled. Patrick made a vow to make sure she did more smiling in his presence than crying from now on. She opened her eyes and looked at him quizzically. Probably wondering why he was staring at her while she ate like some nutter.

He cleared his throat and returned to the conversation. "Corruption. I don't know what you've been able to pick up on between what Colin, James, and myself have been saying around you, but the force has become very corrupt in the last five years, coinciding with the meteoric rise of the Fitzgerald Family here in Tower Hamlets."

"Tower Hamlets? I thought we were in London."

Patrick swallowed. "London is a fairly large city, so they divided it up into thirty-two boroughs. We're in Tower Hamlets, one of the poorer parts of the city."

"So, is London's entire police force corrupt? If it's as large as you say, you'd think that would take a lot of work."

He shook his head. "Only ours, it seems. Mickey Fitzgerald is a smart bloke. He keeps most of his business dealings and crimes centralized here. That way, anything he does occurs in the jurisdiction of the local police and then he can get away with it a lot easier. Consequently, since the Fitzgeralds have moved into town, the crime rate has increased and the safety of the area has gone down. Try to remember that before you go running off by yourself again. You're not exactly in the safest part of London. Five years ago, maybe, but now," he shook his head, "the borough is becoming almost unrecognizable."

She gave him a sympathetic smile. "I'm sorry. If you didn't like the corruption here, why didn't you transfer to another borough? Didn't you like being an officer?"

He shook his head. "After all the pressure to cave to Fitzgerald's demands, and watching all of my former colleagues in the force cave, I became very disillusioned with wearing the badge. If our small little borough could become corrupt, what was going on in the other boroughs? I didn't want to find out. I put in my resignation and set up my investigation agency with James. And we've been doing pretty well, if I say so myself."

"And James was also an officer?"

He nodded. "He was. He and I were partners at the end. When he also became disillusioned with the force, we came up with the idea to start the agency together. We found the flat we're living in, moved in, and set up our office, since we couldn't afford to rent a separate place. London is bloody expensive."

"Do you solve a lot of murders? I keep picturing you as Sherlock Holmes."

Patrick laughed. "No, definitely not Sherlock Holmes. We do a lot of cheating spouses. You wouldn't believe the number of men and women who'll pay exorbitant amounts of money to get at least one picture of their significant other shagging someone else. We make a very good living on just staking out and following someone for a couple of days and getting the money shot."

"Wow. I had no idea that that was a thing."

"Yeah, and if we're not doing a cheating spouse, we're finding a missing dog or missing money from a till. It's usually all quite boring."

"Then how did you pick up a case that involved taking down the major crime syndicate in your borough?"

He quickly took a bite of his food. "Colin, actually," he said after swallowing. "His solicitor's office is desperate to build a case against Fitzgerald, and they're trying to do whatever they can to have it ready in the event he actually gets arrested."

"And they need someone outside of your borough's police to help out."

He pointed his fork at her. "Exactly. And a few days ago, this girl, Megan, fell into their lap. She'd been sleeping with Fitzgerald, but then had a change of heart a few months ago and began putting together loads of evidence against the bastard."

She stopped her fork halfway to her mouth. "Wait, if she called your dad wanting to turn in evidence and be a witness, what were you doing at the airport?"

He smiled, wryly. "Well, the bitch got cold feet, apparently, and called from Heathrow saying she was going to hop the first plane out of the country. Colin called me and begged me to run to Heathrow and pick her up. And I did, and that's how I met you and fucked up the entire case."

They sat quietly for a few minutes, both eating, before she spoke.

"I'm sorry for messing up your first big case. If I wasn't in a such a hurry and not looking where I was going, I never would have crashed into Megan, switching bags, and you never would have mistaken me for her. And she would probably still be alive."

He shook his head. "It's not your fault, so please don't think it is. I'm the one who fucked up. I was so focused on finding the bag, I didn't pay attention to anything else. All I wanted to do was prove to Colin I could handle this case."

"Why do you call your dad by his first name? Is that something they do here in London?"

"I don't want to talk about it," he said gruffly, focusing more on his plate.

"Earlier you and James were arguing about how this case was personal to you, same with you and Colin. Something about your mom?"

He coughed. "Look, why don't you finish your breakfast and we can go back to the flat and check in with James, yeah?"

Her face fell, and she concentrated on eating her breakfast.

They finished their meal without either one of them saying anything else.

CHAPTER 11

EVELYN

Upon returning to the flat, Evelyn was floored. She couldn't believe this was the same place she'd stayed the night before. The floor no longer looked like the substitute for the trash can. The couch, while still the ugliest thing she had ever seen, no longer had food and empty bottles surrounding it. She was pretty sure she could see the kitchen counters sparkling from the front door.

"Wow." She resisted the urge to pinch herself to make sure she wasn't still laying in the bedroom sleeping.

James emerged from the back of the flat, yellow rubber gloves on, an apron around his waist, and a mask across his mouth, brandishing a scrub brush.

When he caught sight of Evelyn, he reached up and pulled the mask off his face to hang around his neck. "You like?" He gestured around the flat.

"I do. It's amazing. How did you manage all of this in the short time we were gone?"

"Let me tell you, it was no easy feat. And don't go into the bathroom yet. That's not ready for a lady. Patrick, mate, how the fuck did we ever let that room get so bad? I'm half expecting to find a nest of rats or cockroaches or something in there."

She glanced back at Patrick as he walked into the flat and shut the door.

"I don't know. Maybe it's because we're rarely here anymore. We're always coming and going and sleeping in the car on a stakeout."

"Touché," James answered. "Oh, Evelyn, before I forget, I went to the girl two doors down and gave her a sob story about my sister being in town and how the plane lost her luggage. She lent me about a week's worth of clothes for you to borrow. She seems to be about your size, so I hope that will help you."

She looked at the man in front of her in awe. This man barely knew her. She had a brief conversation with him in the hallway in the middle of the night, and he had not only found her clothes for her stay, he had cleaned the entire flat for her. "Thank you. I don't know what to say."

James flashed her a smile that made her weak in the knees. "When you realize this one is not as bad as he seems, remember I'm the one who got you clothes and shag me, not him."

Before she could react, Patrick brushed past her and headed into his room. "I'm going to change." He didn't bother to turn around to speak to them before slamming the door.

"What's his problem?" She turned back to James.

James shrugged. "Fuck if I know. He's been very touchy lately."

"I've noticed. What's up with that? I asked him at breakfast, and he completely ignored me and shut down."

The smile fell off his face. "Well, if he doesn't want to tell you, then it's not my place. But if you wait, I'm sure once he gets to know you better, Patrick will tell you anything you want to know."

She sighed and looked back toward the shut door. For every answer she was getting, she had even more questions. And now he was locked in that room with her stuff and if she was going to be out here, alone, while James finished the bathroom and Patrick did, whatever Patrick was doing, she could at least work on some research for her thesis and—

"Fuck a duck!" She exclaimed.

"What's wrong?" he asked.

"My parents! My professor in charge of my program! The director of the dig! They're all expecting me to be in Greece right now! I was supposed to email or call my parents. What if the director has already called and told them I never showed up? What if they think I'm dead? Fuck, fuck, fuck!"

"Whoa. Calm down. Why don't you use your mobile and call them?"

"I didn't want to pay for international service. My cell phone is a glorified alarm clock right now."

"Why don't you go over to Patrick's computer and send an email, making up an excuse about why you aren't there? It'll probably be easier through text, anyway."

She glanced over at the computer and began breathing easy again. Why didn't she think of that? This jet lag business was definitely playing with her head.

"Thanks. Don't let me keep you from...whatever it is you were doing."

She smiled at her. "I'm tackling the shower. Give me thirty, and then I'll show you the clothes I dug up for you and allow you to clean up." He flashed her one more cheeky grin before pulling the mask back up to cover his face and retreating to the bathroom.

Evelyn shook her head before turning toward the computer. She walked over, sitting in Patrick's desk chair. No wonder he had a sore back and neck. This chair wasn't exactly the most comfortable on the planet. She minimized all the windows Patrick had open before pulling up the internet browser and logging into her email. After staring at a blinking cursor for ten minutes, she finally composed an email that had just enough truth in it that it would be believable.

Hey Everyone,

I'm sorry I didn't get in contact sooner, but this is the first time I've been able to sit down and compose an email. Remember how I was worried about my connecting flight in London? Well, I was right to worry. I missed my connection to Athens! I've been at the airport all night trying to re-book, and they're having difficulty accommodating all of my travel arrangements.

Unfortunately, I'm stuck in London for a little while. As soon as I know more, I'll let everyone know. Please don't worry about me. The airline has set me up in some nice accommodations. If I had to be stuck somewhere, it seems London is a good place to be stuck. Maybe I'll get some sightseeing in.

Evie

"What are you doing?" Patrick's voice right behind her caused her to jump.

Holding her hand to her chest, she turned to face him. "I'm emailing my parents and program directors so they don't worry about me."

Patrick nodded. "Good idea. I don't know why we didn't do that earlier."

She shrugged. "Probably because we were too busy shouting at each other."

"Quite right. I couldn't help but notice you signed your email 'Evie'. Is that what you're called?"

She nodded. "Yeah, almost everyone I know calls me that."

He seemed to think about that new information and file it back for later. "Duly noted."

She quirked her eyebrows at him and was about to say something when James shouted from down the hall. "Evelyn, the bathroom is safe now. The clothes I borrowed are in a canvas bag which I have set inside the bathroom door. And since I know your toiletries are more than likely somewhere between here and Greece, you may use whatever you find inside the shower. Feel free to commence the cleansing."

"Well, don't let me keep you from tidying up. After all, James worked hard to make our loo worthy of your use, *Evelyn.*"

She looked at him, and tilted her head, puzzled at this emphasis on her full name, especially after she told him everyone called her Evie.

He met her gaze, holding it.

Her heart rate increased as seconds stretched between them as they held each other's gaze before he broke it with a smirk and turned to walk back into his room, closing the door behind him.

As she watched the door close, she willed her heart rate to slow down back to normal. She had no idea what had just happened between them. Nor did she want to think too much about it. The first hot shower and clean clothes she would experience in almost three days awaited her just down the hall. She could analyze whatever it was happening between her and her investigator after she washed away the grime of traveling and didn't smell of blah.

She quickly hit send on her email and headed down the hall, the puzzle of Patrick sitting in the back of her mind the entire way.

CHAPTER 12

PATRICK

Patrick laid on his bed and listened to the water running in the bathroom. He closed his eyes and tried to make sense of the way he was acting. No matter how many times he ran it through his head, he still didn't understand why he had this sudden rage every time James spoke to Evelyn. He had no interest in her as anything other than a client, so why did it matter if James flirted with her?

Because I saw her first, the little voice at the back of his head muttered.

He pressed his hands firmly against his eyes, willing the little voice to shut up. He needed to focus on the case, not on whether Evelyn and James were going to sleep together. He needed to figure out what to do about getting the evidence to the police.

He began running over the names of everyone he knew from the force who were still in Tower Hamlets. Then he started eliminating the ones he knew for sure took bribes from the family to look the other way. And then he eliminated the ones who were on the fence about taking bribes. And finally, he eliminated the bloody chief superintendent because who the fuck saw that coming? That left him with one name. One name, he was certain, would still be clean.

He was about to stand up and go fill James in on what he had figured out when the door to his bedroom flung open, revealing Evelyn, whose hair was still wet from the shower, wearing clothes about two sizes too small.

"Oh, I'm sorry. I didn't know you were still in here. I was going to grab my hairbrush." She gestured at her bag on the floor.

Patrick waved off her apology and gestured to her bags. "Don't worry about it. More importantly, what the bloody hell are you wearing?"

She bent down to retrieve her bag and set it on the bed. "Well, apparently, James is terrible at discerning when women are even remotely the same size." She pulled out her hairbrush and began combing through her unruly hair, the T-shirt pulling even tighter against her chest and riding up a little, revealing a sliver of her stomach. "I hope you guys solve this case sooner rather than later, because I don't know how long I want to walk around London looking like this."

He gave her a once-over and then resumed his position of lying back on the bed and staring at the ceiling. "It's not so bad. If you're going for the Julia Roberts in *Pretty Woman* look."

She scoffed and then something soft crashed into his face. He brought his hand up and lifted a pile of his T-shirts, looking at her. "What was that for?"

"Consider that me helping make this room match the rest of your flat." She smiled.

He waited until she was zipping her bag back up and depositing it on the ground before throwing the shirts back at her, nailing her right in the head.

She sprung back up and tried to glare at him, attempting to not smile and failing.

He went to lay back down, humming Roy Orbison's 'Pretty Woman' when the clothes came sailing back at him. He ducked out of the way this time, letting out a laugh as he dodged his dirty laundry.

She half growled, half laughed in frustration, causing Patrick to look up at her. He had to admire the way her nose scrunched up so nicely when she narrowed her eyes and pursed her lips in frustration. He wanted to lean over and—

"So," he said, a little louder than he intended, "if you're done in here, we should go out and find James. I just thought of a solution that will get us on the path to getting you wherever it is you want to go. Whether it's on to Greece or on your way back to the States."

Her face lit up with that bit of news, and he had to pretend he didn't notice her eyes were the most expressive part of her, and it made his heart skip a beat.

"Really? What did you figure out?"

He shook his head. "I'll tell you out in the living room with James. That way, I only have to tell it once."

She nodded and walked into the living room.

He closed his eyes, counted to ten, and then followed her out.

In true James fashion, he was already in the living room, perched on the side of the couch where Evelyn was sitting, chatting her up, in the ten seconds Patrick stalled in his room. He moved to his desk, pulling out the chair, and turned it to face them, before sitting down.

"Evie was just telling me you have a solution to our little corruption problem."

Patrick tried not to cringe when James addressed her in such an informal way. "Yes, I did. After mentally going over every officer I know in Tower Hamlets and trying to figure out who wouldn't be in the Fitzgeralds' pockets, I came up with one name."

James leaned forward on the arm of the couch. "Really? I've spent all morning going over the names, and I couldn't think of one. Who was I missing?"

"Well, maybe you know something I don't, but I came up with Harry."

James was silent for a minute. "Harry. I completely forgot about the bugger. He's been chief inspector for so long he slipped my mind. However, if the chief superintendent has fallen to Fitzgerald, how can we be sure Harry hasn't?"

Patrick shook his head. "I'm sure he hasn't. You don't know Harry like I do. He wouldn't do that. He's one to uphold the law above all else."

James sat back for a few minutes. "If you're sure, then he's the only chance we have of catching these bastards."

Evelyn chose that moment to speak up. "I'm sorry, but I'm feeling a little left out here. Who's Harry?"

"Harry was my mentor when I joined the force," Patrick replied. "He showed me the ropes, and he was the senior officer they partnered me with. He became the father I always wished I had. He's a great guy, and it disappointed him when I left the force, but he also understood why I needed to."

"Are you sure you're not allowing your sentiments for this guy get in the way of your judgment? Don't get me wrong. I trust your judgment, but I want to make sure you're absolutely, positively sure this guy isn't going to sell us out to the Fitzgeralds before you bring him in on whatever it is we're doing. I'm not even sure what it is we're doing, and I want to be filled in on that, by the way." Evelyn pointed her finger moving it between the two men.

Patrick didn't hesitate. "I trust him. I don't know what it is, but my gut is saying this is our one shot. He's the only person in the police office here who's honorable enough to stick with his beliefs and not accept bribes from the Fitzgeralds. He wouldn't do that."

Patrick waited as Evelyn looked at James for confirmation. He gave her a subtle nod, and she turned back to Patrick.

"If you feel this strongly, and you along with James, both trust him, then I say we go for it. Like I said, I trust you both. It's crazy because I don't even know you, and really, I don't have much of a choice anyway, but I trust you."

Patrick gave her a small smile. "Great. Believe me, this will be what we need, and he'll be our ticket to blowing this case wide open."

He reached over to his desk and found his mobile. He scrolled through the list of names until he found Harry's. Hitting the send button, he listened while it rang.

"Hello?" Harry answered.

He smiled, hearing the voice of his old mentor and father figure. "Harry? It's Patrick."

Harry chuckled. "Patrick, how are you, mate?"

"I'm doing well, Harry. How are you?"

"Not bad, not bad. And to what do I owe the pleasure of this phone call?"

Patrick swallowed. "I'm calling you about a case I'm working on. I was wondering if you'd be able to help me out."

"Anything, anything. What can I do for you?"

"Well, the case has a layer of confidentiality surrounding it, so I don't want to disclose too much over the phone. Is there any way we can meet and discuss this?"

Harry was quiet for a few minutes. "Of course, of course. But can you give me any kind of hint as to what the case entails, so maybe I can prepare a little before we meet? My brain isn't what it used to be. Help an old man out."

Patrick didn't respond right away. He needed to think about this. And maybe get James's opinion. He reached over and grabbed a pad and pen and scribbled a note on a page, holding it up for James to read.

"Fitzgeralds?"

James nodded.

He scribbled again. "*Megan?*"

James shook his head in the negative.

"It's about the Fitzgeralds," Patrick told Harry.

Harry got really quiet for a really long time. Patrick almost thought he'd lost the call.

"What about the Fitzgeralds?"

"I can't tell you right now, but I can when we meet in person. I will tell you this could change everything."

"Uh-huh. Well, then, I'll meet with you and see if I can help you. How about later tonight? Say, around eleven? And we should meet somewhere public. That way we know the walls won't have ears."

"Er, okay." Patrick was confused. "Where is it you want to meet?"

"How about The Southbank, on the promenade?"

"Yeah, yeah. We'll meet you there around eleven."

"We?" Harry asked. "Who else is coming with you? I was under the impression it would be just the two of us."

"Nah. I'm bringing a couple people with me. People who need to be there."

"Who?" Harry sounded a little harsher, but Patrick shrugged it off.

"James Moore. You remember him when we were all officers, yeah? He's my partner. And my client, Ev—"

He broke off when James began slashing his hand next to his throat. "And my client will be there as well."

"Okay, well, I guess it would be okay to bring them. I'll see you at The Southbank at eleven."

Before Patrick had a chance to respond, Harry disconnected the call.

Patrick stared at his mobile for a few minutes before setting it back on the desk.

"Well, what did he say?" James asked.

"We're to meet him at The Southbank on the promenade at eleven tonight."

James quirked his eyebrow. "Did he say why we were meeting at such a public place?"

"He said it would be better to meet in public. That way, the walls wouldn't have ears."

James laughed. "You're fucking kidding, right?"

Patrick shook his head. "Nope, that's what he said."

James shook his head. "I don't bloody believe it."

Evelyn looked back and forth between the two men, confusion etched on her face. "I don't understand? What's so funny?"

James and Patrick exchanged a look, and James gestured for Patrick to go ahead and explain.

"Here in London, we have CCTV: Closed-Circuit Television. Basically, we have cameras all over the bloody city, showing what everyone is doing. Every move someone makes is being recorded when they're out on the streets of London. So, when Harry said he wanted to meet us at the Southbank Promenade so the 'walls wouldn't have ears,' that's ironic because we're going to be meeting somewhere that literally has eyes and will leave a record," Patrick stated.

"Then why are we meeting there?"

"Fuck if I know." Patrick shrugged. "Look, let's not read too much into this. He's agreed to meet, and he's agreed to help. We'll have an ally in the police department, and we'll bring down Mickey Fitzgerald."

James stood. "Listen, mate, you need to slow down and gain some perspective. Just because we have an ally in the department doesn't mean we'll be bringing the Fitzgeralds down immediately. It may take some time. You can't expect justice overnight."

"And why the bloody hell not? We have the evidence! We have quite literally a bloody head in a box. We have an officer to arrest him and press charges, and a solicitor to prosecute him. Why shouldn't I expect things to move quickly and for us to get rid of the fucking Fitzgeralds once and for all?"

"Because life doesn't work like that. Just because, on paper, it looks like we have an open-and-shut case, it doesn't mean we really have an open-and-shut case. There are so many factors that could work against us. We need to slow down and figure out if we're really doing everything, we can to make sure we don't get screwed over in the end." James gave Patrick an intense look.

Patrick stood. "I don't need the negativity. If you don't think we can accomplish this, then I need you to stay out of my way. This is the first chance we've had to make any progress, and I won't have you buggering it up."

The two men stood in the middle of the living room, staring at each other. You could cut the tension in the room with a knife.

James was the first to speak. "Listen, mate, I'm not going to get in your way, not intentionally anyway, but I'm not going to stand back and watch you get hurt. I'm going to be the voice of reason. I'm going to tell you when you're doing something stupid. I'm going to slow us down when I think we're going to do something rash. You're my best friend, and I'm not going to lose you to the Fitzgerald family or to your obsession. Do you understand?"

Patrick narrowed his eyes and breathed heavily through his nose. "Yeah, I understand."

"Great. So, what do we need to do to prepare for tonight?"

Patrick relaxed when James changed the subject. "We need to get Evelyn something appropriate to wear first, I think." He gestured to her.

She had been previously ignored during their spat.

James looked at her, giving her body a once-over. "I don't see anything wrong with what she's wearing right now."

She stood, placing her hands on her hips. "Well, I'm voting with Patrick that I need new clothes. So, it looks like you're outvoted."

"You'd think a bloke would get a little more thanks for going out of his way and finding you a perfectly good wardrobe for your stay in London, but I guess being a gentleman is a thankless job these days," James said dramatically.

"These clothes are two sizes too small."

"Her clothes are obscenely tight."

Patrick and Evelyn spoke over one another.

James held his hands up in defeat. "Alright, alright, I get the hint. We'll go out and get you some new clothes. Maybe on the way back we should take Evie to get some fish and chips at the place you love. Then come back here and talk strategy. How does that sound?"

Patrick shrugged. "Sounds good to me."

Evelyn nodded. "Sure, as long as during that strategizing meeting, you two fill me in on everything, and I mean *every-thing*, going on. If I'm going to be involved, I want to have an equal say in things. And in order to have an equal say, I have to have equal knowledge."

The two men exchanged looks. After a few more seconds, they both shrugged and turned to Evelyn.

"Fine. We'll tell you what's going on and will answer any questions you have. Within reason," Patrick conceded.

"But—" Evelyn started.

Patrick held up a hand and shook his head. "Within reason or nothing at all."

She sighed, crossing her arms across her chest, and Patrick's eyes were immediately drawn to how the shirt pulled tight against her breasts, accentuating them.

Apparently noticing where Patrick's gaze had landed, she let out a huff of frustration and lowered her arms, placing her hands on her hips. "Fine, within reason. Now can we go get me some clothes so I can breathe again? I'm afraid if I take anything more than shallow breaths, the button on these jeans is going to pop off and kill someone."

Patrick's gaze snapped back up to hers at the comment, and he couldn't help but start laughing. Soon, Evelyn and James joined in, the tension in the room dissipating. As soon as the three caught their breath, James gestured to the door, and they all exited, still smiling at her comment.

CHAPTER 13

EVELYN

The three of them returned to the apartment with full bellies and several shopping bags of clothes.

"I'm pretty sure I just spent my first month's food budget on a new wardrobe." Evelyn set the bags on the couch.

"Well, we'll feed you. Don't worry." Patrick walked to the fridge and put some food inside they had purchased at the supermarket on their walk back. "I think this is the most food James and I have had in our flat in months."

"Well, I'm probably not going to be here for a month, so it may end up being a problem for me if I end up going to Greece rather than back home."

Patrick froze, his back stiffening.

She cocked her head to the side, but before she could question his strange behavior, Patrick shook his head and turned around.

"Well, we can send some of this food with you when you leave, yeah? That way you won't starve." Patrick walked back into the living room.

"Thanks. That's really sweet of you." She paused and narrowed her eyes. "Who are you, and what did you do with Patrick?"

He looked stricken, but when she laughed, he joined in with her.

"Haha. I know I've been a complete arse, but I can be nice when I want to be."

She shook her head. "Nah, I don't believe it. James, I think we have a case of an invasion of the body snatchers here."

He took two steps back to the kitchen island, picked up the dish towel, and chucked it at her, who caught it as it got close.

"Children, children," James said with mock authority, "we need to focus on what it is we're going to do tonight."

The reminder of their situation sobered the group instantly. It was becoming easy to forget circumstance forced them together, and they were not just getting to know each other like normal young adults.

Evelyn sank onto the couch as Patrick took his spot in his desk chair. James took a seat on the floor, sitting cross-legged.

"So, where do we start?" Evelyn asked.

"Let's discuss tonight first, and then we'll answer any questions you have," James replied.

"Within reason," Patrick added, pointedly.

"Within reason," Evelyn parroted back.

"Tonight, we're going to meet at the Southbank Promenade at eleven. How much should we disclose to Harry?" James asked.

"I say we tell him everything," Patrick stated. "We know we can trust him, and we'll need him in the loop so we can get an arrest."

Evelyn shook her head. "I disagree. Shouldn't we keep some knowledge to ourselves? What if he turns out to *not* be trustworthy? Do you want to reveal all your aces so early in the game?"

Patrick frowned. "We've already been over this. Harry is like my father. He won't betray us. He's the most loyal and upstanding man I know."

"That's great, and I'm sure he is, but what harm is it if we keep some stuff to ourselves? Like the chief superintendent being in the pockets of the Fitzgeralds? Or Megan's head being delivered to your father? Or whatever else you found in that bag? I'm just saying maybe we should be a little more cautious." Evelyn rambled off key points.

Patrick opened his mouth to respond, but James interrupted him. "The lady has a point, and I'm wanting to agree with her. I say we only reveal what's absolutely necessary to get him to agree to be our man on the inside. Once we know for sure he's on our side, we can let him in on the things we've left out, little by little."

Patrick sighed. "Fine. Since I'm outvoted, I guess we'll do it your way. But what *do* we reveal at the meeting tonight?"

"We reveal that you're working with a solicitor's office to bring down the Fitzgeralds. We have the required evidence. We just need someone inside the Municipal Police Service to make the arrest and file charges. The solicitor's office will do the rest."

"How do we explain Evelyn?" Patrick gestured to her.

"We don't. We just say Evie's identity is on a need-to-know basis. That we're bringing her along because she's essential to the case, but we can't reveal how just yet."

Patrick turned to Evelyn. "Are you okay with that?"

She nodded. "Yeah. You know, I'm starting to think it would be fine if you left me behind. I mean, this will probably turn out to be pretty dangerous, right?"

Patrick furrowed his eyebrows. "How so?"

"Like, what if he has a gun? Doesn't this have the potential to become a shootout?"

Patrick shook his head. "Not likely. We have very strict gun laws here, and most police officers don't even carry a gun. More than likely, we'll be fine. Plus, we'll be meeting in clear view of the CCTV cameras. No one would be stupid enough to do anything like that on camera."

"But those guys at the airport yesterday, they had guns," Evelyn argued.

"Love, they're career criminals working for a major crime syndicate. Do you think they care about our strict gun laws?" James asked.

"Yeah, I guess you're right," Evelyn sighed. "Even knowing all of this, I'm going to be nervous the whole time. I'm not used to being in the middle of a criminal investigation."

"What are you used to?" Patrick leaned forward.

"Sitting in the library with my laptop and a pile of books, researching."

"I knew it!"

"No one likes someone who gloats."

"What do you like to do for fun?" Patrick asked. "Because that does not sound like fun."

Evelyn shrugged. "It's actually a lot of fun for me. I don't get out much. Since going to grad school, I've sort of distanced myself from my friends and become really engrossed in my research. The one thing I've been looking forward to was going to Greece and working on that dig. This trip is the first time I've ventured outside of my comfort zone and outside of the country. Actually, really traveled on my own. My mom was *so* worried that something would go wrong before I left. I kept reassuring her I'd be fine. How ironic that I find myself wanted by the mob."

"Don't worry," Patrick whispered to her, "we'll make sure you get to where you're supposed to in one piece."

She smiled. "I really appreciate the thought, but don't promise something that you may not be able to deliver. If these people are as dangerous as your dad, you, and James are implying, it seems the odds may be stacked against us. But let's not ponder on that. Tell me about this mysterious event that has you and James yelling at each other."

Instantly Patrick lost any humor in his face and put on a blank mask, hiding all of his emotions. "I don't want to talk about it."

James sighed. "C'mon, mate. She has the right to know."

Patrick whipped his head around to look at James. "No, she doesn't. I'm drawing the line here. I'll answer anything else, just not this."

She huffed. "Fine. Can you at least tell me what Mickey Fitzgerald looks like? Do you have a picture I can see?"

"Ye—" James started.

"No," Patrick interrupted.

"Patrick!" James shouted. "C'mon. She should at least know what she's up against."

Patrick shook his head. "No, she doesn't. I want her to know as little as possible because, if for some reason the Fitzgeralds outsmart us and capture her, if she knows nothing, maybe, just maybe, they won't kill her."

"So, I'm supposed to not know anything? Then what's the point of even coming tonight if you want to keep me in the dark?"

"I can't risk leaving you alone in the flat. What if the building is being watched? If you're with us, we at least have a chance to prevent anyone from taking you. Leaving you behind would leave you vulnerable," Patrick explained.

"I'm not some damsel in distress, you know. I can take care of myself."

"No, you can't," Patrick pronounced each word harshly. "Not against these people. Trust me. I would feel much better if you were to never leave my sight."

She growled in frustration. "And here we are, back to being an ass. I really thought we had moved past this. That we made some sort of progress in the last few hours."

"If caring about whether you live or die makes me an arse, then I'm the biggest arse in Great Britain and proud of it."

"You're infuriating!" Evelyn shouted.

"You're impossible!" Patrick shouted back.

"Oh my God, just sleep together already!"

That shut the two bickering adults up as they turned in shock at what James had said.

He shrugged his shoulders. "Seriously. If the two of you have it off and get it out of your system, maybe we could move past this mutual attraction and be productive."

"What?" she screeched. "You think that, I, that he, that we..." She shook her head.

Patrick turned to James. "Thanks a lot, mate. I need some air." He stood and walked out the door, slamming it behind him.

Taking her cue from Patrick's quick exit, Evelyn gathered up her shopping bags and bolted to Patrick's room.

When Evelyn emerged from Patrick's room, changed into appropriate clothing and ready to head out, Patrick had already returned to the flat. She had no idea how long he'd been there, but he was sitting and working at his computer. She had holed herself in the room, on the bed, with her laptop and research and was plugging away on her thesis. Just because she was stranded in London didn't mean her professors would excuse her if she didn't meet any of her deadlines. She wouldn't have a lot of the firsthand knowledge and research she was hoping to have by participating in the dig.

He had looked up when she walked into the room and gave her a small smile. She returned it and could feel a weight lift off her shoulders. They were good again. Sometime between breakfast this morning, and the teasing over the clothes in the bedroom, they had fallen into a rapport. To then dissolve into a shouting match was a little disheartening. However, the smile was a good start. Hopefully, they could continue to get along as the evening progressed. Or else it would be a long, long night.

They decided parking at their destination would be too difficult, so they opted for the Tube, which allowed Evelyn to tuck the experience away as a typical tourist thing to do in London that she could report later to her parents.

The Southbank promenade was bustling with people, and it was hard for the trio to find a place to stand where they wouldn't get run over by passersby. Evelyn looked out at the river as the moon reflected over the water. Behind her, the London Eye turned, and the multicolored lights of the County Hall shone. She didn't know there could be something so beautiful in the middle of such a busy city.

After what seemed like an hour, they finally found a spot near one of the old-fashioned-looking lamp posts that allowed them to get out of the crowd and hopefully allow Harry to notice them. The promenade was long and, even this late at night, was full of tourists.

"How is he ever going to find us here?" Evelyn had to shout so they could hear her over the crowd.

Patrick shrugged. "I have no bloody idea. I'm more concerned about how many people will overhear us here."

"Having second thoughts, mate?" James shouted.

Patrick shook his head. "No, not at all. I trust there's a reason Harry wanted to meet us here."

They waited in silence for a while.

"Favorite superhero." James broke the silence that had fallen around the group as they waited.

"What?" Evelyn asked.

"I'm pretty partial to Superman, myself. Indestructible he is. Plus, he has the Fortress of Solitude. You can't beat that."

"Spider-Man," Patrick smiled. "Fucking badass scientist who also kicks major ass. But is also human and can be defeated, unlike your choice, who can only ever be defeated by some rock only billionaires can buy."

James scoffed. "Exactly. That's why he's, as I said, indestructible."

"That takes all the fun out of superheroes if you can't fear for their safety. You read or watch something with Spider-Man, and you're on the edge of your seat hoping the villain won't defeat him. With Superman, as long as there's no kryptonite, there's no tension."

Evelyn smiled, watching the two men banter back and forth. You could tell they had this particular debate often, and that James started it in order to work as a distraction. It was working.

"You both are wrong," Evelyn spoke up. "The superior superhero is obviously Iron Man. He's a billionaire, not unlike Batman, however, he's also a badass scientist like Spider-Man, and he has the added bonus of the shrapnel floating in his chest which, if his arc reactor ever stops working, not only is his suit useless, the shrapnel will enter his heart and kill him."

The two men stared at her, and James started laughing. "I knew I liked you from the moment we crashed into each other in the middle of the night. But Evie, my sweet, sweet Evie, how very wrong you are. Let me tell you all the ways in which you are and why you should change your answer to Superman."

"Not a chance." Evelyn laughed. "We all know nothing you're going to say is going to change my mind. Iron Man is better than Superman for the crucial fact he is Marvel. Marvel beats DC any day of the week."

"Fuck yeah it does," Patrick agreed, holding his hand up for a high five, which Evelyn gladly slapped, "two against one, mate."

James shook his head. "I don't know how two very smart people can be so very wrong about something like this. DC is obviously better. We have Superman *and* Batman. Plus, the most recognizable villains."

"Marvel has recognizable villains," Evelyn retorted.

"Yeah? Name some."

"Doc Oc."

"Green Goblin."

"Loki."

Evelyn and Patrick looked at each other and smiled. They were on a roll. Completely in sync. Something fluttered inside Evelyn's chest as she held his gaze. She tried to push it aside and focus back on the conversation. She didn't have time to focus on whatever this feeling was inside. But for the first time since the airport, she thought of Patrick as attractive. Probably because below all the snarky, broody exterior, he was just as much of a nerd as she was. And that was definitely something she wanted to focus on later. Much later.

"Loki isn't exactly a villain, though. More like an anti-hero," James retorted, bringing her back fully to the conversation.

"I'm sure I could say the same about DC villains," Patrick volleyed.

And so, the three of them stood in the middle of the promenade and loudly debated all the merits of each and every superhero and their respective universe. Every once in a while, Evelyn caught Patrick glancing at his watch, frowning, as the time continued to creep past the agreed upon meeting time. Around eleven forty-five, the crowd had thinned out a bit and the noise level reduced. The trio, who had grown tired of standing, sat on a bench overlooking the Thames. Evelyn, still not on the right time zone, was struggling to keep her eyes open as their conversation slowed down.

"Mate, I don't think he's going to show." James leaned around Evelyn to talk to Patrick. "We've given him forty-five minutes. Evie here is going to fall asleep on this bench, and we still have the ride on the underground back to the flat. Let's go, and you can call him in the morning to find out why he didn't show."

Patrick vehemently shook his head. "No. Let's give it a little more time."

James sighed and leaned back.

Evelyn decided that if they were going to sit and wait, it wouldn't hurt to rest her eyes for a few minutes. She closed her eyes and relaxed for the first time all day. She thought about all the stuff she'd experienced since landing in London and couldn't believe she'd only been in town for a little over twenty-four hours. The rapport between them making it feel as if she'd been in town and known the boys for weeks. The boys. When did she start thinking about them as 'the boys'? Probably sometime between shopping and them all meeting back up about an hour before they were supposed to meet Harry.

She involuntarily started leaning to her right and, before she could catch herself, something warm and soft stopped her. Smiling, she burrowed herself into the warm, soft wall and relaxed even more. Whatever this wall was, it was comforting and smelled really nice. She tried to figure out what it was she was leaning on, but soon her mind decided to enjoy the warmth and not question it.

CHAPTER 14

PATRICK

Patrick looked at the sleeping girl on his shoulder and then looked up at James, who shrugged.

"I told you she was tired."

Patrick sighed and looked at her again. He almost shook her awake, but decided he would wait until she needed to be up. She was only here because he insisted, she had to be here. If he hadn't, she would be back at the flat, sleeping soundly in his bed. He shifted his arm, trying not to wake her as he wrapped it around her shoulders. He moved his body a couple of inches to the left until their sides were touching. He pulled her toward him until her head rested in the crook of his neck, and she relaxed again. He looked up to see James looking at him, eyebrows raised.

"You're telling me you're not attracted to her at all?" James gestured at their intimate positioning.

Patrick glared at him. "There's no attraction. We've been friendly. This is what a friend would do when their other friend just happens to fall asleep on their shoulder."

"So, if I were to fall asleep on your shoulder, you'd put your arm around me and let me snuggle into your neck?"

Patrick scoffed. "Of course."

James smirked. "Good. I'm glad, we've cleared this up because I've decided I'm going to shag her before she leaves."

Patrick couldn't help the rage that boiled up in him, his face forming a scowl. His arm tightened around Evelyn, pulling her toward him, almost possessively. He opened his mouth but stopped himself short before declaring his claim on her. What the fuck?

James laughed and pointed at him. "No attraction, my arse. You want her. Admit it. You've fancied her since the moment you grabbed her at the airport. Don't try to deny it. You're my best friend. I know you better than you know yourself."

Patrick sighed. "I'm not admitting to anything. Besides, I don't have the time for anything right now, and she's going to leave in a few days, hopefully, so there's no point in starting anything."

"I never said you had to be in a relationship with the girl. Just a one-off. It's been a long time since you've had a shag, and you're way overdue. And what better than a girl who's only in the country for a little bit? It can be a little wham bam thank you ma'am, and then she's on her way and you'll never have to see her again."

Patrick shook his head. "For someone who claims to know me better than myself, you really don't know me. I could never do that to someone I know. Some girl I pick up at a club? Sure. One night, never call her again. But by the time I'd get to the point where I'd be able to sleep with her and have her gone, I'll have known Evelyn for days. She would be an acquaintance, possibly a friend, and I could never do that. It will be much simpler if we remain not intimately involved. Too many emotions I don't want to deal with."

"You know, you're allowed to be happy."

"I know."

"Okay. Just making sure you're aware, since you seem so fucking set against doing something for yourself."

"I'm not set against doing something for myself. I just said, in any other circumstance, I would take the leap. See if anything would come of this. But, I can't. Not during this case."

"*Sooo*, why can't I shag her, if you're going to let her leave thinking you're just friends?"

Patrick smirked. "Because, mate, I saw her first."

They both started laughing, Patrick trying to not move his body so he wouldn't wake Evelyn.

As their laughter died, James wiped at his eyes and grew serious again. "How much longer are we going to wait? It's been over an hour. I don't think he's going to show. I know how much you hate to admit it, but maybe we should leave. Evie has already checked out. She has the right idea."

Patrick closed his eyes. "Maybe you're right. Maybe we should—"

"Holy shit."

Patrick opened his eyes and looked over his shoulder to where James was looking. Walking up the sidewalk toward them was Harry. It was well after midnight, and the Southbank Promenade was, while not deserted, certainly less crowded. Patrick gently shook Evelyn, and she lifted her head off his shoulder. She opened her eyes and looked at him, blushing, before pulling away.

A pit in Patrick's stomach grew at the sight of the man walking in their direction. While he was confident, they had made the right choice coming here tonight, there was a nagging feeling that maybe his confidence was a wee bit misplaced. And that feeling, the one that lingered in the back of his consciousness, made him realize he should be ready for any scenario tonight.

Because nothing was off the table.

CHAPTER 15

EVELYN

Evelyn opened her eyes as her soft wall moved. Looking up, she realized she wasn't leaning against a wall at all. She was actually leaning against Patrick, who was looking at her. Her face warmed, and she looked away before moving down the bench from him, leaving some space between them. She rubbed the sleep out of her eyes and turned her head in the direction the boys were looking.

An older man, with graying hair and wearing a dress shirt with slacks, was walking toward them. She looked around. The Southbank had emptied quite a bit since she'd fallen asleep. It was almost deserted. James and Patrick stood, the latter offering his hand to help her get to her feet. She accepted it and tried to hide the heat that filled her face as their hands touched. As soon as she was on her feet, she dropped his hand and busied herself with dusting off her pants as they waited for the man to finish his approach.

The man stopped in front of them. "Patrick, mate." He smiled. "It has been too long."

Patrick returned his smile. "Harry, it's good to see you."

The two men closed the gap between them and embraced.

"I wish we could have got together under better circumstances," Harry said as they pulled apart.

"Yes, but I do thank you for taking the time to meet with us. I had no idea who else to call."

"Nonsense. You know I'd do anything for you." Harry turned toward Evelyn and James and smiled. "James, it's good to see you as well." He extended his hand, which James accepted. "And you, I don't think I've had the pleasure."

Before Evelyn could respond, Patrick spoke. "This is my client, and she wishes to stay anonymous, if you don't mind."

Harry's hand dropped back to his side. "I don't mind at all. It's a pleasure to meet your acquaintance, Miss."

Evelyn opened her mouth to speak, but was, again, interrupted by Patrick.

"She's happy to meet you, too. We didn't think you were going to make it. We were just about to leave."

Harry coughed. "Well, I got here at eleven, like we agreed upon, but I had such a shit time trying to find you through the crowd. I went and got a cuppa and waited until the crowd thinned out."

Something wasn't right. Evelyn couldn't put her finger on it, but her gut was saying Harry was full of bullshit. She didn't know him, so maybe he was always squirrely like this. Plus, Patrick didn't seem to want her talking, so she'd just keep her mouth shut. James nudged her. She looked at him and he subtly shook his head and returned his gaze to Harry. She got the message loud and clear. There was something off. It wasn't just her imagination. James noticed it too. But unfortunately, Patrick wouldn't want to hear it, so they couldn't question Harry in front of him. He'd become defensive of his mentor. He would have to put together the pieces himself. This man wasn't who Patrick wanted him to be.

For his part, Patrick was looking confused as well. "So, you left us waiting here for over an hour? Why have us meet in such a public place if you didn't want people around?"

"I have my reasons," Harry barked. "Now, enough with the questions. I'm here, aren't I? It's late. I have work in the morning. Tell me about this case."

Patrick closed his eyes for a second and then opened them, looking a little wearier than before. "Well, a few days ago, a case was brought to me from the solicitor's office—"

"Colin?" Harry interrupted.

"Yes," Patrick replied slowly. "Anyway, the solicitor's office gave me this case, dealing with the Fitzgeralds—"

"Why didn't they bring it to the police? Aren't we more equipped to handle a crime syndicate than two young, inexperienced private investigators?"

Patrick narrowed his eyes at that, and Evelyn could see him visibly tensing up. He looked like he was going to yell or say something he might regret, and they had all agreed earlier that evening they would remain levelheaded and calm, in order to maintain the upper hand. She reached out and gently laid a hand on his arm. He jumped, but then relaxed. He looked over his shoulder and gave her a brief smile before turning back to Harry.

"You know why he came to us instead of the police. I don't have to waste my breath spelling it out. Do you want to hear about the case or not? You're right, it's late, and we would all rather be in bed right now."

"Please, continue. I promise to not interrupt anymore."

Patrick took a deep breath and slowly exhaled.

Evelyn moved to remove her hand, but he stopped her, taking her hand.

"As I was saying, the solicitor's office brought this case to me a few days ago. A former lover of Mickey Fitzgerald's came forward, saying she had sufficient evidence that would put Fitzgerald behind bars for a long time. Well, when they went to meet her, she lost her nerve and decided to flee the country, taking the evidence with her. I met her at the airport and retrieved the evidence. All we need is someone to make the arrest and press charges."

"And that's where I come in?" Harry asked.

"Yes. We'll need you to arrest Fitzgerald and make sure there are charges brought up against him, and Colin and his team will do the rest."

Harry brought his hand to his chin and began rubbing it. "What kind of evidence do you have, exactly?"

"Photographic evidence," Patrick responded.

"I don't know, Patrick. This seems awfully risky, what with circumstantial evidence. Why would I risk my career, and my life, by arresting Mickey Fitzgerald, only to have him back on the street within twenty-four hours?"

"He won't be out on the street in twenty-four hours. We have some pretty solid evidence, and he's going away for a long, long time." Patrick's grip on Evelyn's hand tightened as he struggled to maintain his cool.

She gave him a reassuring squeeze as James took a step closer to them, closing her in between the two. He was obviously getting uncomfortable with the current situation and suspected something was going to go wrong, and soon. And, to be honest, the bad feeling Evelyn had at the beginning of the meeting had only intensified as it continued. The tension between the four of them had only begun to grow. And if she was feeling off about the situation, the boys, being investigators, were more than likely also feeling it. Which was probably why she was currently sandwiched tightly between them.

"Let me see it then," Harry responded. "Let me see this hard-core evidence you have. Convince me you have a case."

"I won't be showing you anything until I can be assured, you're with us."

"So secretive. C'mon, Patrick. You're like a son to me. I was there for you when your father wasn't. You can trust me. You know I have your back."

"I'd still like your word you're on our side. That we can trust you."

"You can trust me. I don't know where all this mistrust is coming from, but I'm guessing it's from James and your American tart. I promise, I'm on your side."

All three immediately tensed at his words. Patrick's grip on Evelyn's hand tightened as James moved in even closer. Evelyn couldn't help but start shaking in fear.

"We never told you she was American," Patrick stated.

Harry sighed. "Oh, bugger. You're right. I suppose you didn't. My mistake. I guess the cat is out of the bag now." He reached behind his back and pulled out a gun, pointing it at the trio. "You'll hand over the evidence and the girl, and I'll let you go."

Patrick looked like he'd been slapped in the face. "What the fuck! I thought you were clean."

Harry chuckled. "Poor naïve Patrick. I was never clean. I'm just an excellent actor. Anyone who is clean on the force is a fool and won't last long. You're lucky you got out when you did, or else your poor father would have been planning two funerals."

"I trusted you." Patrick's voice trembled.

"Yes, and you were a fool. Now, hand over the girl and the bag."

"Do you think we'd be stupid enough to carry that much evidence around with us?"

"No, I guess you wouldn't. I'll just take the girl then."

As he took a step toward Evelyn, Patrick moved in front of her, and James grabbed her, pulling her back. It was as if they'd rehearsed the move as it went so smoothly.

Patrick took a swing at Harry, which Harry easily blocked. He made a lunge for Harry's gun hand.

Evelyn watched the two men struggle for control of the weapon. She couldn't tell who had the upper hand, which made her nervous.

Suddenly, a blast rang through the quiet of the night.

Evelyn screamed, her hands coming up to her ears, startled by the sound.

She watched helplessly as Patrick fell to the ground and Harry ran from the scene.

CHAPTER 16

EVELYN

James let go of Evelyn, and she rushed over to Patrick's side. He was lying on the ground, but he was still conscious. She inspected his body, trying to find where he had been hit.

"Oh, my God," she cried.

Patrick moaned on the ground. He moved his head back and forth.

She gasped.

The left side of Patrick's head was gushing blood. She couldn't even see where the wound was, there was so much blood.

"Fuck, fuck, fuck." Tears raced down Evelyn's cheeks. "What do I do?"

James knelt next to her. "Fucker runs fast. I couldn't catch him. What do we have?"

"Harry shot him in his head. He's losing a lot of blood." Evelyn never took her gaze off of Patrick, who was growing pale and sweating, but he was still mostly conscious.

James ripped his shirt over his head and tossed it at Evelyn. "Use this to apply pressure to the wound. Don't stop, don't ease up. It's important you use as much pressure as you can to stop that blood. I'm going to run and get a cab."

James moved to run into the road, but Evelyn called out to him. "Wait! Why aren't we calling an ambulance to take him to the hospital? Wouldn't that be faster?"

"We're not taking him to hospital!" James shouted, running toward the road.

She turned her attention back to Patrick. She wadded up James's T-shirt and pressed it to the wound as hard as she could.

He hissed.

"I'm sorry," Evelyn whispered.

"It's okay." He closed his eyes. "Bloody hell, this hurts. I always thought getting shot would be heroic, but nope, just hurts like hell."

"I'm so sorry. If it weren't for me, you wouldn't have gotten shot."

He opened his eyes and gave her a half-smile. "What? You think I'd let him take you? Did you think I was going to let you be collateral damage or something?"

She laughed, wiping her cheeks with her shoulders. "Haha. I knew when the time came, you wouldn't let me get hurt. You're a better man than I thought you were, Patrick, Patrick?" She looked down, and his eyes were closed. He no longer seemed conscious. "Patrick?!" she shouted, jostling him. "Wake up!"

He moaned, but didn't wake.

"James! Where are you? You need to hurry!"

James came running back to her. "The cab's waiting at the corner. We need to move him there and keep pressure on the wound at the same time. I can't carry him by myself. Do you have anything that we can use as a tourniquet?"

Evelyn moved her hands to her pants and undid the belt buckle before ripping the belt out of the loops. She handed it to James. They worked together to wrap the shirt around Patrick's head before using the belt to hold it in place. Once the belt was tightened, James moved so Patrick's arm was around his shoulder, and he was supporting most of his weight.

"Love, I need you to get under his other arm and help me move him. We need to do this quickly. I've paid the cab way too much money to get us to where we're going as quickly as possible."

She moved into place as quickly as she physically could. With James supporting most of Patrick's weight, it was easy for her to keep up and help support Patrick. The cab wasn't as far off as she'd thought it would be, and they arrived at it almost instantaneously. The cabbie jumped out of the driver's side and opened up the rear door for them. The three of them managed to get Patrick into the back seat, lying down. Evelyn didn't hesitate before climbing in after him.

"Are you sure you want to ride back there with him? I don't mind."

She shook her head. "I'm smaller. I fit better. Stop wasting time. Let's go. I don't like the shade of white he's turning right now."

James didn't say another word as he shut the back door and ran around the car to get into the passenger seat. As soon as

James was in, the cabbie didn't hesitate before peeling away from the curb, speeding down the street.

Evelyn sat back and moved Patrick's head to rest in her lap. He was burning up and sweating profusely. She started running her hands through his dark hair, wanting to show him some comfort but stopped herself short. She didn't want to hurt him anymore than he already was.

Up in the front seat, she could hear James talking on his cell phone, but she couldn't make out what he was saying or who he was talking to. She instead focused on the man lying on the seat next to her.

They weren't in the cab for long before they pulled up in front of a building. James was out of the cab before it had even come to a complete stop. He ran around and threw open the door. She climbed out as the door to the building flew open and an older woman came running out, pushing a metal gurney. Evelyn jumped out of the way so she wouldn't get run over by the cart. James and the woman easily transferred Patrick to the gurney and ran inside. Evelyn quickly followed.

Evelyn found herself in a waiting room. There were non-descript chairs lining the walls, a counter, and several potted plants. She looked around. She couldn't see James, the woman, or Patrick anywhere. She looked toward the doorway to the right and surmised they probably went that way, but the hallway was dark, and she really didn't want to go exploring. She'd had enough adventure for the night. James would come out and find her and explain what was going on. Wouldn't he?

She moved to one of the chairs and took a seat. As she sat down, she started shaking. It took her a minute to realize she was sobbing uncontrollably. The events of the last thirty minutes hit her all at once, and every emotion she had been holding in overwhelmed her. She was on their radar. They knew who she was. The mob wanted her, and they sent a police officer to kidnap her. In public. In front of those closed-circuit television things Patrick had told her about. And with a gun! Patrick got shot making sure the mob didn't kidnap her.

What the fuck had she gotten into? All she wanted to do was go home. Fuck Greece! Who needed to go to *another* foreign country, into more unfamiliar lands, with even more strangers? All she wanted to do right now was curl up in bed with her mom and cry and never leave. Tell her mom she was right she should have never left. It's a dangerous world out here, and she found herself in the middle of it.

She moved to bury her face in her hands and noticed they were covered in blood. Patrick's blood. She cried even harder. She wrapped her arms around her body and slipped to the floor. She curled up on the cold, hard linoleum and listened to the quiet of the strange building she was in. Yet another situation she had no control over since arriving in London.

Somewhere in the back of the building, she could hear a man scream. And scream and scream. She recognized it as Patrick. He sounded almost inhuman and in so much pain. The screaming was relentless and growing more and more frantic. Evelyn moved her hands to her ears and closed her eyes. She started rocking back and forth, humming the tune of her favorite Beatles song, as the tears continued to roll unchecked down her face.

"Evelyn," a voice called as a hand gently nudged her. "Evie, wake up."

She blinked open her eyes and noticed the sun was peeking through the windows of the lobby. She sat up and grimaced as her back popped.

She looked at James from her place on the floor. "What's going on? What time is it? How's Patrick?"

James lowered himself to sit next to her on the floor. He rubbed his face, which was showing a past five-o'clock shadow. "It's late, or early, I guess. I would guess it's around five. Patrick's doing okay. He's resting, but he's out of commission for a while. The good news is, he wasn't hit. The bullet just grazed him. He was fucking lucky. The bad news is, the wound was deep, and he lost quite a bit of blood, but my mum was able to stitch him back together. And my mum says he probably has a concussion from hitting the ground. We're waiting for him to wake up so she can make sure he's coherent enough to send home. Where we will be tasked to make sure he doesn't move for a few days, while his body recuperates from the blood loss and recovers from the concussion."

She blinked, trying to process everything. "Wait, your mom? She's a doctor?"

"Veterinarian. This is her clinic. I didn't know where else to take him, and she lives in a flat above the clinic. Which, I want to apologize, we should have let you up there, and you could have slept in the guest room rather than on the floor."

"It's okay. You had more important things to deal with than my sleeping arrangements."

"Do you want to go up there and take a shower and freshen up, or something?"

She shook her head. "I'm okay. I'd like to see Patrick, if that's okay?"

James nodded. "Of course."

He stood and offered his hand, which Evelyn gladly accepted. As she stood, the full effects of having slept on the floor for hours hit her. James took her by the hand and led her through the doorway and into the back of the clinic, where all the exam rooms were. He took her into the first room on the right, and there was Patrick, lying on the exam table, sleeping.

Since the clinic was a veterinary clinic, it wasn't a normal exam table. It was completely metal, with metal legs and wheels. In order to make it more comfortable, they had placed lots of blankets on the surface, and there was a pillow placed under his head. He wasn't wearing a shirt, and his head had a large white bandage wrapped around it. He wasn't as pale as he had been the night before right after he was shot, but his breathing was still shallow.

She brought her hands to her mouth to stifle a sob.

James wrapped his arm around her shoulder and pulled her to him. "He's going to be fine, Evie. He's fucking lucky the bullet just grazed his head, right around his left temple. The wound really looked much worse than it was. Head wounds bleed a lot, making them look more urgent than they really are. If he were actually shot, it would have been worse. Much, much worse."

She filled in the blank that James wasn't going to say. Dead. He would have been dead. She would have lost one of her only friends in this country. Someone who drove her crazy but also who was someone she really wanted to get to know better.

"There's a chair right over here. I can't promise how comfortable it is, but it's probably loads more comfortable than the floor you slept on."

She nodded, still not trusting her voice. She moved out from under James's arm and pulled the chair up right next to the table Patrick was lying on. She sat and stared at him.

"Since you're back here with him, I'm going to run upstairs and take a shower and try to freshen up a little. Then maybe you should, too, considering..." he trailed off, gesturing at her.

She looked at her hands. Patrick's dried blood still covered them. She'd totally forgotten about that. She nodded. "Okay. That's a good idea."

"That phone in the corner is connected to a phone in my mum's kitchen. It's leftover from when I was little and she needed to check on me while she was down here working. If you need anything, or if something happens, pick it up, and the other end will ring."

She nodded again.

He placed a hand on her shoulder. "I promise, everything is going to be okay. Try to relax. After we're both cleaned up and refreshed, we'll sit down and talk about what happened."

"Yeah, and we need to figure out what to do next. Because I don't think we had a backup plan if this one went pear-shaped."

"We didn't. Patrick didn't want to make one. He was so sure—" James broke off, shaking his head, "we'll talk when I get back. I promise. try to relax, and definitely try not to worry."

He turned and walked out of the room, leaving her alone with Patrick and her thoughts. Everything they had planned relied one-hundred percent on Harry not being a back-stabbing bastard. They weren't counting on him betraying them. Patrick had been so sure of his loyalty; they didn't even try to research and find someone else. Patrick's father was counting on them to find someone to arrest Fitzgerald, and they failed. For now, at least.

Patrick's father. Someone needed to tell him Patrick got hurt. Right? Her parents would want to know if she'd been shot and was being patched up by a veterinarian. But would Patrick's father? Patrick and Harry both had alluded to a strained relationship between the two men, and two days ago, when they were in his flat, their relationship didn't scream warm and fuzzy. Patrick called him by his first name, for Pete's sake.

She wouldn't be telling any of the events of the past twenty-four hours to her parents any time soon. As far as they were concerned, her trip to London involved sightseeing and eating lots of fish and chips, alone, in the solitary space of a hotel room. When this was all over, when they figured out what they were doing, she was going to have to have the boys take her to a few places to take some pictures and get brochures and then have them help her alter the time and date stamps on them, to make her lies more believable. She hated lying to her parents, but telling them she was almost kidnapped twice, would not go over well. She could guarantee that. They would never let her leave the house again. Which, at this point, wouldn't necessarily be a bad thing, but she knew eventually she'd get over the trauma of this trip and want to venture out again. She might be eighty, but she had to think it could happen.

She looked back at the man lying on the table, and her heart ached. He jumped in front of a man with a gun for her. He wrestled a man with a gun for her. He got shot for *her*. They didn't know each other well, only been acquainted for forty-eight hours, and yet it was beginning to feel like there wasn't a time when she didn't know him. Yes, their personalities didn't mesh well and their stubbornness clashed with the others, but she had to admit, it had become kind of fun to verbally spar with him. He looked kind of cute when he was being frustrated and furious with her. Working him up had become quite the pastime.

Looking at him now, she wished he'd wake up and spar with her. She didn't even care if he woke up and resented her for getting him hurt. She wanted him to wake up so she knew he was okay.

She reached out and took his hand. It was cold, which made sense. James said he had lost a lot of blood. She wondered how long it would take for him to recuperate from an injury like this. Especially since he wasn't in a hospital, and she was pretty sure he didn't get a blood transfusion. She was ninety-nine percent sure animal blood wasn't compatible with human blood. But she was a historian, not a scientist. She hoped James hurried back. She had so many questions. And he was the only one with answers. Well, and his mom, who she still hadn't met. She'd seen her briefly last night when she and James wheeled Patrick in from the cab. And then she was gone.

Evelyn sighed and held Patrick's hand between the two of hers. She rubbed her hands over his. "C'mon, Patrick. You need to wake up. Please. Wake up and let me know you're okay."

She moved her chair closer to the table and rested her head against his body. He didn't smell right. Gone was the rich, woodsy smell that had become comforting the last few days. A clinical, antiseptic smell had replaced it. She closed her eyes, taking comfort in the rising and falling of his chest with every shallow breath he took. She allowed that feeling to lull her to sleep.

CHAPTER 17

PATRICK

There was a weight on his chest, making it difficult to breathe. He was cold. Freezing. Except in the spot where the weight was. That was warm. And his entire body ached. His head was full of a fog, and he couldn't quite clear it out and think properly. He tried to remember what had happened, but the fog wasn't allowing any thoughts through. He focused and then remembered. Meeting Harry at The Southbank and Harry betraying them. Harry trying to kidnap Evelyn. Getting shot. And then nothing else after that.

Fuck. Am I dead? He started to evaluate and take an inventory of everything. He was breathing. Yes, he could definitely tell he was breathing. That was a clear sign he wasn't dead. But he couldn't wake up. His eyelids were heavy and glued to his cheeks. He needed to wake up. He needed to open his eyes.

What if Harry had ambushed James and Evelyn after he got shot and the Fitzgeralds had captured Evelyn and they were torturing her right now while he lay on the pavement?

Wake up, Patrick, he urged himself. *Wake the fuck up!*

His eyes flew open, and first thing he noticed was he was no longer on the pavement near the Thames. He was in a room somewhere. His eyes adjusted to the dimly lit room, which was when he noticed the reason, he was having trouble breathing was because someone was sleeping on him. Their hands were on his, and their head was on his chest. He turned his head slightly toward the person and breathed a sigh of relief. Evelyn. She was fine and keeping vigil over his sickbed. He wondered where they were and how long he had been out. They weren't in hospital because there would be more machines and more people. Definitely more people. He turned his head to the other side. On the wall there was a giant poster of a dog running through a field of grass. He knew that poster. They were in James's mum's veterinary clinic.

He closed his eyes against the headache forming. He had been so confident everything would go their way. He didn't even know where to even start with coming up with a new plan. And James and Evelyn were going to look to him to lead, and he was fucking useless.

He pounded his free hand on the metal cart, causing the whole thing to shake. Jostled by the movement, Evelyn sprung up from where she was sleeping on him with a gasp.

Her head whipped over to look at him, and she immediately started crying. "Oh, my God, you're awake!"

Patrick winced, but nodded. "Yeah, I'm awake," he whispered, struggling to even do that. He tried to sit up, but she stopped him, placing a hand on his chest. Her warm touch on his cold skin made him keenly aware of the fact he was shirtless.

"Stop," she said, softly. "You need your rest, and trying to get up right now doesn't constitute resting."

"I need to bloody well get up, is what I need to do. We don't have time to rest. I need to get started on a new plan. We need to figure out what we're going to do about getting you home. We need—"

"Patrick, you were shot in the head. Well, technically, the bullet grazed you, but fuck it, for all intents and purposes, we're going to say Harry shot you. The important part is you've lost a lot of blood, and you have a concussion. What you need to do is rest and do what James's mom says. When we get back to your flat, we can start planning what James and I can do next while you get better."

Patrick shook his head. "You can't—"

"I don't want to hear about what I can or can't do. You were shot. You. Were. Shot. You lose your vote about what's going to happen. Your new job is to relax and heal and not strain yourself. I don't want you to kill yourself over this. It's not worth your life. Mickey Fitzgerald is going to go to prison, eventually. You don't need to be the one to personally do it."

"Yes, I fucking do," he yelled, sitting up and immediately regretting it. He brought his hand up to his head, wincing. "I need to be the one to bring him down. It has to be me. No one else."

"Why?" She brought her hand up to lay on his shoulder. "Why does it have to be you?"

"Because he fucking killed my mum!"

Silence fell over the small room. The only sound was his heavy breathing and the ticking of the clock on the wall.

"What? Is that why Harry said last night your father would have had to plan two funerals?"

Patrick closed his eyes and got as comfortable as he could on the metal gurney. "Yes."

"When?"

"A little over a year ago."

"I'm sorry, Patrick. I'm so sorry. I've made a complete mess of this for you. You were hoping to use Megan to get Fitzgerald, and I was a complete klutz and fucked the whole thing up."

"Don't blame yourself for this mess. We don't know for certain anything would have been better if you weren't here right now. If anyone is to blame, it's Harry."

She nodded and wiped away her tears. "God, I'm so tired of crying. I don't usually cry this much, so please don't think I'm always this emotional."

"Considering you were almost snatched last night and watched someone get shot, I think you're holding up pretty fucking well."

"You didn't see me last night in the waiting room."

Patrick reached out, taking her hand. "You're holding up pretty fucking well. I'm standing by that statement."

"If you don't mind me asking, why did Fitzgerald kill your mom? Was it because you and your dad were working against him?"

"It was a case of mistaken identity. He had a hit out on a female solicitor who had something against him. His asshole goons saw my mum leaving my father's office late one night and thought she was the solicitor. Gunned her down right there on the street."

"Oh, my God."

Patrick closed his eyes, tightening his grip on Evelyn's hand. "Dad came running out of the office when he heard the shots, but by the time he made it to her, she was already dead. No time to even call for an ambulance. It was shortly after that Colin and I began working harder to bring the Fitzgeralds down. We want our city to be safer."

Evelyn rose, and standing on her tiptoes, wrapped her arms around him in a hug. He winced when she brushed his head but ignored the pain and brought an arm around her to return the hug.

"Ah, um." Someone cleared their throat behind them, and they leapt apart, turning toward the door. James stood there, still in the clothes he wore the night before, but looking freshly shaved and showered. "Sorry to interrupt this touching moment, but Evelyn, you should head upstairs and wash up."

Patrick looked at her and noticed, for the first time, the blood on her hands and how disheveled she looked.

"Yeah, okay." She took a hesitant step toward the door.

"Out the door, take a left, first door on your right leads up to the flat. My mum will show you where everything is."

She nodded, looking once more at Patrick, before exiting the room, leaving the two men behind.

"How are you feeling?" James asked.

"Like utter shit, but I'll get over it. Good thinking bringing me here rather than the hospital."

"It was pure instinct and adrenaline. I didn't even start thinking coherent thoughts until this morning. Poor Evie slept on the floor in the waiting room all night because I didn't even think about making her get up and go sleep in my mum's flat. All I could think about was getting you here and making sure you didn't fucking die on us."

"Well, thanks, mate. I don't even know how to thank you for saving me."

"Don't thank me. Thank my mum. She was amazing. She stitched you up. There was so much blood, I didn't think that—" He choked up.

Patrick closed his eyes. "I'm sorry for scaring you."

"Only you would apologize for someone shooting you."

Patrick opened his eyes. "I can't believe Harry fucking shot me."

James looked at him, concerned. "How are you feeling? Emotionally, I mean. The man was basically your father."

"I'm trying not to think about it right now. At the moment, I don't think I can handle the situation. I think once we get back to the flat and I have time to process what the hell went down last night, the full weight of the betrayal will hit me. But right now, my head fucking hurts and all I want to do is go home and lie down in my comfy bed and make a plan for where we go from here. Because we've fucked up, James. We don't have anyone else to arrest Fitzgerald. We don't have a backup plan. And we've screwed over Evelyn. She's stuck here and can't go home or to Greece, and that's on us."

James nodded. "Yeah, I've been thinking about Evie and her situation, and it makes me feel worse than anything else. We promised her we'd meet with Harry last night and then she'd be on a plane in a couple of days. And now..."

"And now we don't even have a timeline. When can we get out of here?"

"As soon as mum convinces Evie she needs a long hot shower, rather than just scrubbing your blood off her hands, she'll be down here to discharge you, on the grounds you will go home, relax, and *not* go chasing after criminals."

Patrick smiled. "Your mum knows me too well."

"That she does. And you will go home and relax. I'm going to see to that." He grew serious. "You're lucky that bullet just grazed you. There was so much blood, I thought for sure the bullet had actually entered your body. I've never been more scared in my life. My mum didn't have any anesthesia she could use on you, only animal grade, so she had to work on you without any painkillers. It's something I never want to experience again."

Patrick looked at his friend, and his chest tightened. He really didn't know how serious everything had been last night. But looking at all the dried blood on Evelyn's hands, and listening to James describe how his mum had fixed him up, it was sobering, to say the least. He could have died last night. He could have died, and his dad wouldn't know he really did love him. He would have died, and his dad would have had to bury him next to his mum, thinking he wished he had any other man as a father than him. How fucking selfish was he?

"Hey, don't you dare start feeling fucking guilty about anything that happened. It's not your fault. You thought we could trust Harry. I trusted your judgment. We were all responsible for deciding to go last night. You weren't solely responsible for the events that transpired. Harry betrayed us. You didn't."

Before Patrick could respond, the door to the room opened, and James's mum walked in. "So, let's see about getting you home."

CHAPTER 18

EVELYN

James opened the door to the flat and let Evelyn through. She rushed into Patrick's room, picked up the bag of clothes she'd bought the day before, and rushed into the bathroom to change. While she had showered at the clinic, she could still feel the dried blood on her skin. Patrick's blood. She would never be able to associate the outfit she had been wearing with anything other than Patrick getting shot, so she might as well throw it in the garbage. She threw on her new outfit quickly and walked back to the bedroom as James was settling into a chair and Patrick was settling back against his pillows under his comforter.

She looked around the room and was about to settle herself on the floor when Patrick spoke up.

"Here, why don't you sit next to me? You've sat on the floor enough the last twenty-four hours."

She eyed the small spot on the bed next to him. They would have to be awfully close in order to both fit there. They had spent a lot of time in close quarters lately, and Evelyn really wanted to sit down and analyze her feelings about everything, but there wasn't time. She decided, for once, to just enjoy the moment.

She moved toward the bed, sitting on his right side. Their legs were touching and, to make matters even more intimate, he moved his arm around her shoulders, pulling her close to him.

"Do you mind?" he asked quietly, nearly whispering in her ear. "I've found your presence comforting, and I've come to enjoy having you close like this."

She shook her head. "I don't mind." If a hot guy wanted to flirt with her, then she was going to go along with it. She could over analyze every little thing after her life was no longer in danger.

"Oi," James called out, "best mate still in the room. Please don't forget that."

"Noted."

She leaned closer to Patrick, and he began running his hand up and down her arm.

"So," James spoke up, "where do we go from here? What's our next step?"

Patrick sighed. "We need to find a new police officer to arrest the Fitzgeralds, but I don't even know where to start. Are there any officers who are clean anymore? Or are they all in Fitzgerald's pockets?"

"There has to be," James replied. "I refuse to believe every officer in Tower Hamlet is crooked."

"But last night, Harry implied every cop was crooked. He said either you're crooked or you're dead. At least that's what I took out of his ranting," Evelyn commented.

"Yeah, that's what I understood, too," Patrick agreed.

James shook his head. "What if Fitzgerald and his friends just *think* all the police are in his pocket? What if there's someone who's a double agent, so to speak?"

"But how will we know? How will we determine who's worth trusting? We thought we could trust Harry, and look how that turned out," Evelyn questioned.

"I can do some research, and hack into computers with personnel files and start weeding through every officer in the borough until we find one who's trustworthy. Unfortunately, doing that will take some time. In fact, it could take weeks," James replied.

"Don't worry about the time frame. Just focus on being thorough and finding someone. How certain will you be once you find someone that they're clean?" asked Evelyn.

"Ninety percent. I don't think I can be any more certain. We will have to hope they don't show up to a meeting with a gun and take us all out."

Patrick sighed. "What if we don't find someone? If you go through everyone in there and every single cop is in that man's pocket, what then? We need a backup plan for our backup plan. We need to plan for the unthinkable."

The three were quiet.

"What if we draw him out and make him commit a crime in a different borough? Use jurisdiction in our favor. Then we'll have the other borough's officers arrest him. He doesn't have all of London under his thumb. Someone will have to arrest him," James piped up.

Patrick's face lit up like a Christmas tree. "James, you're bloody brilliant. But how do we draw him out? Get him out of his comfort zone, so to speak?"

"Me," Evelyn spoke up.

"What?"

"No bloody way!" James and Patrick shouted over each other.

"They want me. What if we use me as bait to draw him out? And his crime is attempted kidnapping, or even kidnapping. You guys can have the local police on notice, and they can swoop in and arrest him before he even has a chance to take me."

Patrick was vehemently shaking his head next to her. "No. We're not using you as bait. It's too dangerous and too risky. What if the officers don't believe us? What if they don't get there in time? I'm not going to sit back as Fitzgerald takes you and fucking murders you."

"I agree with Patrick, sweetheart. It's too risky."

"It's only a backup plan, right? We're counting on the fact you guys will find someone here who isn't dirty, so if you do, we won't ever have to use this plan. If you don't, won't we be desperate? And don't desperate times call for desperate measures or whatever?"

Patrick shook his head. "I'm still not liking it. At all. We'll find another way. We'll draw him out in a different way, if it comes down to it."

"Yeah, there are always more ways that involve not sacrificing a life."

She sighed. "Fine, but if you can't think of anything, my offer stands."

"We won't be using it," Patrick stated firmly. "We'll figure something out."

James nodded. "We'll think of something when the time comes. But you're right. Hopefully, we'll not have to use it. We'll find an officer who isn't crooked. We'll find someone who will help us. In fact, I'm going to go start the search now. If you need me, I'll be on my computer." He stood and walked out of the room, taking the chair with him.

Evelyn and Patrick were left alone, sitting on the bed, his arm around her.

He turned to her. "Hey, I know I've said it before, but I'm sorry for being an arse the last few days."

She turned toward him. "It's okay. I get it now. This case is personal, and you were frustrated it wasn't going the way you hoped. And you took it out on the person you thought caused the problems, me."

"You amaze me. The way you can understand a situation. Mind-boggling."

"I would have figured out the reason sooner if you had been open and honest with me when I was asking questions yesterday, rather than filing it under things I didn't need to know."

"I'm sorry. It's all so incredibly personal and painful for me to talk about."

"What changed?"

"What do you mean?"

"What changed between yesterday and today? What made you finally open up to me?"

"I don't know. Maybe my near-death experience? Mortality really puts things into perspective. I don't want to be an ass to you anymore. You helped save my life. And for that, I'll be forever grateful."

She shook her head. "I didn't do much. I held a T-shirt to your wound."

"Which helped slow down my bleeding. I don't care what you say, or how serious, or not, my injury turned out to be. You helped save my life. And I don't know how I'll ever repay you for that."

"You don't need to. I'm glad I did it."

"Me, too. Because it's given me a chance to do this."

Patrick leaned in and closed the small gap between them. Their lips met, lightly at first, but Patrick applied a little pressure, and Evelyn returned the kiss. Patrick brought his good arm up to the back of her head, cupping it, allowing the kiss to deepen. Evelyn's heart raced. She'd been kissed before, but there was something about this one that made it unlike her other first kisses. It was almost as if she were sharing it with a close friend, but she barely knew Patrick, so that was impossible. Right?

The two drew apart, short of breath, resting their foreheads against one another, eyes closed.

"Wow." Evelyn breathed.

"Yeah. Took the words right out of my mouth. I don't know why I was so reluctant. I should have done that day one."

Evelyn opened her eyes, pulling away from him slightly. "You've wanted to kiss me since day one? You seemed so annoyed and put out by me even existing."

"Yeah, I wanted to kiss you. You're fucking gorgeous. But I have a one-track mind. I've been so obsessed with nailing

Fitzgerald and getting my revenge for my mum's death, I kind of decided I had no time for a relationship. But then you come into my life and you're gorgeous and sweet, and all I can think about is what it would be like to kiss you and hold you, and I can't have that in my life right now. Plus, you were supposed to leave in a few days, and it wouldn't have been fair to either of us if I started something we would have to end so quickly."

"So, you were an ass to try to drive me away."

"Right in one. Plus, I learned *very* quickly you're even more attractive when you're riled up."

"I'm guessing your near-death experience last night also changed your mind about kissing me?"

"Of course. That, and the fact your time table has been moved back a bit. You're now stuck in the country for a little while longer. I might as well take advantage of it. Unless you have any objections."

"I have absolutely no objections. I have been kind of attracted to you as well, but you've been such an ass. I never wanted to act upon it."

"Well, I'm glad we have a mutual attraction." He yawned. "I'm sorry, but I think I'm starting to hit my limits here. I think I'm going to have a lie down."

She brushed a kiss on his forehead. "Okay. I'll leave you to rest for a bit then."

"Lie down with me?"

She shook her head. "Maybe later. Right now, I really need to work on my thesis. I still have deadlines I need to make. Rain check? I mean, you're kind of taking over the space you gave me to sleep on."

He laughed at that. "I'll hold you to it."

"Deal." She stood. "Get some rest. You need it. Mrs. Moore said you need to rest a lot so you can replenish all the blood you lost last night."

"Alright. I'm not going to argue with you. See you soon."

"See you soon." She scooped up her backpack and duffel bag and walked toward the doorway. She turned around to look back and Patrick had already slid down so his head was on his pillow, lightly snoring. She smiled and closed his door so they wouldn't disturb him and he could get a good sleep, something he hadn't had since she arrived.

"Is he sleeping?" James asked from over in the corner on his computer.

"Yeah. He was out the second his head hit the pillow. Any luck yet?"

"I've only been able to look at a handful of officers so far, corrupt as fuck."

"Of course. Well, I'm going to go sit in your room and work on my thesis so I won't bother you. Oh, and James?"

"Yeah?"

"For the record, even if Patrick wasn't interested in me, I wouldn't have shagged you."

As her words struck him, James' mouth popped open, and he struggled for a comeback for the first time since they'd met.

A wide smile spread across her face as she turned. She smiled all the way down the hall to his room to work.

CHAPTER 19

EVELYN

Evelyn stared at the blinking cursor on her laptop. It had been three days since they returned from their ill-fated meeting with Harry, and she should be writing more of her thesis, but her brain wasn't cooperating. How could she focus on ancient sleeping rituals when her, whatever you wanted to call it, was recuperating in his room? No matter what she tried, she couldn't get him to open up to her. She had a feeling this whole completely shutting down thing had to do with a lot more than just with the betrayal of a beloved mentor. If only he would *talk* to her, then she might be able to find a way to help him. However, despite everything that had happened, she was still virtually a stranger, so she really didn't blame him for not opening up.

She minimized her writing program and opened her internet browser. Obviously, writing about healing treatments at the Asclepeion, and how they related to healing treatments of modern medicine, wasn't going to happen right now. Instead, she opened her email. Once she waded through all the junk mail that clogged her inbox, she smiled. There was a new email chain from her sisters. She clicked on it and didn't even have to read a complete sentence before she began laughing hysterically.

"I didn't know Ancient Greece was so funny."

She jumped, turning toward the corner of the living room.

James sat at his computer, turned around in his chair, looking at where she sat on the couch, smirking at her. She had forgotten he was even in the room. He was so quiet sometimes.

"I've quit writing for now. I'm checking my email. My sisters and I have this really long email chain going right now."

James fully turned his chair to face her and leaned back. "Yeah? Is it jokes? Please tell me your email chain is just sending puns and dad jokes back and forth to one another."

She laughed. "No, it's not jokes. Most of the time it's mundane things, like what we are eating or what book we're reading right now. But right now, we're speculating on the love life of a very popular, and hunky, Hollywood celebrity."

"Celebrity gossip via email. Seems slow."

She shrugged. "I didn't want to pay the exorbitant international cellular fees, or else it would be text messages. Email works. Besides, it's a great distraction right now."

He nodded sagely. "Yes. From the stress of watching your new boyfriend get shot in the fucking head."

"He's not my boyfriend." She focused her gaze on her laptop. "At least, I don't think so. I don't know what we are."

She looked at the blinking cursor on the screen after she hit reply. She wanted to make a witty comeback to her sisters, but nothing was coming to mind. What she really wanted to talk about, she couldn't. She considered her sisters her very best friends, and all she wanted to do was tell them she was starting a new relationship with a man who jumped in front of a gun for her like he was a fucking superhero. But she couldn't.

"Don't look so glum, Evie," James said, pulling her out of her thoughts. "It's only been a couple days, there's plenty of time to define whatever this is."

She sighed, shutting her laptop, she would reply later. "I know. It's just, this is all unfamiliar territory for me. And it doesn't help that whenever I go into the room to check on Patrick, he's asleep."

"Well, he *was* shot in the head and received a concussion for his efforts."

"I know. And I'm not mad about him sleeping so much. I'm *glad* he's sleeping. He should be resting as much as possible. But sometimes I feel like he's maybe faking his sleep, in order to get out of talking to me."

He laughed. "Love, he's not that great of an actor. I think you're just building the situation up in your head because everything is so unknown. Just give it time."

She leaned her head back on the couch she was quickly beginning to love and understand why the guys kept it around, despite its sad and disgusting façade. "You're right. All of this is probably stemming from the fact that I'm stuck in this apartment with just the two of you, and the last few days I've been mostly on my own."

He grimaced. "Yeah, my fault, really. Since the computer can run the algorithms, I need it to on its own, I don't really need to be here, and we really need the money..."

"You don't need to explain yourself," she interrupted. "I understand."

"Hey! Why don't you come out with me tonight?"

"Another stakeout?"

Since they had been back, James had been out every night on a job. She wasn't sure if he was actively seeking jobs or if they really had all these jobs lined up before.

"Yeah, it'll be fun! We can stock up on crisps and biscuits. Enough tea and coffee to keep us awake, but not too much where we're going to need to take a piss every half hour. I'll even let you have a turn using the binoculars."

She laughed, shaking her head. "You know, I'm lonely, but I don't think I'm sitting in a MINI Cooper for hours waiting for the money shot lonely quite yet. But thank you for the invite."

He rose from his chair, picking up his backpack as he went. "You're welcome. Is there anything I can get you before I leave?"

She shook her head. "I'm good. I might make myself some cup noodles later and see if Patrick will actually eat any of it."

"If you need anything, you know how to reach me." He began moving toward the door, but stopped. "Oh, I called Patrick's dad earlier to fill him in on everything. He said he might stop by at some point. But he was very vague on the when. I thought I should make you aware if he comes while I'm gone."

"Thanks for the heads up. I'll make sure I let him in."

"Have a good night, Evie." James opened the door and left, the apartment immediately feeling quieter in his absence.

She picked her computer back up and opened it. She quickly typed a response to her sisters. It was vague and focused on the topic at hand. Despite their protestations, she was pretty sure that the two stars were, in fact, dating. She sent the email and minimized her browser.

She tried to force herself to open her document, but instead found herself staring at the closed door of Patrick's room. She stared at it, as if she could will him to wake up and want to spend time with her. Which was ridiculous. James was right. Patrick was doing exactly what he was supposed to be doing. But why did it make her feel so helpless?

This whole "being in a relationship," or whatever you wanted to call what she and Patrick were doing, was completely foreign to her. While she dated a bit in college, there was no one she was ever really serious about. She had definitely never slept with a man before this trip, literally or figuratively, and now she found herself sharing a bed with someone she barely knew, and it didn't feel weird, in fact, it seemed almost natural. It was as if she were Alice having fallen through the rabbit hole. She landed in London and became an almost completely different person. Evelyn in Iowa would never have been comfortable sparring with a man one day and then sharing his bed the next.

She was still debating whether she should try to wake Patrick or actually work on what she needed to work on when there was a knock on the door.

She froze.

No one ever knocked on the door unless they ordered take-away, and she was pretty sure Patrick wasn't in his room ordering food.

James had reassured her their address was unlisted for everyone's safety, so it couldn't be a client. And she was pretty sure Patrick wasn't in his room ordering secret takeaway.

Her heart raced with all the possibilities of who could be behind that door. Visions of a Fitzgerald goon, led there by Harry, busting down the door and kidnapping her while Patrick slept in the other room began playing through her imagination.

"Hello?" a male called through the door. "It's Colin. Anyone home?"

She breathed as she realized it was Patrick's dad. She stood and opened the door. Standing in the hallway was Colin. His hair that was styled impeccably when she met him on her first day in London was mussed, and he was wearing his dress shirt untucked from his slacks. In his hand, he held a bag of takeout.

"Evelyn," he greeted. "James called me and filled me in. I brought some curry and the hope my son will allow me to see him."

"Yes, he told me he had called you before he left. Please, come in." Evelyn stepped aside to allow Colin entry into the flat. She shut the door behind him and turned around.

The two of them stood awkwardly just inside the doorway.

"So," Colin said, "where's Patrick?"

Evelyn gestured to the closed bedroom door. "Laying in his room. Where he has been since we've come home."

"And he's…"

"He's okay. He's pretty upset about everything. He seems to be in pain, but I honestly don't know. He won't talk to either of us."

"Yes, that seems on par with my son. When his mother died, he threw himself into work, and he didn't talk to me for months, which wasn't unusual for him. I was never the best father, but at least, when my wife was around, I got to see him in passing. But Patrick tends to close in on himself when the going gets tough."

"Patrick told me about his mother. I can't believe it's so similar to my situation. Mistaken identity. The Fitzgerald lackeys must be completely face blind."

"Yes, well, that's not completely true with what happened to his mother. I told him it was a case of mistaken identity for him to not have to worry about anything. The truth of the matter is, his mother was specifically targeted. I'd been working on trying to take down Mickey Fitzgerald and his firm for quite some time. At one point, I was getting fairly close to closing in on him. He must have decided it would be prudent to send me a message I could never forget, so he had my wife murdered. After that, I moved and backed down on the case. Then Megan fell into my lap, and I couldn't pass over this opportunity. And as you can see, this second attempt is going just as well as the first. That's why I'm here. I need to tell Patrick we're backing off the case. I can't lose my son the way I lost my wife."

"Fuck you."

Evelyn and Colin both turned to look in the direction the voice came. Standing in his doorway, well, more leaning on the doorjamb, was Patrick. He was shirtless and his sweats hung low on his hips. The bandage on his head stood out starkly against his skin, and his face looked haggard. His eyes were filled with tears.

"Patrick," Colin started.

"I heard the door open and then voices. I was worried Harry had come to finish the job. But no, it's my own father come to twist a knife into my gaping wounds."

"Patrick," Colin tried again, taking a step toward his son.

Patrick shook his head and moved back into his room, shutting the door behind him.

Evelyn moved to go speak with him, but Colin held up a hand, stopping her.

"No, I must go." He handed Evelyn the bag of food. "I bought enough for everyone. Please help yourself. I'm going to go try to fix things with my son."

Evelyn took the bag of curry from Colin and watched as he didn't even bother knocking on Patrick's door before letting himself in. She took the food to the kitchen, plated herself up a serving, and went back to the couch. Once settled, she reopened her laptop and pulled up her thesis. She could at least try to get some work done and pretend she wouldn't be hearing every word Patrick and Colin had to say to each other in the bedroom.

CHAPTER 20

PATRICK

Patrick had just made it to the side of his bed when his door flew open, allowing his dad entry.

"I don't recall inviting you in," he bit out.

"I wasn't about to ask permission. I knew you wouldn't let me in, and I need to talk to you."

"So, you can lie to me more?"

"I lied to protect you. I knew you'd run into the situation half-cocked, hellbent on some sort of revenge if you knew the Fitzgeralds had targeted your mum. I knew if I told you they killed your mum because of me, you'd hate me. Know that I lied out of a place of love."

"You're right." Patrick's eyes burned with his unshed tears. "I would have hated you if I'd known. And lying to me didn't stop me from wanting revenge against Mickey Fucking Fitzgerald. The bastard killed my mum. Doesn't matter the circumstances."

"I should have realized you would have wanted revenge regardless. If I'd admitted that to myself, I would have never hired you to help with this case."

"Of course, I want revenge! I'm pretty sure I've even mentioned it to you, but you wouldn't have realized it because you were too busy with work, which has always been more important than your family."

"And if you're not careful, you're going to turn out exactly like me."

Patrick scoffed, rolling his eyes.

"It's true. I've seen it. Your dedication to this job is no different from mine to my own."

"Only I don't have a wife and son to neglect."

"Because you haven't taken the time to look for someone. When's the last time you went on a date?"

"Fuck you. I'm nothing like you. And I think that's what bothers you the most."

"You're everything like me, and I think that's what bothers *you* the most."

Patrick didn't have anything to respond with. Maybe his dad was wrong. Maybe he was right. Either way, he was distracting him from the situation.

"That girl out there," Colin pointed at the door, "is counting on you to get her home. In fact, I distinctly remember telling you to drop this case after I had a head delivered to my door, and, as expected, you ignored me and continued on. You're letting her down, and you're putting yourself in danger. They could have killed you, Patrick, and you can't even begin to imagine how much that would have destroyed me. Drop the case. Take the girl on a tour of London. Get her home safely."

"You expect me to not do anything now that I know Fitzgerald had mum killed? If anything, I want to take the whole bloody firm down even more. I'm not letting Evelyn down. I'm saving her life. Harry was going to take her to the Fitzgeralds. I stopped that. Sure, she's not on an airplane home, but you said it wasn't safe to send her anywhere. We don't even know if the Fitzgeralds have any connections in America or not. You told me to keep her here and keep her safe. I'm living up to my end of that bargain. She's still here. She's safe."

"You need to drop the case."

"Fuck that. I'm in too deep now, Colin. I'm seeing this to the end."

Patrick watched as his father's shoulders drooped in defeat. He knew he'd won at that point. Colin wasn't going to say anything else about it. Patrick sat on the edge of the bed before bringing his legs up, allowing himself to sit with his back against the headboard. Just the small amount of energy he exerted to move about the room and argue with his father had completely drained him of energy. He was exhausted.

"I left some takeaway with Evelyn. Please make sure you eat. You need your strength in order to heal." He moved to the door, but as soon as his hand was on the handle, he turned his head to look back at Patrick. "I love you, son." Not waiting for a response, he turned the knob and exited the room.

Patrick closed his eyes and listened to the muted sounds of Evelyn and Colin saying goodbye to one another. His head was pounding, and his chest was heavy with emotion. He swallowed down the lump in his throat. He wasn't going to cry.

The door to his room opened, and without opening his eyes, he knew it was Evelyn.

"Do you want any food? I can bring you in a plate."

He didn't know if it was the fact, she didn't need to ask him how he was feeling or the fact her voice was so kind. The sob he'd been holding in broke through. He could feel her before he even knew she'd crossed the room as she eased herself onto the other side of the bed and wrapped her arms gingerly around his torso.

She laid her head against his shoulder and placed her other hand gently on his cheek. "Shh, it's alright," she whispered into his ear.

"They killed my mum," he sobbed.

"I know."

The two sat in silence in each other's embrace as Patrick let his emotions wash over him. Once he finally stopped crying and had himself under control, he shifted them so they were lying so he could wrap himself around her body, pulling her against his chest. Lying in bed, arms wrapped around Evelyn, the tension left his body. He leaned his head forward and buried his nose in her hair. She smelled of his shampoo and that stirred something inside of him. Not only did it comfort him, but it also awakened something inside of him, causing him to feel slightly possessive.

His dad was right. It was his job to protect her, to make sure she got home safe. And he needed to do everything in his power to make sure the Fitzgeralds didn't do to her what they did to his mum. There was no way he was going to let the firm use her as a means to get him to drop the case. He was in this for the long haul. The Fitzgeralds were going to be taken down and brought to justice. No more collateral damage. Those days were done.

"I'm not going to let them kill you," he whispered against her head.

She hummed sleepily in agreement, and that was all the acknowledgment he needed in order to relax the rest of the way and drift off into a dreamless sleep.

CHAPTER 21

EVELYN

Evelyn opened the door to Patrick's room. It was dark inside, even though it was midday. It took a few seconds for her eyes to adjust to the dim light after being in the brighter living room.

Her gaze immediately found the bed in the center of the room. Patrick was on his side, covers pulled up completely over his head.

"Patrick?" she called out tentatively.

No response.

She sighed. She took a step back and closed the door behind her. She walked back to the couch and picked up her laptop, settling it in her lap.

"Is he sleeping again?" James asked from his spot in front of his computer.

Evelyn looked up from her own computer. "Yeah, he is."

He sighed. "Has he even moved from his bed at all since his dad left the other day? Because I'm wracking my brain, and I don't think he's ever even emerged from his room."

"He uses the restroom, otherwise he just sits up in bed and eats whatever I put in front of him. Either he's not a picky eater or he's not even really paying attention to what's in front of him."

"Has he showered?"

She hesitated before answering, wrinkling her nose. "I don't think so."

He let out a disgusted groan. "How do you share a bed with him if he hasn't showered in nearly a week?"

"Believe me, it's becoming difficult. I think he's taking this 'take it easy' thing a little too seriously."

"Has he started talking about it to you yet?"

She shook her head. "No, in fact, he's taken great lengths to ignore me even more ever since his father talked to him. James, the things they said to each other..." She trailed off, remembering the two men yelling at each other. "It's pretty obvious the two have problems they need to work out. Didn't he say Harry was more like a father to him?"

"Yeah, he was closer to him than anyone else in his life."

"So, essentially, his father betrayed him and then shot him."

"It's a fucking mess. Almost Shakespearean. He should really open up about it and talk with someone. I keep hoping it will be you. What do you guys talk about in there?"

"Nothing really, not since the night his dad left, actually. He just kind of lies there and sleeps on and off. When I try to engage him, he clams up and refuses to say anything. He just stares at the wall. The only time he talks is to occasionally ask if you've found anything yet."

"What a great relationship you have. Are you sure you don't want to upgrade to the non-broody Brit?" He smiled and gestured to himself.

She picked up one of her pencils and threw it in James' general direction, laughing. "I'm sure. I'm really, really sure. It's just," she paused, all the glee she was feeling just seconds ago draining out. "I'm just starting to get worried about Patrick."

"You need to get him to talk. You need to force the issue and convince him he needs to get everything he's feeling off of his chest. And then make him take a fucking shower. And hopefully, after steps one and two, he'll decide to join the land of the living because we're getting really close to having to take the next step."

She set her computer on the coffee table and leaned forward. "You found someone?"

"Maybe. I don't know. Someone I've found seems promising. I need to run a few more checks on him. He seems clean right now, but I've been at this stage with a few other blokes and they failed out at the next step."

"But this is the first *actual* progress we've had all week." She found herself growing antsy.

"It is. Maybe when Colin calls next, we'll have something to tell him for once." He rubbed his eyes with the palms of his hands.

"Have you slept?"

"Yeah. I've gotten a few winks here and there."

"I hope this all pans out because if it doesn't, your lack of sleep will have been for nothing."

"At least there's been nothing from the Fitzgeralds since Harry's betrayal. It's been rather convenient for both our research and Patrick's recovery," James pointed out.

"Yes, but is it a good thing or a bad thing they're being quiet?"

He shrugged. "I don't know, and at this point, honestly it doesn't even matter. We're doing our best, and I'm feeling great about our plan and what we've accomplished so far. Besides, if Plan A doesn't work out, we have the backup plan."

"Do you want to be the person to tell Patrick we're implementing the backup plan? Because I sure don't."

"Good point. We'll make this plan work before we have to tell him we're sending you out as bait to catch Fitzgerald in the act."

They each went back to working on their computers. In the past few days, she had finally been able to get a lot of work done on her thesis, and she was actually ahead on some deadlines. It helped she was basically under house arrest. She hadn't left the flat in a week, not since *that night*. With Patrick healing and moping in his bed and James either attached to the computer or doing jobs, it left no one available to assist her with going out and making sure she didn't get kidnapped. Not that she was totally eager to get out and do anything. Even so, cabin fever was a real thing.

"I called my program yesterday," she stated, breaking the silence without looking up from her computer. "I told them I wouldn't be able to make it."

James stopped his typing. The creak of his chair indicating he had turned it toward her. "Oh, Evie. I'm sorry. I can't even begin to explain how terrible Patrick and I feel about you missing out on your program."

She shook her head. "It's fine, really. I gave them a story about being stuck in London for a family emergency, and they moved me to the next session at the end of July."

"Brilliant!" James exclaimed. "Well, brilliant that you get to still do your program, not that you have a set leaving date. I don't want you to get the wrong idea. I enjoy your company."

"And I enjoy yours as well. I'll be sad to leave, but I've been looking forward to this trip for so long, I really want to make sure I get to go on it."

"Have you talked to your parents yet?"

She shook her head. "Not yet. I was going to video call them, and then I was going to just call, but I've chickened out. I think I'm going to shoot them an email and call it good. I never lie to them. I just know if I try to verbalize it, they'll be able to tell I'm not telling the truth."

He pointed at the computer in her lap. "You should email them right now. Get it over with. Like ripping off a plaster."

She sighed and opened her email. She typed up a story about being stuck in London because of some error, and how the airline is making it right. She was staying in a hotel funded by them and getting lots of sightseeing done before she needed to leave for the next session. Before she could second guess herself, she hit Send.

"There. I did it."

"Good job. Shall I reward you with a sweet?"

She laughed. "No, but after we wrap up the case you and Patrick can take me around the city so I can build up enough evidence to support the massive lie I just told my parents."

"Deal."

With lying to her parents out of the way, Evelyn reopened her thesis document. At least with being trapped in the apartment with nowhere to go for the next month she'll at least be traveling to her program with a mostly finished thesis, if the last week was any sign of how much work she would get done.

She sighed and stared at the document open on her computer screen and the books spread out on the coffee table before her. She needed a break, and honestly, to get out of the apartment for some fresh air.

She stood to stretch, and looked over at James, who was engaged fully in whatever it was he had to do on the computer to make sure this man was the one they'd been looking for. She didn't want to bother him any more than she already had. He was their only hope for getting this thing moving.

She looked at the closed door to Patrick's room. Her only hope for getting the hell out of the flat for an hour was behind that door, and she was going to make it her mission to pull him out of his funk and get him to take her anywhere but here.

CHAPTER 22

PATRICK

Poor Evelyn. His father's words echoed through his brain. *You're letting her down.*

He knew he was, yet he couldn't get himself to act on anything. He hadn't even asked her how she was handling everything. Watching him get shot. Being stuck here without an end date in sight. He'd promised her he'd have her on a plane in a couple days, but here they were, over a week since she'd been stranded, and she was still here. What did she tell her parents? Had she even told her parents? These were things he was sure she'd told him at one point, but the last week was such a blur. He wasn't even sure of anything anymore. And all of this wasn't even taking into consideration his newfound intense feelings of keeping her safe at all costs.

The door to his room opened, and the object of his thoughts walked in, giving him a small smile.

"You're awake."

"Yeah, I am. I have been for a while now."

"Why didn't you come out and join us? Mrs. Moore said you were done with bed rest. There's no reason to stay cooped up in here. It would probably make you feel better if you got up and moved."

"I wasn't in the mood to be social."

Evelyn sat on the edge of the bed. "Want to talk about whatever's been bothering you?"

"I'm fine."

"You're not fine. You've been in here moping for a week. I think you'll feel better if you talk about what's bothering you."

"I don't want to talk about it. I'm tired." He wrapped the covers up around him. "I'd like to be left alone."

She ripped the covers from him.

"Oi, what the fuck!"

"You're not tired. You're using that as a defense mechanism and as a way to get rid of me. I'm tired of you avoiding me, Patrick. I'm tired of you pushing James and me away. You need to talk about what's bothering you or you're going to fall deeper into this depression."

He sat up, glaring at her. "I'm not going to talk to you about my feelings. We're not going to sit in here and plait each other's hair and have heart-to-hearts. If that's the kind of person you think I am, I'm sorry to disappoint you, sweetheart. I'm not touchy-feely. And even if I were, you'd be the last person I'd open up to. I don't even know you that well."

He waited for her to get angry and storm off, hurt, but he was surprised when she stayed on the side of the bed, looking at him with a sympathetic gaze.

"Bullshit."

"What?"

"Bullshit. Don't try to pull this crap on me, Patrick. You can't push me away like that. I'm onto you, remember?"

He sighed and lay back on the bed. "Can't you just leave me alone? You've done enough, allowing Colin to come in here last week and go off on me. Just let it go and allow me to have this time to feel sorry for myself, yeah?"

"No. I'm done letting you feel sorry for yourself. You smell."

"What?"

"You haven't showered in a week. You're starting to smell, and if you don't do something about it, I'm going to sleep on the couch."

"You can't be serious?"

"Completely serious. You've stopped taking care of yourself. I know we said you needed to take it easy, but this is fucking ridiculous."

He winced at the profanity. She'd rarely used such language since she arrived, so he knew she was serious if she was pulling out all the major swear words.

"Please," she begged. "Please talk to me. Your mentor, your *father figure*, betrayed you. He shot you. Yell about it, scream about it. Throw something against the wall. Break something. Just do *something*. Keeping these emotions bottled inside isn't healthy."

"I don't want to talk about it," he gritted. "I don't want to yell or scream or anything. I just want to lie here, in my bed, and do nothing else."

"Seriously? Seriously? That's it? You're just going to lie there and give up? What happened to the Patrick who was out for revenge? Where's the fire? Where's the passion? You're going to let one minor setback get you down and let your mother's killer walk the streets?"

"Minor setback? I was fucking shot! Do you think I want to give up? Harry was the only family I had. I trusted him with my life, and he tried to take that away from me. Getting shot did nothing but remind me what dangerous work I'm doing and showed me I'm—"

"Human?" Evelyn supplied.

"Yes! And I don't like how vulnerable this injury has made me. I don't like I wasn't able to protect you or stop Harry from leaving the promenade."

"Good. These are all valid feelings. Thank you for finally opening up. I've been waiting all week for you to talk to me. Everything sucks. And your father figure shot you. Remember that conversation we had before we met up with Harry? The one about superheroes?"

He nodded.

"You're not a superhero, Patrick. You're not Superman or Spider-Man. You're Patrick, a regular human man who has feelings and vulnerabilities. I am here for you. I hope you know that. To listen to you, and comfort you and be whatever you need during this time. However, that all being said, you need to get the hell out of this bed and continue living your life. Start thinking about what you can do next. We still have a shot to bring Harry down with the rest of the Fitzgeralds. James is pretty damn sure he has a lead. He's finishing up as we speak. Please get out of bed and join us. Help us bring them down."

He sat on the bed, deep in thought. "You make some valid points, but I don't think I can. I'm not ready to trust anyone outside of this flat. Can you please leave me alone? I'll understand when you don't come back in for bed tonight."

He lay down, pulling the covers up and over his head, summarily ending the discussion. The bed shifted as She stood, and he listened as she moved to the door.

"You know, the reason I started having feelings for you was because of how strong and assertive you were. I'm having trouble melding the you from a week ago with the you I see right now. The Patrick who saved me from the airport wouldn't let Harry defeat him. He'd go out there and take him down. By lying here in this dark room, you're letting the Fitzgeralds win. You're allowing them to get away with all of the horrible things they're doing in your city. Think about it. I hope I see you out there soon."

She opened the door and left the room, allowing him to close his eyes and reflect on all of the things she'd said during her visit.

CHAPTER 23

EVELYN

Evelyn sighed and leaned against the bedroom door. She didn't know how else to get through to him. And she was no closer to leaving the damn flat than when she went into the room.

She pushed away from the door and reached into her pocket. There was still some money left over from what she took out the day she was supposed to only have a layover in London, since James insisted, they pay for all of her food while she was here. She was confident she could remember the way to the restaurant where they stopped for fish and chips the week before. She could easily walk down there, get supper for the group, and return. It would be easy, and she'd be quick. James and Patrick wouldn't have to worry about her.

"I'll be back in twenty minutes." She slipped her shoes on.

"What?" James looked up from his computer. "Where are you going?"

"I'm going to pick up some supper."

James stood. "I'll go. Why don't you stay here and keep working on your paper?"

"James, I've been stuck in this apartment for a week. I need to get out and get some fresh air. I need to see something other than these walls."

"Then I'll go with you."

"Stay here and finish up whatever you're doing. I'll be fine. I'm only going to the fish and chips place we went to when I first got here. I'll be there and back before you know I'm gone."

James stood in the living room, looking unsure. After a minute, he finally sighed. "Fine, but take my mobile. If you run into any trouble, call Patrick, and we'll come find you, okay?" He handed her his phone.

She took his cell and put it in her pocket. "Deal. Now, get back to work. I'll be back in a jiffy."

She opened the front door and walked out. She practically ran down the hall, down the stairs, and out into the street. Once her feet touched the sidewalk outside the apartment building, she stood there and lifted her face to the sky.

She closed her eyes and took a deep breath. Fresh air. The sun was getting a little low in the sky, and there was a soft breeze, making the summer evening feel absolutely wonderful.

"Gorgeous night for a walk, isn't it?" a male voice said from beside her.

She jumped and opened her eyes. Standing next to her was a middle-aged man dressed in a dark black pinstriped suit. His jet-black hair was slicked back, accentuating his graying sideburns. He looked at her with emotionless gray eyes, although his mouth was turned up in an attempt at a smile.

"Yeah, it's beautiful."

"Ah, an American. What brings you to London?"

"Visiting my boyfriend." She really was getting good at this lying thing. She should look into acting or something when she got back to the States.

"Really? How does an American lass end up dating a British lad?"

"Internet. We met in an online group, really hit it off, and started dating. This is the first time we've been able to meet in person."

"And you're out here without him? If I'd flown thousands of miles and across an ocean to be with my online paramour, I wouldn't want to waste one second without him."

"I got hungry, and he needed to catch up on some work he's neglected."

"Ah, so you're out here all alone?"

She stopped smiling. There was something about the way he asked the question. It didn't seem like a question a stranger on the street being nosy would ask. It was something else.

"I, um, need to get going. I promised I wouldn't be long." She moved around him, making sure she seemed confident about where she was planning to go.

The man moved and blocked her path. "What's the hurry, Evelyn? I thought we were having a delightful conversation."

She froze. "How do you know my name?" She started backing away, looking around for a way out of the situation.

"I know everything about you, Evelyn Stevenson. And I think you know all about me, which, I have to say, is a bit of a problem. Which is why you're going to have to come with me."

"I know nothing about you! I don't know who you are!"

"You're a terrible liar. Did you know that?" The man took a step toward her. "But it's okay. It won't take long for me to get what I need from you."

She turned to run, but he grabbed her and pulled her toward him. She struggled, kicking her legs and wiggling, trying to get free. She opened her mouth to scream, but he held a cloth up to her face, covering her mouth and nose. She smelled something sweet, like almonds, before everything went black.

CHAPTER 24

PATRICK

Patrick lay in his bed, staring at the ceiling.

Evelyn had been right. Of course, she was.

He was too busy lying in bed feeling sorry for himself to take any sort of action. All the fight had left him when he started really thinking about what his dad had said. He was becoming his father. Obsessed with the job, and it was becoming detrimental to his personal life.

However, his solution to the problem, lying in bed, staring at the ceiling, feeling sorry for himself, was ruining everything just as much. He was in danger of destroying the budding relationship he had with Evelyn before it even started, just by the power of doing nothing. He needed to change. He needed to get out of bed and finish this damn case. The sooner the case was over, the sooner everyone he cared about would be safe. And the sooner he could shift his focus back to smaller jobs and make room in his life for other things.

Like Evelyn.

He sat up, rubbing his face. The skin was greasy, a byproduct of not washing since his injury. If his face felt this bad, he knew the rest of his body was just as disgusting. He probably smelt terrible. Another fact Evelyn had gotten right. He needed to take a shower before he apologized to her. Or groveled at her feet for forgiveness. Whatever it took to get her to never look at him the way she had before storming out of his room.

Just as he moved to get out of bed, the door to his room swung open and a distraught James came storming into the room, as if he was searching for something.

"What's wrong?"

"I need your mobile." James held out his hand.

"What? Why?"

"Just give it to me."

Patrick shook his head and reached over to the nightstand, grabbing his phone and tossing it to James.

James immediately opened it and dialed a number. He listened to it ring and ring and ring.

"Fuck." He immediately dialed it again.

"Who are you calling? More importantly, why aren't you using your own phone to do it?"

"I'm calling Evie. She has my phone."

Patrick froze in bed. "Why would you need to be calling Evelyn? Shouldn't she be here, safe in the flat?"

"She wanted to get some fresh air, so I let her go pick up dinner from the chippy down the way. I thought it would be fine. She'd be back in ten minutes, twenty tops. That was over an hour ago." He hung up and dialed a third time.

Patrick stood. "Why the hell would you think letting her leave the flat on her own was a good idea? The Fitzgeralds want her. They tried to take her when we were *right there*. They wouldn't hesitate taking her when she's alone! What were you thinking?"

"I don't know. Maybe that the poor girl had been cooped up in this flat for a week straight and deserved to go out? She was so confident everything would be fine, I let her go."

Patrick went at him, his anger fighting with the growing panic. "Why didn't you go with her?"

"I was busy looking into the officer who I'm pretty sure is our guy. And I thought she could handle going down to the corner alone. She is an adult."

Patrick grabbed James by the collar and pushed him against the wall. "I trusted you to take care of her!"

"And I did! I'm sorry. I thought—"

"Well, hello there, Detective Miller," a voice came through the phone, interrupting their argument.

Patrick grabbed the phone out of James's hand and put it on speaker. "Who is this? Where's Evelyn?"

"Evelyn can't come to the phone right now. She's a bit, detained, at the moment."

"Put her on. I want to talk to her."

"*Tsk, tsk, tsk.* So demanding. So hotheaded. Harry warned me you'd be hard to negotiate with. Just too damn stubborn."

Patrick winced at the name of his former mentor. "Put her on the phone."

"I'd love to, but unfortunately, my associates are busy having a conversation with her right now. But never you mind. You'll have your precious Evelyn back before the night is through. And when she returns, she'll have a message for you, and I expect you to take the message *extremely* serious."

The line disconnected, and Patrick and James were left staring at the phone. Patrick pulled his arm back to throw the phone against the wall, but James caught his arm and stopped it.

"Don't do that. What if they drop Evie off somewhere and she needs to call us?"

Patrick relaxed his arm. "You're right." He threw the phone on the bed instead. "This is all my fault." He ran his hands through his hair. "If I'd gotten out of the fucking bed like she asked, repeatedly, or talked to her, she never would have felt the need to go out alone, and Mickey *Fucking* Fitzgerald wouldn't have her right now."

"You don't know that. He's obviously been watching the building if he managed to get her the second she walked outside. If you were with her, nothing would have been stopping him from taking the both of you or killing you and taking her. This isn't your fault."

"It's completely my fault. I did this. I was too busy feeling sorry for myself. We need to do something. We need to find her."

"We don't even know where to start looking. Look, I'm almost done running algorithms on this officer who I think is our ticket to getting the bastard behind bars. You need to go take a shower and start smelling human again. I need to finish up my research. And wash your sheets while you're at it. It stinks in here. Let's regroup in an hour. We will figure this out."

"An hour? She could be dead in an hour!"

"He's not going to kill her. Didn't you hear him? He's sending her back with a message for you. Shower, and we'll regroup in an hour."

James left the room, presumably to return to his computer.

Patrick watched him walk away before sliding to the ground, pressing his fists to his eyes. First, his mother, then Harry, and now Evelyn. Was he destined to lose everyone he cared about to Mickey Fitzgerald?

His chest tightened. It was becoming harder to breathe. Gasping, he looked frantically around the room. He stood, moving around his bed to the lamp on his side table. He picked it up, ripping the cord from the wall, and threw it against the wall. It made a rewarding crash. It was satisfying and made him feel slightly better, so he looked around again, picking up the nearest object, and throwing it, too, against the wall.

And another, and another, and another, until he curled up in a ball on the floor and wept.

CHAPTER 25

EVELYN

Evelyn woke up in a seemingly empty room. Her head was fuzzy, and there was a terrible taste in her mouth. She blinked as she looked around the dimly lit room. It was small, with bare concrete walls and a small metal door directly across from her. It was sparsely furnished with only a table and a few chairs against one wall and the chair she currently sat in.

She closed her eyes as she struggled to catch her breath, her heart hammering inside her chest. Someone had kidnapped her. She had barely stepped outside the building for a minute before she'd been kidnapped by who she could only assume was Mickey Fitzgerald. She would never hear the end of this from Patrick.

She tried to move her hands, but they were bound behind her back. She looked at her feet. They were tied to the legs of the chair. It was like she was a character in a Nancy Drew novel, and not the Nancy Drew heroine, more like one of her hapless friends who always ended up needing to be saved.

The door across from her opened and two men entered, briefly letting in a bright light. One was the man who'd abducted her. The other was one of the men from the airport. They shut the door behind them and stood in front of her.

"Ms. Stevenson, so glad you have finally decided to join us. We have some questions." The man who'd abducted her walked over to a corner and dragged a chair from the table to in front of her and sat. "There are two ways this can go down. You can answer all the questions I ask, truthfully, and then I'll return you to your detective unharmed. Or you can be difficult and we'll be forced to pull the answers from you in any way necessary. What will it be? Are you going to cooperate?"

She nodded slowly. She thanked every god in existence that Patrick had kept her in the dark about anything having to do with the Fitzgeralds. She'd be able to cooperate, tell the man what he wanted to know, without compromising the case in any way, and be back home in one piece.

"Great. I'm glad. Now, where's the bag?"

"I don't know."

"See, this is what I was talking about. This is the perfect example of you being difficult." He made a hand signal to the other man in the room, who pulled out a pair of pliers from his back pocket and took a step toward her.

"No, I am. I am cooperating. I really don't know. I gave the bag to Patrick when I first met him, and I haven't seen it since. I don't know what he's done with it. I swear," she screamed.

Fitzgerald held up his hand, halting his associate. "Now we're getting somewhere. The fact you don't know its exact location is disappointing, but we can work with this. What did that *slut* put in the bag you don't know the location of?"

"I don't know. Patrick wouldn't let me see anything in it."

"So, I'm to believe that when you switched bags in the airport you didn't look into it? Weren't you curious?"

"I just wanted my bag back and to get on my airplane. I didn't care what was in the bag."

"And in the last week, the detectives haven't told you anything about what was in it or even looked inside yourself?"

"Patrick has made it abundantly clear anything having to do with the bag is on a need-to-know basis, and I'm not on the list of people who need to know. He's done a great job at isolating me from the case he's trying to build against you. In fact, I didn't even know what you looked like until now."

He brought his hand up and started stroking his chin. "Hmm, smart man, keeping his cards close to his chest."

For a minute, Fitzgerald sat there, staring at her. She couldn't read what his eyes were saying, but it seemed as if he were trying to work out a difficult puzzle.

"I cannot believe it," he murmured, almost to himself, as he continued to stare at her.

"What?"

"The resemblance is uncanny. You and Megan could be siblings." He stood and moved closer to her as he spoke. "Except, you would be easily labeled the more attractive sister, by far." He leaned in, his face close to hers.

His expensive cologne smelled bitter and had been applied liberally.

"Maybe," his accented voice was low so only she could hear it, "we don't use you to send a message to those lads. Instead, I keep you here to warm my bed at night." He ran a finger down her cheek, and her heart sped up.

But, as quickly as he'd leaned in, he was gone, moving away from her. "Except, a promise *is* a promise. Jimmy, rough her up a bit, pin this note to her, and drop her off on our good detective's front step."

He turned to leave the room.

"Wait! I answered your questions. I did what you asked! I thought that meant I wouldn't get hurt."

"I said you wouldn't get tortured. I never said anything about you leaving here unscathed."

As he walked to the door, the phone she had forgotten about rang in her pocket, causing him to stop. He turned around slowly and walked back to her. He reached into her pocket and pulled out the cell, smiling when he saw who was calling.

"Now, this will be fun. Make sure you do a good job. Really send those boys a message. I'll take care of the investigator."

He walked out of the room, carrying James's phone.

The door closed behind Fitzgerald, and she looked at the man in the room with her. He was smiling at her as he moved closer.

She closed her eyes and waited for the pain to come.

CHAPTER 26

PATRICK

Patrick walked out of the bathroom feeling slightly better after showering and shaving for the first time in a week, but he was still on edge. He'd be much better when they found Evelyn and had her back with them.

"Have you finished your research yet?" He moved into the living room.

"I have. This guy is completely clean, on paper and digitally. If he's being paid off by the Fitzgeralds, then they've covered it up really well. Which I highly doubt, since the chief didn't even come clean when I ran my thorough search on him. I think we've found our arresting officer."

Patrick allowed himself a small smile. "Excellent. Now what? We can't just call the bloke and beg him to arrest Fitzgerald right now."

"No. I'm sure he'll take some convincing. We need to pull what evidence we're willing to share from the bag and set up a meeting, somewhere private, and start working on convincing him to help us."

"What about Evelyn? We need to get her back. This is going to take too long—"

"I know, but what else can we do? Neither of us owns a gun. We can't start looking for the Fitzgeralds. That's not going to work in our favor. We can't defend ourselves against an arsenal. We need to follow the plan and trust we'll find her in time."

Patrick opened his mouth to argue, but a loud bang against their front door interrupted him.

They looked at each other before moving slowly toward the door. James signaled for Patrick to get behind him and cautiously turned the door handle. He opened it, and they both gasped at the sight before them.

Lying in a bloody heap on their doorstep was Evelyn.

"Evelyn!" Patrick moved forward and knelt next to her.

He moved his hand up to her neck. There was a strong pulse. She was alive. She was just unconscious. He slipped one arm under her knees and the other under her shoulders, lifting her, and brought her into the flat. He went into his room and set her on the bed.

"Is she—" James asked from the doorway.

"She's alive. I just need to see her wounds."

He moved her hair, and his heart ached to see bruises already developing and causing her face to become discolored. As if being used as a punching bag wasn't enough, she had tiny cuts up and down her arms, which were the source of the blood.

"Get me the first-aid kit and whatever we have that's frozen." Patrick didn't take his gaze off of her.

He ran his hand down the side of her face, softly and slowly caressing her. She was here. She was safe. And whoever hit her was going to pay. He was going to make sure of that.

James was back in the room before Patrick even realized he'd left. The two of them began working on dressing all of Evelyn's wounds and stopping the bleeding.

"Patrick, have you seen this?"

He looked up. Pinned to her shirt was a piece of paper. He shook his head.

James took the paper off her shirt and opened it. He read what it said and then handed it to Patrick.

Drop the case, or next time, we'll be delivering her corpse.

Patrick crumpled the note and held it, closing his eyes.

"What are we going to do?"

James began cleaning and bandaging the wounds on Evelyn's arms while Patrick began applying the frozen vegetables to the worst of her bruises.

"Every fiber of my being is saying we ignore it and keep pushing, but then there's the part of me—"

"That says it's just a case and we need to drop it so we don't lose Evie."

"Exactly. Maybe we should take her to the hospital. What if she's hurt internally? Maybe we should have her checked out."

"No, no hospital," came a soft voice from the bed.

They looked at Evelyn, who was slowly waking up. "And you can't drop the case because of me."

"Evelyn." Patrick brought his hand to her forehead. "How are you feeling?"

"Like I've been hit by a truck which, judging from the size of the man who did this to me, isn't that much of an exaggeration."

He smiled. "No offense, but you look like you've been hit by a truck. Does anywhere hurt worse than other areas? Do you think anything is broken?"

She shook her head. "No. Everything hurts equally. He kept saying he was going easy on me. Which, if this is going easy, I don't want to know what would have happened if I hadn't cooperated with them."

"Are you sure you don't want us to take you to the hospital? We can get some x-rays done to make sure you're really okay."

"No. I'm fine, really. And if you take me to the hospital, they're going to call my parents since they're my emergency contacts, and then our whole tourist ruse is up."

"I'm so sorry, Evie," James said from her other side. "I shouldn't have let you go off alone."

"Don't be. I was quite insistent you let me. I can't believe I had barely taken one step outside before they kidnapped me. I'm looking forward to hearing you guys telling me 'I told you so' for the next forever."

Patrick smiled weakly. "I'm glad to see they didn't take away your sense of humor during your abduction."

"I have to laugh about it or else I'll break down, and if I breakdown, I don't think I'll be able to stop."

He sobered. "You terrified me, Evelyn."

She looked at him, tears pooling in her eyes. "I'm so sorry. That wasn't my intention. I wanted to go out, bring back food, and hope maybe it would help get you out of your funk." She looked at him more closely and smiled. "You showered."

"Yeah, I had to. I couldn't go on a rescue mission looking and smelling like a homeless person."

She smiled. "If I'd known all I had to do was get kidnapped to get you out of bed, I would have gone out for food a week ago."

He shook his head. "You're ridiculous." He gazed into her eyes.

"I know." She returned his intense gaze.

James cleared his throat. "I'm going to go out there and leave you two kids alone."

He left the room, closing the door behind him.

She shifted over in the bed, and Patrick took it as an invitation to settle in next to her. He lifted his arm, and she tucked herself against his side, laying her head on his bare chest.

"I was so scared," she whispered. "He said he was going to let me go, but he's a hardened criminal. I didn't think I could believe him."

"I was scared, too," Patrick whispered back. "I thought Fitzgerald had succeeded in taking another person I cared about away from me, permanently." He tightened his arm around her and planted a kiss on her head. "Please don't go out alone again."

"Done. I never want to leave this flat again. Maybe even this bed. I think you had the right idea. Let's just hide away here, forever."

He chuckled. "I don't think I had the right idea. I think you were right to make me get out of bed. I was being foolish and cowardly, hiding away in here. You and James were busy working on the case while I wallowed."

"Well, to be fair, James made progress on the case. I made progress on my thesis. Let's give credit where it's due. Tell me more about how you're feeling."

"Hurt. Betrayed. Not depressed about it anymore, necessarily. Sad, maybe, would be a better word. Like it'll take a long time for me to trust new people again."

She gave him a small smile. "All of which are perfectly normal and okay feelings to be having. I don't know why you were hiding out in here. We could have helped you work through them, you know."

"I know, but I wasn't feeling very logical, you know? I guess I wanted to wallow. I've never really done that before. After mum was killed, I threw myself into my work. I never mourned. And I guess Harry betraying me and getting shot kind of piled on top of the suppressed emotions, and I guess I kind of imploded."

She leaned up, giving him a peck on his lips. "I get it, and I'm sorry I wasn't more sensitive to your needs."

He shifted them so they were both lying on their sides, facing each other in the bed. He ran his hand up and down her arm and her side, careful to avoid her injuries. "Don't apologize. I was a mess, and you were right to point that out to me. I wish I'd had the sense to get out of my funk on my own and not because my, um, female companion had gotten kidnapped by my arch nemesis."

She laughed. "Female companion?"

He shrugged. "We've never really defined what we are to each other, and I don't want to say we're in a relationship, especially since in the last week I've been nothing but an arse to you."

"You've been hurting, both physically and emotionally. I'll give you a pass for this one. How's your head?"

"It hurts still, but nothing like it was before. It's nothing I can't handle."

She gently touched his forehead, leaning forward. She placed a soft kiss near where his injury was. She pressed another kiss on his cheek, and then another on his jawline. She looked at him, meeting his intense gaze before bringing his head down so she could give him a proper kiss.

Their lips touched, and he eased them into a gentle kiss, mindful of the injuries on her face. She opened her mouth, and he took advantage, deepening the kiss.

Reluctantly, he pulled away as things were becoming more heated.

He pressed his forehead against hers, closing his eyes. He ran his hand softly through her hair and cupped her cheek. "We should stop before this goes any further."

"But—"

"You're hurt. We have plenty of time to go further later, when you're better. You're here indefinitely, remember?"

She let out a soft puff of breath as she silently chuckled. "You're right."

He pulled away, and he moved her until he was on her other side and he was spooned behind her, his arm around her waist, holding her tightly against his body. Her warmth reassured him she was okay.

"Why do you call me Evelyn?"

"Well, last I checked, it was your name."

"I know that, but, well, I mean, I told you everyone calls me Evie, and James even calls me Evie, but you always make it a point to call me Evelyn. I was wondering why."

"Well, it's like you said. Everyone calls you Evie. I don't want to be just anyone."

"Wow, excellent answer."

He planted a kiss on the top of her head. "I'm glad that you think so."

They fell quiet again and enjoyed lying in the bed together.

"Don't give up the case," she said finally.

"What?"

"Don't give it up. You guys have worked so hard, and you finally have leads and evidence to bring the man who killed your mom to justice. Don't give it up because of me."

"I'm not going to put your life in danger. I can't sit back and ignore a very credible threat to your life in order to get someone arrested. My dad ignored the warnings, and it got my mum killed. I don't want to take the chance the same will happen to you. There'll be other chances to catch Mickey Fitzgerald. Believe me. I'll just let some other fool do it."

"But you guys are so close! You need to do it. Meet with the police officer James found. Find out what he can do for you. You have to do at least that. James spent a week finding him."

"Fine. We can meet with whoever James found, and then we clean our hands of this whole thing. I don't think you've had a chance to look in a mirror, but, no offense, you look terrible. And I don't want to take a chance you could end up looking worse, or even dead, because I was selfish and wanted to see out my vendetta personally."

She turned so she was facing him. "I don't need to see a mirror, thank you. I was there. I can imagine what I look like. Let's take the case one step at a time. I don't want you making any final decisions right now. We've all had a very emotionally trying week. Between the head, the betrayal, and my abduction, we've all been on high alert on an almost constant basis. Just promise me you won't give up because of me."

He brushed her hair off her face. "I promise."

She burrowed deeper into the covers. She moved slightly so her head came to rest on his pillow. He moved so she was nestled into his body, her head tucked into his neck, his chin resting on her head.

"I'm so tired. I may never leave this room again. You guys are on your own. Come and get me when it's time for my plane to leave in three weeks."

"What? You've booked a plane?"

She looked at him. "Yeah. I'm pretty sure I told you sometime in the last few days. My program rescheduled me for the end of July. I fly to Athens from here in about three weeks."

"Oh."

"Hey, you knew I'd have to leave eventually."

"Yeah, I know," he said flatly. "I've never really thought about you actually leaving, though."

"Well, I don't leave for almost a month. Let's make the most of the time we have together. As...companions."

"Yes, companions," Patrick agreed absentmindedly.

"For the record, I'm starting to wish I didn't have to go," she whispered.

He wrapped his arms around her, pulling her closer to him until her head was in the crook of his neck. "I wish you didn't have to leave, either."

CHAPTER 27

EVELYN

When the two finally emerged from Patrick's room, James was sitting on the couch reading the paper, barely able to contain the grin on his face.

"What are you grinning about?"

James folded the paper and set it aside. "It's my job as the best friend to be a bit cheeky, so I'm going to perform that duty with gusto."

Patrick sighed as he pulled a chair out for Evelyn. "I'm too tired for riddles, James. What on earth are you talking about?"

James looked absolutely giddy, clapping his hands, wearing a goofy grin on his face. "Bow chicka wow-wow." He waggled his eyebrows.

Patrick sighed and opened his mouth to respond to him, but James continued on.

"Oh, I'm not done. You two were so adamant you weren't going to shag. You were all, 'No, James, I'm not interested in her like that,'" he raised the pitch of his voice in a mocking tone, "but I should have put money on it, because you two totally shagged."

It was Evelyn's turn to bury her face in her hands. Her face burned in embarrassment. She was about to protest, but, again, James interrupted to continue on his tirade.

"Now, seriously, I'm happy for you two. I could sense the attraction and the sexual tension from day one. I'm glad you guys finally acted on it. Are you going to do a long-distance thing when she leaves in a few weeks?"

Patrick and Evelyn glanced at each other.

"Well, first off, we didn't shag. Who do you take me for, James? The girl was just abducted and abused just a few hours ago."

"You didn't shag?" James's face fell, seemingly more disappointed about their lack of sex than he really should be.

"We didn't shag," she confirmed, "and we haven't really discussed what's going to happen when I leave."

"We're going to focus on the now and then figure out where we stand in a few weeks."

"Well, now I'm disappointed with my skills as an investigator because I can't believe I was so wrong. Let's move on before I embarrass myself further. Where do we stand on the whole Fitzgerald thing? Because, as I'm looking at you, Evie, I'm really thinking we need to drop the whole bloody thing."

She brought her hands up to her face, touching the bruises. Her face hurt, but her eyes weren't swelling shut, so she knew she wasn't too bad. She still didn't want to look in a mirror.

The way Patrick and James were reacting to her, she wasn't sure she wanted to see the extent of her injuries. She looked at her bandaged arms. Yeah, she didn't want to know the full extent of her injuries.

"We've decided to stay the course," Patrick said.

James's eyes widened. "You're fucking kidding."

He shook his head. "Evelyn insisted."

James's head whipped over to look at her. "Evie, you need to rethink this. They've threatened your life. They've already captured you once, and even though you look like hell, no offense, they were fairly easy on you. I don't even want to imagine what they'll do if they get you again."

"But they're not going to get me again. Like I told Patrick, you guys are so close to bringing them down, to arresting Fitzgerald, it would be stupid to give up now."

James looked at Patrick, who shook his head.

"She's got a point. We're very close to breaking this wide open. If we can get this done now, we can put this behind us. If we drop it, how many more innocent people are going to get hurt before someone else gets to the point we are now?"

"There are many private investigators in the greater London area, Patrick. We can go and anonymously drop off the bag of evidence and all the research we've done on their doorstep. We would move ourselves out of the danger zone, and the Fitzgeralds would still be on the brink of getting taken down. Or have you forgotten what they did to poor Megan?"

Patrick looked like he was going to consider it, but before he could agree, Evelyn spoke.

"You guys, don't. You can't give the case to someone else. This is personal. You have to see it through to the end."

"Not if your life's in danger. James has a point. We can give this case to someone else. We don't have to be the ones to actually follow through on it. We can sit on the sidelines, taking you sightseeing, while someone else is in the line of fire for Fitzgerald. Wouldn't you rather enjoy your last few weeks here, seeing the Tower instead of being cooped up in this flat, worrying if you step out the door, you'll get snatched?"

"How is sightseeing out in *public* any safer than continuing on with the investigation?"

"Because we won't actively be trying to destroy the Fitzgeralds. We'll be dropping the case, just like they want."

"But, your vendetta—"

"Fuck my vendetta. Look where it's gotten us so far. My father had a severed head shipped to him, my father figure fucking betrayed us, and then fucking shot me, and you got kidnapped and injured. Nothing good has come from me seeking vengeance for my mother's murder. Nothing. I'm not going to sit back and watch another tragedy occur while I attempt to take down the largest crime syndicate in London. I'm sorry, but I can't watch anyone else I care for get hurt, or worse. I can't take the chance I'll open that door and find your head in a box next."

The room fell quiet after Patrick's rant. He was breathing hard, trying to rein himself in.

James turned and looked at her, raising his eyebrows, but said nothing. He was leaving it up to her. He was on Patrick's side. She knew that. She seemed to be outnumbered. But how could she make the boys see they were making a mistake? That they were going to regret dropping the case? She took a deep breath and exhaled slowly.

She had her work cut out for her. "I didn't take you for cowards."

Both men's head whipped over to her, their eyes narrowing. Jackpot.

"We're not cowards," James replied.

"No? You're giving up at the first sign of trouble. You guys have worked tirelessly on bringing down the Fitzgeralds, and they send you a note telling you to give up or else, and you're going to listen to them? What the hell is wrong with you? You can't let them win."

"We're not letting them win, and you keep forgetting they *murder* people. We're not giving up," Patrick stated.

"You are doing exactly what they want you to do. And when you do, Fitzgerald is going to spread it all over town how easy you two gave up, and no one will want to hire you. You'll be known as the detectives who quit when it gets hard."

Both men scowled. It seemed to be working.

"Think about your business."

Patrick shook his head. "Fuck my business. We can rebuild our business. You could die. Do you understand that? They've threatened your life. Why don't you understand?"

"I understand. Believe me, I understand. I was with them, remember? I was there. They had me. They're really fucking scary. But you know why I'm not worried? Because I have you guys. I know you two won't let anything happen to me."

"Have you forgotten you got kidnapped on my watch?" James pointed out.

"Only because I was insistent to go out on my own. It was all on me, not on you two at all. I wish you'd stop blaming yourselves."

"We blame ourselves because it was on us to protect you, to make sure you were safe. We dropped the ball."

"And now you know how stubborn I am, and you'll now no longer drop the ball. You know what the stakes are, and you know the risks, and what to expect. You won't let anything happen again. The situation we're in is not a joke. And we've all learned it the hard way. But with everything that's happened with Harry and me, wouldn't you rather see it through? Why would you give this to someone else after everything we've gone through?" And then she remembered the conversation they had way back that night at the promenade. "Would Superman or Spider-Man give up?"

The boys were silent and then looked at each other. Evelyn could tell they were having a silent conversation. The way they looked at each other, the expressions in their eyes changing, their eyebrows moving up and down, at the way they could communicate with each other without saying anything impressed her. It was truly a testament as to how close they were.

"Fine, but you're going to listen to us this time and do what we say. No more venturing out on your own, no more being stubborn, and no arguing if we tell you to do something you don't like. If we're going to defy the Fitzgeralds, we're going to do it in a way that keeps you safe."

"I'll do whatever you say. I learned my lesson the hard way." She touched her face.

"I don't want to make it sound like we're ordering you about. We're doing this for your own good. We care about you, and we want you to live and make it to your program," Patrick explained.

"Yeah. I get it."

"Good." He turned toward James. "What did you find out during your scan of all the local officers?"

James smiled. "I thought you'd never ask." He walked over to his computer desk and picked up a stack of papers. He handed the stack to Patrick. "Joseph McCleary."

Patrick began rifling through the papers.

"He's been a member of the force for less than a year. He's a total rookie. He's young and itching to prove himself. He's stayed out of the Fitzgeralds' pockets because they don't think he's going to last. Which means they don't see him as a threat, either. He's currently the only officer in Tower Hamlets who isn't being paid off by the family."

"Do you think he'll meet with us? Do you think he'll help?"

"This case is something he'll jump at. I guarantee it. He's so desperate to prove himself, he'd love to be the officer who arrested Mickey Fitzgerald. The press alone would make him giddy. An early promotion to sergeant would be the icing on the cake."

"How do we contact him without raising red flags everywhere?"

"Easy. We send him an encrypted email asking him if he's willing to meet. Then we send another with a location and time."

"Do we tell him why we want to meet?" Evelyn asked.

James shook his head. "We don't tell him anything other than we have something for him that will make his career. He's so obsessed with his career that he'll bite."

"How sure are you this will work?" Patrick asked.

"Ninety percent."

"The other ten percent?"

"That he'll think we're taking the piss and not meet with us. Also, if he does meet with us, he won't want anything to do with the case because of the dangers associated with it. If the solicitors can't get Fitzgerald behind bars and bring down the entire family with him, then this whole thing will paint targets on not only our backs, but his since he's the one who will arrest him."

"So, you're certain he's not going to meet with us and betray us?"

"I get why you're concerned. And I can't guarantee with one hundred percent certainty, but I've done the research. I've run my algorithm twice on him. He's come back clean both times. He's so new to the force, he hasn't had time to become corrupt. He's mostly been on patrols and follow-ups on suspicious activity. Unless Fitzgerald has decided in the last five hours to get him on their payroll, and he accepted, we're golden."

"Send the email then."

"Are you sure?" Evelyn questioned.

"Yeah. I mean, at least this time we've done some research. We're prepared. We're not going to go into this blindly like we did last time. We're going to learn from our mistakes, remember?"

"Yes. We'll learn from our mistakes, and everything will be fine."

James walked back to his computer. "Constable McCleary," he read aloud as he typed. "We are a pair of local investigators. We have a case we think you will want to see. It's a career-making opportunity. In fact, if you don't agree to meet with us, you might find it to be a career-ending mistake. Once we hear from you that you're willing to meet, we'll send you another message with a time and place. We look forward to hearing your reply."

"Sounds good," Patrick said.

"Excellent. And send."

"Now what?" Evelyn asked.

"Now we wait."

CHAPTER 28

PATRICK

"Bloody hell, this is the stupidest thing I have ever seen," James exclaimed.

"It is not. It's awesome."

"This would never happen in real life."

"That's because it's not real life," Evelyn said.

"But why aren't they questioning what's going on? I mean, aren't they a little suspicious that they walk down into a basement and there are all these weird trinkets lying around?"

"James, shut up. You'd think you'd never watched a movie before in your life," Patrick said.

James huffed. "Of course, I've seen a bloody movie before, but I can't stand movies when they're full of idiots. I mean, why can't horror movies have some intelligent people for once? The characters never use their brains. And these people don't even understand they're walking into a trap."

"You understand this movie is a parody, right? The filmmakers are making fun of the horror genre." Evelyn leaned against Patrick on the couch.

"I don't fucking care. If you're going to parody something, at least add an element they're all missing. And every movie in the genre is missing the smart person."

"Just shut your trap and watch the movie." Patrick turned his attention back to the film.

James narrowed his eyes, but watched the film.

It had been a few hours since they'd emailed Constable Mc-Cleary, and he still hadn't responded. They were becoming anxious, and rather than risking their lives by leaving the flat, they ordered takeaway and put on a movie to distract them from checking the email for a response every two minutes.

Patrick was enjoying the brief moment of relaxation. They were simply three friends, sitting in their living room, watching a terrible movie. He glanced at the woman in his arms, and couldn't stop the smile that spread across his face. She was right. If they solved the case now, and arrested Fitzgerald, they'd be able to enjoy her last three weeks here. If they'd given the case away, they wouldn't have been able to enjoy anything. He would have been wondering what-ifs, and they would still have to look over their shoulders because the Fitzgeralds would still be out there. And even though they'd said they'd leave them alone if they dropped the case, they were hardened criminals, and how much could they actually keep them to their word?

He tightened his hold on Evelyn, drew her in closer to his side. She sighed and cuddled with him, laying her head on his shoulder. He was in trouble. What he was feeling for her was more intense than he was ready for. He didn't know how he was going to ever let her go in three weeks. It would be one thing if he knew she'd be coming back, but she wouldn't be. She'd go to Greece for her six-week program, and then fly back to the States. They'd be reduced to keeping in contact via email or video chat. And he'd read about long-distance relationships. They never lasted. They had these three weeks together, and that was it. And he wasn't sure if he was ready for that to be it. He didn't want their *whatever* to end.

Why couldn't he admit they were in a relationship? If he couldn't even admit it in his head, how could he be expected to admit it aloud? It probably had something to do with the fact he'd never been in a relationship before. He was a lone wolf. Loved the one-night stand, love-them-and-leave-them thing. He'd never had a desire for a serious relationship. Until now. This woman, who he never would have met if he wasn't on this case, was the first to come into his life who could even make him consider giving up his bachelor ways. And that wasn't only scary, it also made him sad. Because, of *course,* it was a woman he had no future with. One who was going to leave him in a few short weeks and he'd never see again.

Fate was a fickle bitch.

"Mate, you okay?" James asked. "You're looking pretty pissed off over there."

Patrick shook himself out of his thoughts. "Yeah, I'm fine. Just thinking about what I'm going to do to Fitzgerald when I'm finally able to confront him."

"You're not going to do anything to him." Evelyn moved away from him slightly. "You're going to allow the police to arrest him, and then we'll sit back and watch his trial like normal citizens of the world."

"You think I'm going to let the police arrest him on their own? I'm going to be there. And when I'm finally face-to-face with him for the first time, I'm going to take out all of my anger and frustration on his face."

She pulled out of his embrace completely. "Wait. Has this always been the plan? You being there with the police?"

"Well, yeah, James and I are going to be right there with PC McCleary when he arrests him. The man needs backup. You didn't think we were going to send him in there alone, did you? That would be sending the poor bloke to his death."

She turned to James. "Is this true?"

"Well, yeah. I thought you knew. I mean, I thought it was a pretty obvious step in our plan. I didn't think we needed to actually spell that part out for you."

She shook her head. "What's stopping the Fitzgeralds from killing all of you the second you step into their...whatever you call their location. Their hideout?"

"Their lair," James replied. "I like to think they have an evil lair where they do all of their evil planning."

Patrick and Evelyn looked at him and shook their heads.

"What? Mickey Fitzgerald is obviously an evil super villain. He has to have a lair. I'm sticking with the lair and ignoring your judgmental looks."

"Well, answer me this. Even with three of you, you're out-numbered. You have to know that."

"It's a chance we're willing to take. We can't let PC McCleary walk into the headquarters—"

"Lair," James interrupted.

Patrick glared at him. "—alone. Three men are better than one, no matter how you look at it."

"But—"

"They're less likely to kill three blokes who walk into their lair than one bloke who walks into the lion's den alone," James stated.

She shook her head. "You know that's bullshit. There's nothing that will stop them. They're murderers. When were you planning to tell me this?"

"I didn't think you needed to be told. I thought you had deduced it on your own. You're a smart woman. I didn't think we needed to spell it out for you," Patrick replied.

"Well, obviously, you needed to. And where am I going to be when you guys storm the castle, so to speak?"

"Colin's," Patrick spoke without hesitation.

"You're going to drop me off at your dad's and have him babysit me while I worry about you as you deliberately put yourselves in danger?"

"Well, we're not taking you with us, if that's where you're going with this."

"Why not? Why can't I be there? Wouldn't four people be better than three?"

"Because it's too bloody dangerous! You would be a distraction, which would be the reason the mission would go wrong."

She moved completely away from him and stood. "Fine. I'll remove myself starting now. I would hate to be a *distraction*." She turned around and walked to Patrick's room.

"Where are you going?"

"To go pack my stuff. You should take me to your dad's now. I would hate to be the reason you blow the case."

"You're being ridiculous and completely overreacting." Patrick followed her. "You know you can't be there with us. I don't know why you're acting this way."

"Because I'm tired of you seeing me as someone who isn't part of the team. After everything, I'm still not good enough to be in the know."

"I didn't keep you in the dark on purpose. You know that. I honestly thought you knew this was the plan. You didn't honestly think we were going to send the poor bloke in alone, did you?"

"No. I thought he'd have his own team to bring in."

"What team? Right now, he's the only one who might be willing to arrest Fitzgerald. He's it. He doesn't have a team. We're his team. James and me. We're it. So, I need you to calm down and start thinking rationally."

"Why can't I go with you? I'll be going crazy sitting in your dad's apartment waiting for you to get back. I want to be there to make sure you're going to be okay."

He stopped in front of her, bringing his hand up to cup her face. "Because if the mission does go wrong, if we're ambushed, if the family lives up to expectations and opens fire on us, I want to make sure you're not there. That you're safe."

She closed her eyes. A tear escaped down her cheek. "Please don't think like that."

He shrugged. "We have to take everything into consideration. Mickey Fitzgerald and his gang are hardened criminals. They may decide to take us out rather than going quietly. We need to be prepared."

"So, you guys could be walking to your deaths?"

"It's a real possibility," he whispered.

She shook her head as another tear made a trail down her cheek. "I don't like it. I don't want you to go."

"We have to."

She moved forward, closing the gap between them, embracing him, burying her face in his chest as she sobbed.

He wrapped his arms around her tightly, rubbing his hands up and down her back.

"Hey, guys," James's voice arose from the background.

They moved away from each other and turned to look at him.

"I'm sorry to interrupt your Hallmark moment, but our elusive PC McCleary has emailed us back."

Patrick took her hand and walked back into the living room. "And?"

"And he's agreed to meet. We've piqued his interest. He wants to meet as soon as possible."

Patrick sat, rubbing his mouth with his hands. "We should meet tonight."

"Are you sure? So soon? It's already late. I think we should meet tomorrow. Fresh minds and all that. Give him more time to read the email and prepare."

"I agree with James. We rushed into the meeting last time, and we all know how that turned out. I think we should meet tomorrow night. Give him twenty-four hours to prepare and give us time to really hammer out a plan. We need to make sure we're the ones in control this time. One hundred percent in control. We don't want to be surprised again."

Patrick sighed. "You're right. Tell him we'll meet him tomorrow night at ten."

"Where? I don't think we should have him come here, and I don't think we should meet in public again. We can't risk getting caught on CCTV and having someone on the Fitzgeralds' pay roll see us. That would blow everything."

Patrick steepled his fingers and brought them up to rest in front of his mouth. "We should meet at the office."

"I forgot about the office," James stated.

"The office?" she asked.

"It's this abandoned building about two miles from here. When we first went into this business together, we joked about setting up our agency there. We visited it and we even talked to an estate agent about buying the building. But holy shit, even as an abandoned building, it was fucking expensive. So, we ditched that thought and decided to use our flat as our office as well," James explained.

"We haven't visited the office in forever, and I don't think anyone will even associate the building with us," Patrick added. "It's the perfect place for a clandestine meeting."

James began typing on the computer. "Alright. I pulled the exact address of the office out of trusty Google and made a nice map. I'll copy and paste it into the message, like so. Voila! We have a response. We have a meeting with PC McCleary at ten tomorrow night at the office. And that's all the message says. And it's sent."

"This feels like a cheesy spy movie," she stated.

"That's what makes it so fun." James chuckled.

"Now that we have to wait until tomorrow night for this meeting, how are we going to keep busy?" Patrick asked.

"Well, let's finish this shitty movie, then the two of you can fuck like bunnies. Tomorrow, we can watch even more shitty movies until it's time to go, if you two can stop shagging long enough to grace me with your presence, that is." James wore a cheeky grin.

Patrick picked up the pillow from the couch and threw it at his head.

James caught it and sent it back, and the three started laughing.

The tension left the room. They settled in to finish their movie.

CHAPTER 29

PATRICK

After the movie ended, Patrick picked up his phone.

"Bloody hell, I'm starving. Takeaway?"

Evelyn sat up and stretched. "Yes, please."

"None for me, thanks," James said, standing from the couch. "I'm off to my mum's for dinner. She wants to spend some time with me while not in an emergency setting. You two lovebirds have fun, yeah?" He gave a wink before exiting the flat, leaving Patrick and Evelyn alone.

Alone.

He couldn't think of a time they had the flat to themselves. Well, not a time when he wasn't wallowing in his bed rather than spending time with her.

"Curry?" he asked, unable to keep the excitement from bleeding through his voice.

"Sure. What's got you so happy?"

He quickly tapped in a delivery order from the curry place down the street into the app on his phone before setting it aside. He turned so he was facing her. "We're alone."

She laughed. "Yes, I watched James leave."

"We have the flat to ourselves. We just ordered in takeaway." He paused, waiting for her to pick up on the significance of the moment.

"Yes." She tilted her head, eyebrows down. "Why are you just stating obvious things? Does your head hurt? Are you having delayed symptoms from the concussion?" She reached out to touch the plaster on his head that covered his wound.

He shook his head, a wide grin spreading on his face. "Oh, sweet Evelyn. Don't you realize? It's our first date!"

She brought her hand back to her lap. "Our first date? We are in your flat."

"Who cares? We can't exactly leave because of being wanted by The Fitzgeralds. And really, we don't need much more than each other and some good food for it to be counted as a date, yeah?"

He could practically see the wheels turning in her head as she came to this realization.

"Best date ever," she declared.

He chuckled. "You're having a laugh."

"I'm serious. I don't need to leave the house or put on make-up. Best. Date. Ever."

"Well, then." He rearranged himself on the couch, tucking one leg under his body before resting his elbow on the top of the cushion, leaning his head against his hand. "Tell me more about your life in Iowa."

She also rearranged herself, mirroring his position. "Shit, I feel like I'm being interviewed on a talk show."

"C'mon. We've done things all wrong. We've skipped so many basic things. I want to know about your life. Outside of," he gestured with his free hand, "all of this."

"Okay, well, what do you want to know?"

"Everything."

"I'm the oldest of three sisters. My sisters, Elizabeth and Michelle, are easily my best friends. In fact, my entire family is very close. Elizabeth and I chose to go to Iowa State because of its proximity to our home. Going far away really wasn't something we desired to do."

"And yet you decided to travel halfway around the world."

She smiled. "I did. This was me getting out of my comfort zone. And boy is the universe flashing all the signs about how I probably should have stayed home. In my rut."

"But then you wouldn't have met me."

Her gaze met his. She smiled softly. "You're right. I guess there's been *something* decent about this whole debacle."

"If you're so close to your family, it must really be killing you lying to them about everything."

"You don't even know. It's why I haven't called them or video chatted. I'll just cave like a house of cards the second I look into my mom's eyes."

He could feel jealousy start to creep up. "You're very lucky to have the family you do."

She readjusted her position on the couch so she could move closer to him. She took his free hand into her own. She said nothing, just took his hand in hers. That one small action meant the world to Patrick in this moment.

He cleared his throat. "What are some things you do for fun in Iowa? I looked it up in a quick web search shortly after you came, because honestly, it's a place I was never aware of. And all I got were pictures of corn. Is your entire state made of nothing but corn fields? Do you live on a farm?"

She laughed. "No. I don't live on a farm, and our entire state isn't made of corn fields. We have some large cities, but the population of our entire state is equivalent to the population of Los Angeles."

"The weather must be pretty mild if you have vast amounts of farms."

"Wow, already talking about the weather. This date must be fizzling out."

"Evelyn, I'm British. There's nothing more we like to do than talk about the weather."

"Well, in that case, our weather is not mild. We have brutally cold winters, with several days below zero Fahrenheit. And our summers are hot and muggy, which helps our corn grow."

"And you spend all summer inside with all your glorious air conditioning I've seen in films."

"No, we spend our summer catching lightning bugs in jars, wading through creeks, and going to the State Fair to eat cotton candy the size of your head."

He scoffed. "You're having me on. It's not really the size of your head."

"It really is. So much sugar."

There was a knock on the door, interrupting them. Patrick reluctantly let go of her hand and stood. He opened the door to retrieve the takeaway and returned to the couch.

He and Evelyn moved in tandem spreading out the food on the coffee table. They were so in sync, it was as if they had done this several times. It was so fucking domestic, he couldn't help but imagine that this was what life could be like if she could just stay.

He shook his head and brought himself to the present. No use imagining things that couldn't happen. It only led to heartbreak.

"So, I've talked about myself, what about you? What was it like growing up in London?"

"Well, no creek stomping and catching lightning bugs, for one thing."

She laughed as she took a bite of her dinner. "Well," she said after she swallowed, "I imagine growing up in the city would be quite different than growing up in rural Iowa. Have you always lived in Tower Hamlets?"

"No, I grew up in a more posh neighborhood, but not too posh, more middle class. It was all quite boring. I went to school, and I obeyed my parents, until about secondary school when I really realized my dad was never around and I began to resent him."

"Yeah, I gathered he wasn't around much from everything you and he have said since I've known you. Were you and your mom close?"

"Yes, but probably not as close as you are with your parents. But we were close enough. She was my only parent most of the time."

"What made you want to become a police officer?"

"Rebellion. My dad wanted me to be a lawyer like him, and my A-levels were okay, but not great. I didn't think University was my thing, so I signed up to be in the police. Went through training and was placed here, in Tower Hamlets."

"Where you met James."

He smiled. "Where I met James, and we became the only two fucking sods with morals in the whole borough."

"And the rest is history?"

"The rest is history." He set his fork aside having finished his meal. "You know, starting this business with James was like having a dream come true. I finally had something I could call my own. Something I could control. And I don't even care that I have to spend night after night in a fucking MINI Cooper waiting to get a picture of some asshole cheating on their spouse. I don't answer to anyone, and it's fucking amazing."

She moved closer to him, having finished her meal. She reached over and placed her hand on his cheek, gently caressing it.

He moved his head so he could place a kiss on her palm.

Her gaze immediately flew up to his. Her eyes were so soft and full of emotion.

He leaned forward and closed the gap between them, capturing her lips with his.

She returned the kiss, moving the hand she had placed on his cheek until it was on his shoulder, pulling them closer together.

He brought his arms around, settling his hands on her waist, before running his tongue across her lips. She opened to him, deepening the kiss.

She moved her hands, dragging them up the back of his neck until she tangled them in his hair, all the while being careful of his left side, which was still tender to the touch even a week later.

He moaned as her fingers massaged his scalp. He brought his hands down to the hem of her shirt, inching it up. His hand met with the bare skin of her back. It was warm and soft. He started moving it up her back. When he met the strap of her bra, she froze.

He pulled back, letting his eyes focus, and frowned.

Her eyes were wide.

"What's wrong?"

"Um, I think we left something very important out of our 'getting to know you' session."

"What's that?"

She pulled her lower lip between her teeth and looked down. She was quiet for a long time.

"Evelyn, whatever it is, you can tell me." He worried he did something wrong, or she was going to tell him she was dying of cancer, or she was a prophet and the world was going to end in the next five minutes.

"I don't have a lot of...experience," she finally said, almost haltingly.

He breathed a sigh of relief. Not dying of cancer. "That's fine, love. It's not a big deal."

"Except it is," she insisted, "because when I say I don't have a lot of experience, I mean..." She paused, taking a deep breath, still keeping her gaze on her lap. "I mean, I'm a virgin. And I don't think I'm ready to have sex. At least, not right now. At this moment."

He looked at the beautiful woman in front of him, who just opened up to him about something so deeply personal, something she was clearly embarrassed to admit, and was completely in awe of her. He didn't think he could like her any more, and this happened. She was so fucking brave.

She must have read into his silence something he didn't intend, because she began to move away from him. "If this is a deal-breaker for you, it's fine. I can just sleep on the couch—"

He placed his hand on her arm, stopping her. "It's not a deal breaker. Not at all." He pulled her closer to him, cupping her face between his hands. "I like you, and I enjoy getting to know you. Do I want to have sex with you? Fuck yes. Am I willing to wait and move at the pace you're comfortable with? Also, fuck yes."

She gave him a tentative smile. "Are you sure? You're not going to yell at me and call me a prude?"

Fire burned behind his eyes. He knew immediately with the specificity of the statement someone had said that very thing to her in the past. "Who the fuck would even do that? Whoever did that to you was wrong and an arsehole." He took a breath, composing himself. "Yes, Evelyn, I'm sure. Intimacy doesn't just mean shagging. It can also be sharing your deepest thoughts and fears. And we've been doing that. I can wait until you're ready to move to becoming physically intimate."

She leaned forward and placed a soft kiss on his lips. She pulled away almost as quickly as she began. "Thank you."

"No thanks needed. Truly." He brushed her hair out of her eyes. "Shall we move to the bed? To sleep?"

She nodded, and the two of them worked together to clean up their dinner.

As they moved through their nighttime routine, which had become synchronized like clockwork over the last week, Patrick could feel the same thoughts from earlier creeping back into his mind.

What if this could be forever?

They settled into bed, and he turned off the light.

She moved until she was settled with her head on his chest.

"If you had made it to your program, what would you be doing right now?" He ran his hands through her hair.

"At this exact moment? I would probably be sleeping."

He laughed. "No, just in general."

"Well, I would be working at the ancient site of Epidaurus, helping excavate and rebuild the Temple of Asclepius."

"So, you would be like Indiana Jones?"

"Not quite. More research, less exploring. Only Greeks may do the actual digging, so I would be doing a lot of dirt sorting. And research."

"What's special about the Temple of Asclepius?"

She smiled. "Oh, so much. When people got sick, they traveled to Epidaurus to visit the Temple. You see, Asclepius was the god of healing. And they believed he visited in your dreams and healed you. So, people came and slept in his temple in order to be healed."

"Wow, how fascinating. Did it work?"

"I mean, it's pretty widely agreed the priests and doctors basically dosed the people with hallucinogens so they all said Asclepius visited them in their sleep."

He laughed. "Is that all Epidaurus is known for? Drugging people into believing a god was visiting them in their sleep to heal them?"

"No. They're also known for their amazing theater. I've read if you sit all the way at the top, you can perfectly hear whatever is being said on the stage. And the person doing the talking at the bottom doesn't even need to raise their voice. Trying it out was something I was really looking forward to."

"You'll still have a chance. You're going there at the end of summer, yeah?"

"Yeah."

He noticed a change in her. Thinking about her trip had seemed to bring her down a little. "Tell me about your research. Is it all about Asclepius?"

"No, actually. It's about healing myths in Ancient Greece in general."

And then she was describing her research and everything she had done so far. Her foul mood quickly dissipated, bleeding into excitement as she talked about her work. He enjoyed listening to her talk about something she was obviously passionate about, even though he didn't fully understand everything she was saying.

Eventually they both grew tired, so they rolled over, and he wrapped his arms around her body, pulling her in close.

He pressed a kiss against the shell of her ear before whispering, "I think I've caught feelings for you."

"I think I've caught feelings for you as well," she whispered back.

Smiling at her answer, he closed his eyes and drifted off into a peaceful sleep.

CHAPTER 30

EVELYN

"You guys thought this would make a good office?" Evelyn stared at the dilapidated building they stood in front of.

The single-story building looked as if all it would take was a strong wind, and it would fall over, if it hadn't been made of pure, undecorated concrete. The door was held closed with a chain, but it seemed it was only there as a formality, since the two large windows on either side of it were missing their glass. The roof also seemed like a formality, as it was missing several parts and looked as if, at one point, there were tarps draped over them, but they were long gone.

"It has character," Patrick defended.

"See why we were confused about it being so bloody expensive? We thought they'd be happy to get rid of it, but the fuckers were greedy and wanted loads of money for it. Way more than we offered," James said.

"The estate agent actually laughed at our offer. She thought we weren't being serious. She thought we were having a laugh."

"What did you offer?"

"Twenty pounds," they said in unison.

Evelyn laughed. "You know what? This building looks like it's worth twenty pounds. I don't know why she wasn't taking you seriously. How much did they want for this pile of concrete?"

"Half a mil," Patrick said.

"You're joking." She couldn't believe it!

"One hundred percent serious."

"Ridiculous. So, are we having our meeting out here?"

James shook his head. "No. We're having it inside. Not in public, remember?"

She turned back to look at the building. "You want me to go in there? There are probably mice."

Patrick smiled. "Oh, there are loads of mice and rats. But don't worry, they aren't spies."

"I'm not going in there. I'll wait out here for you to finish."

James shook his head. "We can't let you do that. We're not letting you out of our sight, remember?"

"I'll wait in the car." She pointed at the MINI Cooper at the curb. They'd brought a getaway car, so to speak, in case they needed to leave quickly. They didn't want to have to find a cab again. "I'll even lock the doors. Completely safe."

It was Patrick's turn to shake his head. "Remember, we're supposed to not listen to you when you're being stubborn.

You're coming with us. It'll be okay. I promise to protect you from the rats and the bugs and whatever spooks live in there."

"It's haunted?" She took a step back from the building.

"Well, yeah, I'm sure it is. The building is old. I'm sure there are a few things haunting the inside."

She turned and tried to make a break for the car, but Patrick grabbed her around her waist, throwing her over his shoulder. She struggled for a second before giving up.

"Sorry, love, we were just taking the piss." Patrick walked them toward the building. "The worst thing in this building is the amount of mold growing from the lack of roof and the wet London weather. I'm sure there are mice and rats, but they won't bother you, I promise." He set her down through the window before climbing through himself.

James followed shortly after.

"Alright, let's light these torches and set them on the floor over here, pointing up, to illuminate the room." Patrick pulled the flashlights out of the bag they'd brought.

She took the flashlights and started setting them up around the room while Patrick and James began pulling out photocopies of items they'd found in the duffel bag. That afternoon, they'd decided they'd needed to bring some of the evidence with them in order to convince PC McCleary to help. And for the first time, she had seen what they had. After all the photographs and fake money, she knew, for a fact, they had an excellent chance of bringing down Fitzgerald.

They needed this officer to agree to help them.

She moved back to the men, and Patrick put his arm around her shoulders, pulling her close. After their date the night before, he always seemed to be touching her in some way throughout the day. Whether it was an arm around her shoulders or holding her hand, it was like he wanted to make sure he was keeping her close.

She looked at him and smiled. She was enjoying every second of this new aspect of their relationship. She was going to bask in the glow for as long as she was here.

There was shuffling outside the building, causing all three heads to turn and look toward the windows.

The sound stopped, and the beam of a flashlight illuminated the frame of the window to the left of the door. Patrick removed his arm from around her shoulders and moved her so he positioned her behind him. He was so much taller than her she had to peer around his body to get a view of what was happening.

Patrick and James shifted into defensive stances, each holding a pocket knife, the closest thing they had to weapons in their flat that could do some damage. It wasn't much, and they would never win a fight if the officer brought a gun into it, but it made them feel better to not go into the meeting empty-handed.

The flashlight got tossed through the window, making a large clunking sound as it hit the concrete floor of the building. A man climbing through the window followed closely behind it.

James and Patrick gripped their knives, ready to move into action if the man attacked them. The man bent down and picked up his flashlight before turning around and looking at them.

The lights that were set up around the building helped illuminate his features. He was young, younger than the three of them. He was fit. You could tell he had recently finished all the physical training it took to become an officer. He had blond hair, cropped close to his skull, and he was still dressed in his uniform, like he had just gotten off a shift or he was on his way to start one. And he wasn't very tall. In fact, he was shorter than both James and Patrick.

When he noticed the two large men holding knives, ready to move at him, he held his arms up in surrender. "I come in peace."

"Please state your name," James said, neither one lowering their arms with the knives.

"Police Constable Joseph McCleary. I believe you are expecting me. You have the distinct advantage of knowing who I am, as I have no clue who you are." McCleary was still raising his hands.

James and Patrick slowly lowered their knives, but didn't put them away.

"Sorry," Patrick said. "We can't be too careful, not with the case we're about to share with you."

PC McCleary shook his head. "I understand. I would have done the same. When I arrived at the building, seeing its state, I almost walked past it. I only have my baton on me, and I was worried this was going to be an ambush. But my curiosity got the better of me. I need to know what this case is and how it will make my career."

James and Patrick took a couple of steps forward, making the gap between them and the officer smaller. Patrick reached behind him, grabbing Evelyn's hand, and pulled her along, making sure she stayed close.

"My name is Patrick Miller, and this is my business partner, James Moore. We are local private investigators. We've been working on a case against the Fitzgerald family. Are you familiar with them?"

He nodded. "I'm pretty sure everyone knows of the Fitzgerald family. They're not exactly secretive about their activities. What sort of case are you building? From what I've learned in my time on the force, they're untouchable."

"They're untouchable because every police officer in the borough, except for you, is in the pockets of the family," Patrick stated.

McCleary shook his head. "I don't believe you. Every officer can't possibly be getting bribes from them. I mean, the superintendent is the best person I know."

James walked forward, offering him one of the photocopies from the bag.

McCleary took it and shone his flashlight on it. His jaw dropped open as he looked at the photo of Mickey Fitzgerald paying off the superintendent.

"Impossible. If I wasn't looking right at it, I would still say you were full of shit. I just, I can't believe this."

"Like we said, every officer in the borough is lining their pockets with Fitzgerald money in order to look the other way and let the family have the run of the place."

"How do you know I'm not lining my pockets?"

"We've looked into your background thoroughly," James replied.

"Tell me about the case you're building because my interest is admittedly growing by the second."

"We're working with a local solicitor's office to try Mickey Fitzgerald on the crimes he's committed once he's arrested. We have enough evidence to put him behind bars for the rest of his life. The trouble is, we don't have anyone to make the arrest and press the charges," Patrick said.

"Until now."

"Until now," Patrick confirmed.

McCleary studied the photo for a few seconds before lifting his flashlight and shining it around Patrick and into Evelyn's face. "Who's the girl? What's she got to do with the case?"

"The girl is none of your business. You don't need to know anything about her. Let's just focus on the case."

"If she has something to do with the case, I'm going to have to know. Looking at the fading bruises on her face, she is either tied to the case or you're beating the shit out of her, and I'm going to have to take you in on suspicion of assault. So, which is it?"

Patrick's hand tightened on Evelyn's. "She's involved with the case, and until I know we can trust you, that's all you'll know. The last person we met with wasn't exactly trustworthy, so we'll be keeping things close to our chest until the right moment. I hope you understand."

"Clearly," McCleary stated.

"Good. Now, are you going to help us, or do we part ways now?"

McCleary moved his flashlight back to the picture, investigating it once more. "The rest of the evidence in your possession is this same quality?"

James and Patrick both said, "Yes."

"In the message you sent me, you said this case would make my career."

"If you arrest Mickey Fitzgerald, the media will hail you as a hero and you will get all the credit for breaking up the most notorious crime family in London. You will get the fame, the glory, and the promotions that come along with that title," James explained.

"Or," McCleary went on, "since the three of us will be going into the lion's den to arrest the bugger without backup, we'll gain notoriety as the fools the most infamous crime family murdered because they were stupid enough to think they could bring them down on their own."

"There is a risk we won't walk out of there alive, yes," Patrick agreed. "We'll understand if you walk away now and don't look back."

"What is your plan if I walk out of here right now?"

"We would somehow find a way to get Fitzgerald into another borough, get him to commit a crime, and have that borough's officers arrest Fitzgerald."

"And that officer would get the fame and credit for bringing the man to justice," McCleary added.

"Well, yes."

Evelyn watched as McCleary looked at the photo once more and then at the group.

He handed the picture back to James. "I'm in."

CHAPTER 31

PATRICK

The three friends breathed a sigh of relief as they looked at the man standing in front of them.

"Are you sure? Absolutely positively certain you're willing to do this?" Patrick inquired.

McCleary nodded. "Absolutely. I've been looking for a way to advance my career since I joined the force. There haven't been many cases popping up in Tower Hamlets to really show what I can do since most of the major crimes are committed by the Fitzgeralds, and strangely, we do nothing about those. And whenever I ask about them, I'm always being brushed off by my superiors. This is my chance to make a name for myself and make my borough safer at the same time. I'd be a fool to let this opportunity pass."

James and Patrick turned to each other and shared a look of victory before turning back to McCleary.

"That's good to hear. We have a few details to iron out, like finding where the Fitzgeralds are holed up, but as soon as we know, we'll contact you with a time and place so you can make the arrest."

McCleary nodded. "Do you need my number?" He shook his head and laughed. "Of course, you don't. You already have all of my information."

He took a step toward Patrick, his hand outstretched.

Patrick accepted it, shaking it.

"It was good to meet you, and I look forward to hearing from you soon," McCleary said.

Patrick nodded and released his hand.

McCleary turned and climbed out the window.

Patrick, James, and Evelyn stood quietly and waited for the light to disappear along with the sound of shuffling before they let their guards down and relaxed. Patrick almost couldn't believe what had happened. It was almost too easy. Could things finally be moving in their favor?

"Oh my God." Evelyn moved around to stand next to Patrick. "I just, wow, that went better than our last meeting."

Patrick nodded. "Yeah, I made it through without getting shot. I'd say it went loads better than the last meeting."

James laughed. "Didn't I tell you that with his high ambitions he would take the bait and agree to help us out?"

"Yeah. Good work telling him our original alternate plan of letting another borough take the credit for the arrest and take all the fame and glory. You could definitely see his ego inflating with that one," Patrick replied.

James smiled. "I had a feeling it would push him over the edge, and I was right. I'm pretty sure it was the bit of information that helped make him agree."

"I think you're right," Evelyn agreed. "God, my heart is still beating so fast from when he shone his light on me. I was certain he was going to say something about me and we were going to realize he was a fake, like Harry."

"Me, too, but I didn't appreciate him implying I beat you, though."

Evelyn smiled. "You have to admit, if you didn't know what happened, and the way you were being defensive about who I was, it would give the impression you abuse me."

Patrick sighed. "Next time I take you in public, we need to do your makeup a little better. Make you look less like a domestic abuse ad, yeah?"

"We can try, but I don't think any amount of makeup will fix this."

"You finally looked in a mirror, love?"

"I'm really surprised it still looks as bad as it does. I've never seen so many different colors of blue and green on my face before."

Patrick put his arm around her shoulders, pulling her in close and kissing the side of her head. "The man is a professional. He knows how to hit someone and how to cause certain types of damage. Fitzgerald said to rough you up a little, so he held back. If Fitzgerald didn't give him those directions, I'm sure you would look much worse or be much worse. You should feel lucky."

"I do. I just hope this clears up completely before we have to stage tourism pictures for my parents."

"Evie, I'm a pro at Photoshop, I can fix up anything, so I don't want you worrying about a thing." James moved around the room, picking up the torches they had set out and putting them in the bag.

"I'll keep that in mind. So, what now? What's our next step now that we have found our arresting officer?"

They moved to the window, where Patrick helped her climb through before climbing through himself.

"Now we go back to the flat and start trying to find the evil lair." James stepped through.

"How are we going to do that?" she asked as they got to the car.

Patrick unlocked the car, and they all climbed in. "Well, first we start with you describing, in detail, everything you remember about where you were held, and then we expand upon that with anything else we can find, like from the pictures in the duffel, and hope we hope we find a match."

"But I already told you I was held in a room. An extremely ordinary, plain room."

"Yes, but you'd be surprised at how much you can learn from something like that," James explained. "I'm prepared to amaze you with my internet searching skills.

CHAPTER 32

EVELYN

Evelyn stretched and looked at the clock on James's bedside table. She groaned. It was already early evening. Where had the time gone?

All morning, James and Patrick had sat at their respective computers and shouted street names and locations around town to each other where they suspected Fitzgerald could have his evil lair.

Originally, she had tried to work in the room with them. But after the third time one of their outbursts had made her practically leap from her skin, she'd excused herself to the farthest part of the flat to try to work in peace.

She shut her laptop and stood from the bed. Her bladder and her stomach made her aware of how long she had been sequestered in the room. Time to venture forth and seek sustenance.

She opened the door and immediately ducked into the bathroom. With her immediate need met, she began walking down the hallway. As she did, she noticed it was blessedly quiet. The boys were no longer shouting.

Just as she caught sight of the living room, she stopped in her tracks.

A dozen candles illuminated the room. They seemed to be spread on all the surfaces in the kitchen and living room. Someone had moved the table. She didn't know where, but in its place, they had spread a blanket out.

"Patrick, what's going on?"

He came out from behind the counter wearing an apron. "Fuck. You're early."

"Early?" she asked. "How can I be early when I have no idea what is going on?"

He grinned, gesturing around the room, his right hand encased in an oven mitt. "Date night."

"Date night?"

"Yeah. I wanted to surprise you with another stay-in-the-flat date."

"If you were going to surprise me, how can I possibly be early?" She crossed her arms over her chest, one side of her mouth rising into a half smile as she lifted an eyebrow.

"Okay, okay. This was all a bit last minute, so I may have forgotten the minor detail of telling you not to come out until a certain time," Patrick said sheepishly.

"Where'd you ship James off to?"

"He is on a stakeout. He was frustrated with the lack of progress on finding the secret lair, so he scrolled through the agency's emails until he found something he could knock out easily."

"It's been twenty-four hours since we met with McCleary."

"It has."

"James realizes finding my non-descript warehouse is like finding a needle in a haystack, right? That it's going to take some time?"

"He does," Patrick said, turning back to the kitchen to finish prepping the food. "However, neither of us have any patience, so we need distractions. He has chosen to throw himself into work, whilst I have chosen to woo my lady with my cooking skills."

She walked over and leaned against the counter. "I have to admit, I didn't think you could cook."

He turned to look over his shoulder. "Now, why would you think that?"

"I don't know, perhaps it was the complete lack of food in the flat the day I arrived?"

"Hmm. Yes, I can see why that would lead you to that conclusion. However, I would like to assure you, I am a fantastic cook, and you're going to love what I've made."

"What have you made?"

He turned fully and grinned widely. "Bangers and mash, with Yorkshire pudding. And I've made a tart for dessert."

"I'm going to circle back around and ask you about what the hell some of these foods are, but holy shit. When did you start cooking in order to make all of this?"

"Just about two hours. Nothing I've made is too difficult, and it's all dishes one would find on any British table at any night of the week."

"So, explain. What the fuck is a banger?"

He threw his head back and cackled. Actually cackled.

She frowned. "I didn't think what I said was that funny."

He shook his head, controlling his laughter. "No, it wasn't really. I just find it amusing, is all. A banger is a sausage."

"Why on earth would you call a sausage a banger?"

"Because, love, it makes a bang in the pan."

She shook her head. "I don't know if I'll ever get used to the differences in what you call things here versus in the States."

"Eh," Patrick replied as he spooned the mash into a large bowl before placing two sausages on top. "It's not too different. I think you're figuring everything out just fine. By the time you leave, you'll be a natural." He handed her a bowl and gestured toward the blanket on the floor.

She sat on the floor, careful to not spill her dinner. He untied his apron before grabbing his bowl and a plate with what she guessed were the Yorkshire puddings and walking over to join her.

"What made you think 'picnic in the living room' for our second date?" she asked as she cut her sausage with the edge of her fork.

He shrugged. "Dunno. I guess I was trying to think of something that would make us forget we were stuck in the flat. I can't take you to Vicky Park right now, so I figured I would bring Vicky Park to you."

"Maybe when this is all over, we can go to Vicky Park and have a real picnic?"

He smiled. "Of course. It would be a sin to leave here without taking you to London's first public park."

"Well, that definitely sounds like it would be something I wouldn't pass up if I were here for a planned visit."

She stabbed a piece of the banger, scooped it up with a bit of mash, and took a bite. She closed her eyes. Fuck. He wasn't kidding. He was an excellent cook.

"Good, innit?"

She opened her eyes to find him watching her with a cheeky grin on his face. "It is."

"Now, Evelyn, I've thought we've come so far in our relationship that it wouldn't be so difficult to give me a compliment."

"We have. It's just, I'm pretty sure your ego is big enough. You really don't need me stroking it with compliments."

He bit his lip and looked like he was about to burst out into uncontrolled laughter.

"What on earth..." She trailed off, realizing immediately what was making him react the way he was. "Oh, for fuck's sake. What are you? Twelve?"

"Please, can I just say it, just to get it out of my system?"

"No, because you are a grownup, and you should act like one."

He sighed dramatically. "Fine. Have it your way."

"Now," she said, bringing them back to the date. "I was going to say, before you decided to act like a pre-teen, I can add your cooking to the list of things I'm going to miss when I leave."

He looked at his bowl. "Well, I can teach you how to make all of this before you leave. And maybe we can schedule a night where we cook the same meal and eat it over a video call? Like a long-distance date night?"

She froze, her next bite not quite making it to her mouth. "Long-distance date night?"

"Yeah," he said, his gaze still fixed on his supper. "You know, to vary things a bit."

She set her fork back in her bowl. "You see us continuing past me leaving?"

He finally brought his gaze up to meet hers. "Of course. I would like to give it a try, at least. Do you not?"

"I do, I just wasn't sure where you stood on the whole long-distance relationship thing. I know the other night you said you had feelings for me, but I didn't know if that meant longevity, or just for now."

"Longevity. Definitely."

"Okay, same. Longevity here, too."

He grinned widely. "I'm glad we're on the same page."

"Me, too."

They sat there, staring at each other.

She didn't know who moved first, but bowls were thrust aside, mash spilled on the blanket as they crashed into each other, joining themselves at the lips.

Unlike their previous kisses, this one was more frenzied. She could hardly keep up with whose hands were where.

She broke away to catch her breath as he trailed kisses down her neck.

He moved so he could lay her down on the blanket, shifting on top of her. He recaptured her lips with his, and she gladly returned the kiss with fervor.

He used his knee to spread her legs wide enough for him to settle between them, pressing himself into her.

She could feel his arousal as he moved his hand up to cup her breast through her shirt.

Those two actions caused a panic to rise in her chest.

She was not ready for this.

She pulled away from the kiss, placing her hands on his chest, pushing him off of her.

He immediately moved off of her body, giving her space.

"Are you okay?" he asked, concern lacing his voice.

She nodded. "Yes, it's just I—"

"I know," Patrick said gently, "I know."

She pulled herself into a sitting position and drew her knees to her chest, wrapping her arms around them. "I'm sorry."

He shook his head. "You're sorry? Why are you sorry?"

"For leading you on. For stopping us."

"It's fine. You told me what your boundaries were the other night. I tried to push them. Are you sure you're okay?"

"Yes, I'm fine."

"Then why are you crying?"

She brought her hand to her cheek. It was wet. She wasn't even aware she had started crying. "I guess it's because I feel terrible, and I'm worried I'm fucking up our new relationship with my lack of experience."

He moved closer, wrapping her in his arms and pulling her against him in a hug. She tucked her head under his chin, resting it on his chest. She loved how they fit together, and how this one action immediately put her at ease.

"You're not fucking up our relationship because you don't want to have sex right now," he said, his voice firm.

"In the past..." She started, flashes of angry dates in her undergraduate years calling her a prude flew through her head.

"Fuck the past," he interrupted. "Whatever any other man before said, fuck them. Like I said the other night, there are other ways to be intimate. We can wait until you're ready before we shag. You're worth the wait. And let me tell you, when you're ready? It's going to be fucking amazing."

"What if I'm not ready before I have to leave in three weeks?" she asked, voicing aloud the fear she was holding inside.

"Then we're just going to have to find time to visit one another, right?"

Warmth spread through her body. Never before had anyone understood her insecurities surrounding sex and not being ready. But Patrick did. And that made her fall for him even more.

CHAPTER 33

PATRICK

"Fuck, fuck, fuck." James threw a pencil at his computer screen.

"Still no luck?" Evelyn sat on the couch, working on her thesis.

Her feet were on Patrick's lap, where he was absentmindedly rubbing them as he worked his way through the evidence in the bag, looking at every photograph closely, trying to pick out details in the background that might help them narrow down a location. He knew there had to be a clue in these pictures somewhere, but so far, nothing. Rubbing her feet was a pleasant distraction from the growing frustration he was feeling.

"Do you know how many fucking warehouses have multiple rooms and aren't used commercially in Tower Hamlets?"

"No, I don't."

"Too fucking many." He sighed and dropped his head into his hands.

"Relax. You've only been looking for three days. It took you a week to find McCleary, and you knew where to look. You need to stop putting so much pressure on yourself."

James sighed. "I know, but the sooner we find the evil lair, the sooner we can storm in and take out the super villain."

"Will you please stop calling it an evil lair? We're not living in a comic book." Patrick didn't stop looking at the picture he was inspecting or take his hand off the foot he was rubbing.

"If I keep thinking of this as a comic book, it makes it less scary that we're going to willingly walk into a room full of armed criminals with one police officer with a baton and pocketknives. Remind me again why we think this is a good idea?"

"Because we get to be the superheroes." Patrick kept up with James's comic book analogy.

"Yeah, except when they shoot us, we'll die," James mumbled.

She stiffened next to Patrick.

He looked up from the picture and shot daggers at the back of James's head. He was trying so hard to keep her relaxed and have her forget about the risk they were taking, but James kept bringing it up without thinking.

She shut her computer, removed her feet from his lap, and stood. "I need to go to the bathroom." She scurried off to the back of the flat.

Patrick waited to hear the door shut before turning on James. "You need to fucking stop with the negative shit. I'm trying to keep her calm so she can focus on her schoolwork, and you bringing up the fact we can die isn't helping, at all."

"I'm sorry. I can't help it. It's hard for me to ignore the fact we're essentially walking into a firing squad."

"You don't know that. They could decide to not shoot us as we walk in."

"Do you honestly believe that? Do you really think Fitzgerald isn't going to take one look at us, hear us tell him he's under arrest, and laugh as he signals for his men to shoot us? And then they're going to throw our bodies in the Thames."

"That is a valid scenario. However, I'd like it if you stopped laying out those plausible scenarios in Evelyn's presence."

"I'm sorry. Yeah, I'll do better. I'm just getting frustrated because I'm not finding anything that even remotely looks like it could be the evil lair."

"Stop calling it the evil lair. And I know you're frustrated. I'm frustrated, too. But we need to not think about what can happen when we walk into the hideout and focus on finding the hideout first."

"Have you found any photographs that show any outside details? Because we really need something that shows the outside of the building to narrow my list down."

"Unfortunately, when Megan was spying, she only took photos of the inside of the building."

"Well, bugger. I have a short list. I say we split up and do some old-fashioned investigating. That's my only solution. Normally I'd suggest we go together, but we can cover more ground if we separate and regroup back here."

"That's a brilliant idea, actually. However, we should go out in pairs, not alone. And if one group happens to find the lair, no one acts until after we've regrouped. No impulse invasions. Just make a note of where you found them and move on."

"Agreed. On all points. I'll give McCleary a call and get him here. You take Evie, because you know she's not going to sit back and let us do this on our own. And maybe if you take her, something will jog her memory."

Patrick sighed and watched as she quietly emerged from the bathroom, shutting the door behind her. "You're right. As much as I don't want to take her, there's no way she's going to sit back and let us do this without her."

James picked up his phone. "I'll call McCleary. You go prep Evie."

Patrick followed her to his room. She was lying on the bed, staring at the ceiling.

"Hey." He moved into the room.

She sat up. "Hey."

"So, we've decided sitting here isn't helping our situation, and we're going to do a little field work. Want to join?"

She narrowed her eyes. "Is this a trick? You're not going to drive me over to your dad's and ditch me there, are you?"

He shook his head. "Not a trick. James and I were talking, and we decided we need to go out and see if we can actually find the warehouse where the Fitzgeralds are hiding. But we don't think we should go alone. He's calling McCleary right now, and we decided you should come along with me. Maybe something will jog your memory."

She shook her head. "I've already told you. I was unconscious both times. I was never able to see the outside of the building."

"Are you seriously arguing against coming along? Who are you and what have you done with my girlfriend?" Patrick joked.

Her eyes widened. "What did you say?"

He laughed. "Relax, love, it was a joke. I don't actually believe you've been body snatched."

She shook her head. "Not that, the other part. The part where you called me your girlfriend."

He paused. He hadn't realized he'd said it. It had come out so naturally. He didn't even need to think about it. And now that it was out there, he didn't sense any sort of panic arising like he'd thought there would be. In fact, it felt right.

"Yeah." He smirked. "You're my girlfriend, aren't you?"

She got really quiet, like she was thinking things over, and he panicked. Had something changed in the last forty-eight hours? What if she didn't feel the same anymore? What if she didn't want to adopt these labels? They had talked about being long distance, but they never discussed labels and being exclusive. What if she didn't want to be tied down to just him when there were thousands of miles between them?

"Well, yeah, I guess I am. You've just never said that word before."

"I've always been a little terrified of it, to be honest."

"And now you're not?"

He shook his head. "It's funny, but I said it without thinking about it. It seemed natural."

"And what happens when I leave?"

"Long-distance dates. Remember? Until then, let's just enjoy being together."

She smiled. "Okay. I can do that."

He returned her smile. "Great. Should we get ready to go?"

She shook her head, taking a step toward him, closing the gap before reaching up and pulling him down to bring her lips to his. It didn't take long for their kiss to move from tender and tentative to something more intense.

In the days since they'd admitted there was something there, they had shared some kissing and heavy petting in bed at night, but it never moved past that, and he was okay with taking things slow. This was all unfamiliar territory for him, and he didn't want to fuck things up.

But this kiss was different from all the other ones they'd shared in the past few days. It was intense and full of fire. Hands roamed, and Patrick couldn't help his body reacting to the passion. He moved them until her legs met the edge of the bed, and then he gently maneuvered them onto the mattress, all without breaking the kiss.

They pressed their bodies as close together as they physically could, and as she snaked her hand up the back of his shirt, caressing his skin, he pulled away, panting.

"Love, we need to stop," he said while gasping for breath.

She shook her head. "Please don't stop."

He looked at her, a vision of beauty lying beneath him. "Are you sure?"

"I've never been surer of something in my whole life. Just, be gentle. I've never done anything like this before."

Patrick looked at the woman he held, who he'd grown closer to than anyone else in his life in the short time he'd known her. He didn't want to say he was in love with her, but he had intense feelings for her. She was amazing and kind and beautiful and was choosing him, *him*, to share this crucial moment with.

Not trusting his voice, he nodded and showed her, through his actions, how special she was to him and how he was right. Shagging was going to be fucking amazing.

"Which building did James say was the one we're supposed to be looking for?" Evelyn asked as they approached the street James had sent them to.

"Twenty-five seventy-six," Patrick read from the printout.

They continued walking, looking for the building. As they walked, he noticed each building was identical to the other warehouses surrounding it, and looked like the other five they had already seen that day. He kept that observation to himself. It wouldn't do any good to voice his frustration. They were both feeling it after the day they'd had. Every place they had been to so far was very obviously not where the Fitzgeralds operated their crime syndicate. Two were completely abandoned, and the other three housed small businesses.

"I wonder if James and McCleary have had any luck," she said as they made their way down the road.

He shrugged. "I don't know. I guess we'll find out after we check this one out and head back to the flat."

They continued down the road until they stopped in front of the building they were looking for. It looked abandoned. Patrick held in the curse he wanted so badly to exclaim.

"Well, this was a total waste of time," she stated.

"Now, we can't think like that. This probably saved us time, if you think about it. By going to all these places, we were able to effectively eliminate them from the list of likely locations the Fitzgeralds were operating out of. Now we can go back to the flat, report to James and McCleary, and tell them we weren't successful. Who knows? Maybe we'll get back to the flat and

James will say they were successful, and were able to find what they needed."

"True. But I'm still a little disappointed we weren't the ones to find the warehouse. I mean, I was held there. I wanted to have an 'a ha' type moment and save the day. I guess after my experience these last couple weeks, I've started to think about our lives as being in a spy movie."

"Because of you and James, I'm starting to feel that way, too. Between you talking like Nancy Drew and expecting James Bond to come around the corner, and James talking secret lairs and thinking Superman is going to come flying in, I'm half expecting there to be some sort of exciting, grand, unexpected showdown between us and Fitzgerald."

"Sorry. The last couple of weeks have been completely surreal. I mean, I can't believe what has been going on. I'm still having a hard time wrapping my head around things."

"You're probably going to need to write everything down that's happened in order to make you believe this wasn't all a dream when you return home."

She scoffed. "I'm definitely not going to have that problem. I'll have the image of Megan's severed head etched into my mind forever. Not to mention, it'll be impossible to forget being kidnapped and abused by a major crime boss."

"You're right. With as surreal as it all seems, some dangerous shit has happened to you. Some scary, dangerous shit." He paused and forced a smile on his face, trying to lighten the mood. "If you ever decide to start writing fiction, however, you'd have plenty of experience to build on."

"I've never thought about fiction writing. Maybe that will be my fallback if academics fail me."

"I can see you as a writer. It's a solitary activity and the best part is you can do it from anywhere."

"I might have to consider it. A career I could do from anywhere might not be that bad."

They were almost to the main road when a man stepped in front of them, blocking their path.

"Excuse me, but do you have the time?" He was dressed in jeans and a tight black shirt worn underneath a sport coat.

"Um," Patrick patted down his body, making a bit of a show, "I'm sorry, but we do not. Now, if you'll excuse us." He took Evelyn's hand and tried to move around the man.

However, he moved back into their path. "I'm sorry, but I really must know the time. Don't you have a mobile or something? Everyone has a mobile nowadays."

Patrick's grip tightened on her hand. "Unfortunately, we both left our phones at our flat so we could have a nice walk without interruptions. But we really must be going. We have somewhere to be." He tugged on her hand and tried to move around the man to be on their way.

The man in front of them blocked their path again. This time, lifting his sports coat to show off the gun he had holstered at his side. "I'm sorry, but unfortunately, I'm not going to be able to let you go."

Patrick whipped Evelyn behind his back and, at the same time, he grabbed the pocket knife he was carrying in the back pocket of his denims. He held the knife in front of him and assumed an offensive stance, crouching down with both arms out, ready to fight.

The man in front of them laughed. "You think a puny knife will be any match against us?"

He stood up straight. "Us?"

Just then, Evelyn gasped. He whipped around as she was pulled into the arms of a second man. She screamed as he held her tight.

Patrick moved to attack the person holding Evelyn, but he stopped short when the guy pulled a gun and held it to her temple.

"Ah, ah, ah. One wrong move, and your Yank girlfriend's brains will decorate the sidewalk."

Patrick stopped short and held up his hands. "Please don't hurt her."

"Drop your weapon." The first man had drawn his gun and directed it at the couple.

Patrick hesitated for a second, but one look at his girlfriend's terrified face as they held her at gunpoint solidified his decision, and he set the knife on the ground before straightening and putting his hands in the air.

Both men laughed.

"That was too easy." The first one took a step toward Patrick. "I think the boss has overestimated you both. He thought you were valid threats, but you're both cowards."

Patrick glared and wanted to open his mouth to retort, but feared they would retaliate by hurting Evelyn, so he kept his mouth closed. He tightened his jaw and swallowed his pride.

The men laughed again.

"I can't wait to put you both in front of the boss and see what he has planned for you," the first one stated again.

Patrick looked on helplessly as the man who held Evelyn brought a white cloth in front of her face, pressing it against her nose and mouth.

"Oi!" Patrick yelled, trying to get to her, but the first man grabbed hold of his arms. He watched on, helpless, as she struggled for a second before her eyes rolled to the back of her head and she passed out.

"Easy there, mate. She's fine, just a bit sleepy. We can't have you seeing our operation. And we are under strict orders to not physically harm the girl. But we are under no such orders for you." The man chuckled before bringing his arm back and striking Patrick in the head with the butt of the gun.

He was out before his body hit the pavement.

CHAPTER 34

EVELYN

Evelyn came to with a familiar feeling of fuzziness in her head and cotton in her mouth. She had been knocked out again by chloroform. Her eyelids were heavy as she opened them.

She blinked as her eyes tried to adjust to the bright lights around her. This wasn't the same room she was held in before. This was a much larger room, and she wasn't alone. She was still tied to a chair, but Patrick was in front of her, his arms held above his head with a rope tied to the rafter. They'd stripped him of his shirt, so he was only wearing his jeans and shoes. His head hung limp, his chin to his chest, blood trickling down the right side of his face from a wound on the side of his head.

"Patrick," Evelyn croaked. Her tongue was heavy in her mouth, her throat dry. It was difficult to get anything out. She swallowed and cleared her throat. "Patrick."

He didn't stir.

She blinked, trying to clear her head. But it was difficult. Waking up from the chloroform was much harder than the last time. She must have been dosed heavier. She pulled at the restraints on her wrists, but only succeeded in giving herself rope burns.

She looked around the room, trying to figure out where she was. It looked like a normal warehouse. An *abandoned* warehouse.

"Fuck," she muttered.

They must be in one of the warehouses they visited today and wrote off as abandoned. They hadn't been careful.

She tried to struggle in her restraints again, but the knots seemed to just get tighter and tighter.

"I'd stop struggling if I were you." Mickey Fitzgerald was behind her. "The more you struggle, the tighter the knots will become, and you'll lose circulation to your hands and feet. And it would be a shame to have your hands and feet amputated."

Fitzgerald sauntered into the main part of the room, carrying a metal poker and a cricket bat. He wasn't wearing the tailored three-piece suit he wore the last time he'd kidnapped her. Instead, he wore a black sleeveless shirt and jeans. His hair was still in its slicked-back style, but the change of attire really made him look different. He looked younger. And with the sleeveless shirt, his arms and chest were on display, showing he never missed a day at the gym. If he wasn't a cold-blooded killer, she would have been attracted to him.

She took his words of advice and stopped struggling. She sat still and stared at the man in front of her as her head began to clear. He set down the weapons on a table off to the side before pulling a chair over and taking a seat in front of her.

He sat straddling the chair, folding his arms on the back and resting his chin on them. "Hello again, Ms. Stevenson. I'm sorry we've had to meet again under such terrible circumstances."

"Why are you doing this? I've told you I don't know anything."

Fitzgerald smiled. "Oh, I know. I know you know nothing. And that's why my associates were under strict instructions to not hurt you. It was just an unfortunate accident you were with the person who knows something. Someone who we specifically warned to drop the case he was working on. Someone who blatantly ignored said warning. Yes, it was unfortunate, indeed. But I don't want you to worry. I'm not going to hurt you, nor will any of my associates. You're not the one we want."

"Then what are you going to do to me?"

"Well, first, you're going to watch so you can see what happens to people who don't follow my instructions. Then you'll stay here. As I said in our previous meeting, I find you very attractive, and I love the fire you have. I want you to be mine."

Her eyes widened. "Yours?"

"My new lover, of course. You're so young and fit. I will enjoy fucking you until you're obedient."

"Don't you fucking think about it," a voice growled.

Fitzgerald stood, and Patrick was now awake, glaring daggers at Fitzgerald.

She breathed a sigh of relief. He was alive.

Fitzgerald chuckled. "Well, well, well, look who decided to join us. Welcome to the land of the living, Detective Miller. I was worried my associates were a little too eager with their strike and that you were lost to us. This is a wonderful occurrence."

Patrick struggled with the ropes tying him to the rafter. "Let her go."

Fitzgerald chuckled before moving behind Evelyn's chair. He put his hands on her shoulders, rubbing them, before moving them down in front of her chest, massaging her breasts while planting kisses on her cheek.

She tried to pull away, but couldn't, his embrace too tight around her. She cringed as his tongue slid up her neck and stopped at her ear.

"Get the fuck off of her!" Patrick yelled from across the room as he struggled with his restraints. "Get off of her!"

A tear ran down her cheek before Fitzgerald pulled away, chuckling.

"This is easier than I expected." He moved away from her.

She breathed a sigh of relief, but it was short-lived. Fitzgerald walked over and picked up the cricket bat from the table before moving to Patrick.

"I'm going to enjoy this about as much as I'll enjoy fucking your girlfriend for the first time." He lifted the bat into a swinger's stance.

She screamed as the bat made contact with Patrick's stomach for the first time. And the second and the third. At the fourth contact, she closed her eyes, listening to her boyfriend's yells as she prayed for a way to get out of the situation they were in.

Suddenly, the screaming stopped, and she opened her eyes. Fitzgerald had walked away from Patrick, casually swinging the cricket bat back and forth at his side, as he moved to the table.

"Patrick." She tried to get his attention, but he didn't look at her.

His eyes were trained on Fitzgerald.

She followed his gaze and failed to hold back a gasp. He had picked up a metal fireplace poker. He walked over to a barrel she hadn't noticed before. One of the henchmen must have brought it in and built a fire inside. He stuck the metal poker in the barrel, all the while whistling "God Save the King." It was revolting how casual he was about torturing a man.

Once he was satisfied with how hot the poker was, he pulled it out. The tip glowed an orange-red as he made his way back to Patrick.

Evelyn tried to be brave, but as Fitzgerald brought his arm back, she squeezed her eyes shut. She couldn't watch the man she cared for get impaled. She just couldn't.

Patrick's scream echoed through the warehouse as Fitzgerald pressed the hot metal poker into his side.

She opened her eyes. Her boyfriend hung limply from the ceiling. He was beaten and bloody, and Fitzgerald showed no signs of stopping the torture any time soon. She was pretty sure he wasn't going to stop until Patrick was dead. And it was looking like it wasn't going to be long until that happened.

She moved her wrists and winced when the ropes tightened even more. She growled in frustration. There had to be a way she could get out of these restraints and stop Fitzgerald from killing Patrick. She moved her hands closer together, and her eyes widened as the ropes loosen a little.

She smiled. Struggling brought the ropes tighter together, as she was pulling her hands outward to try and break through the ropes. However, doing the opposite, bringing her hands inward, seemed to have the opposite effect. She began to quickly move her hands in and out—out a little, in a lot—and the ropes loosened. She almost let out a victorious cheer as her first hand broke free, but held it in to not draw Fitzgerald's attention to her. She quickly freed her other hand and, after a quick glance to make sure Fitzgerald was still focused on Patrick, bent down and undid the ropes at her ankles.

She watched Fitzgerald walk back to the barrel to heat the poker. He shoved the instrument into the fire and waited. She looked over to the table where he had traded the cricket bat for the poker. The bat was still there. Keeping her eyes on his back the whole time, she tiptoed over to the bat. She picked it up as quietly as she could and continued on her journey to where Fitzgerald still had his back to her.

She crept up behind him and, as she got closer, she glanced at Patrick, who had lifted his head and was staring at her.

He shook his head. He mouthed the word, "no," his eyes wide with fear.

She ignored him and turned back to Fitzgerald. It was the only way for them to get out of there. She had to try. She had to do it for their safety. She brought the bat up and swung it with everything she had. It made contact with his back. He stumbled and fell to the ground with a curse.

She turned around and ran to where Patrick was hanging, knowing she had little time. She dragged a chair over to him, climbing on it. She began to undo the ropes holding him to the rafter.

"You need to run. You need to get out of here and save yourself. Leave me."

She shook her head as she struggled with the rope. "I'm not leaving you."

"You need to go," Patrick wheezed. "I'm only going to slow you down. Get out of here and go find James. Get him and McCleary here. This is your chance."

She shook her head again and cursed the fact her hands were shaking too much to get the ropes undone quickly. "I'm not leaving you."

She was near tears as she struggled with the rope and let out a whoop of excitement when she could get it loose. "We're almost there, love. We're almost there, and then we'll both get out of here to get James and McCleary here after we get you to the hospital."

"Evelyn, watch out!" Patrick gasped.

"What?" She turned around as Fitzgerald barreled down on her, tackling her off the chair to the ground.

The air left her lungs as her back made contact with the concrete floor, Fitzgerald's hard, heavy body landing on top of her.

"You bitch." He pinned her down, her arms above her head. "You'll pay for what you've done." He let go of one of her hands, slapping her hard across the face. "I suppose it would be best to let your boyfriend watch the first time. To watch as his bitch gets fucked by his enemy." He reached between them, struggling to undo the fly and button to her jeans with one hand.

Panicking, she brought her knee up and, with all her force, smashed it into his groin.

Fitzgerald keeled over, groaning, bringing both hands to protect his manhood.

She took advantage and wiggled her way out from between his legs, crawling away from him.

"Not so fast, you slag." With lightning quick speed, he reached out and grabbed her by her hair, dragging her back to him.

She screamed and kicked as he dragged her across the floor and deposited her at Patrick's feet. He had been screaming at Fitzgerald to let Evelyn go, but his screams were falling on deaf ears.

She looked at Fitzgerald, and icy fear ran down her spine at the look he gave her. Gone was the smug arrogance, replaced with a look of utter evil. She had a fleeting thought that James wasn't too far off when he declared Fitzgerald an evil villain, but the thought was replaced with sheer terror when Fitzgerald reached for the hot metal poker he'd placed in the fire.

She tried to scramble to her feet, but she wasn't fast enough. Fitzgerald approached her in seconds, stabbing the metal poker into her shoulder.

The pain was worse than anything she had ever experienced. She screamed until her throat was hoarse, tears streaming down her cheeks as she sobbed through the pain.

Fitzgerald removed the poker, stabbing her in her other shoulder.

More pain, more screaming, more sobbing.

"You fucking bitch." Fitzgerald removed the poker from her other shoulder. "If you had just done what you were told, you would have remained unharmed. But I guess I'll have to teach you the valuable lesson of respecting the man in your life. I promise, I won't kill you, but you'll be wishing I would by the time I'm through with you."

He raised the poker and brought it down hard across her face, knocking her flat on the ground. The pain was blinding, and the bones in her face cracked. She lay on the floor, trying to curl up into a ball to protect herself, but it was impossible to move.

She was sluggish. Her head swam, and she had never experienced so much pain in her life. All she wanted to do was go to sleep and forget about everything that was happening.

Yes. Sleeping would be good. She should go to sleep.

She cried out as Fitzgerald's boot made contact with her stomach. He kicked her, again and again, jolting her back to consciousness and causing her to struggle for breath. She didn't know how much more she was going to be able to stand.

She could hear Patrick in the distance. He sounded so far away, even though he was right there. Right next to her.

As quickly as it had started, it stopped. Fitzgerald stopped his attack on her, and through the fog, she thought she could hear him moving away. She tried to open her eyes to confirm, but they were swollen shut.

She was able to pry one eye open. Everything was blurry. She could make out Patrick, who remained tied to the rafter. She thought she could see him looking at her, but she honestly did not know. He was mostly a blur. The mere act of holding her eye open became too exhausting, so she closed it, her head rolling back on the concrete.

She moved in and out of consciousness, the only things she was fully aware of were the pain in her head and torso. Somewhere through her haze, she thought there was a sound of a door crashing open and shouting, but she was sure she was dreaming.

CHAPTER 35

PATRICK

Patrick groaned as he woke up. He opened his eyes and was greeted by florescent lights, which could only mean one thing. He was in the hospital. He groaned, and immediately regretted it. Everything about his torso ached. He brought his hands to his face and rubbed. He was trying to remember how he got here. The last thing he recalled was Evelyn passing out at his feet, hearing a loud noise, and then nothing. He must have finally succumbed to his pain and passed out.

He looked around the room. Colin was asleep in the chair beside his bed.

"Colin." He winced as his throat burned when he tried to talk. Colin didn't move. "Colin," he said a little louder. Still nothing. "Dad," he said as loud as he was able.

Colin stirred, opening his eyes. "Patrick, thank God you're awake. How are you feeling?"

"Like I've been hit by a truck. How long have I been here?"

"A couple of days. They had to put you in a medically induced coma for a day so your injuries would have time to heal, and we've been waiting for you to wake up."

"What's the prognosis?"

"You'll live. You had a collapsed lung and a couple of broken ribs. You needed loads of stitches, but you'll be fine."

"Where's Evelyn?"

"She's here, but she's in the intensive care unit. She was worse off than you were, unfortunately."

"I need to go see her." He struggled to get up.

Colin put a hand on his shoulder, pushing him down. "You're not going anywhere. You need to rest."

"I need to make sure she's okay." He still tried to get up.

"Even if you could get down there, they're not allowing anyone but family to see her."

Patrick shook his head. "She has no family here. I need to go down there so she's not alone."

"They flew her parents in. They arrived the morning after you were admitted."

Patrick froze. "What?"

"Are you ready to hear what happened?"

He nodded, settling back into the bed.

"James and that police officer, PC McCleary, called in the CIA after they discovered you both were taken by the Fitzgeralds. Turns out, they'd been tracking the Fitzgeralds for a while. They had nothing concrete to bring them in on yet. When they got word from James of an international kidnapping, they stormed the warehouse where you were being held, since, by some miracle, Mickey Fitzgerald's lackies didn't leave your mobile lying on the ground where you were taken. They arrested everyone who was there, including Fitzgerald himself. They rushed you both here. Since Ms. Stevenson is an American citizen, the embassy was notified, along with her parents, since they were listed as her emergency contacts. They were flown in, and they have been by her side ever since. James was able to talk to them and discern her condition is pretty serious. Besides her shoulders both being impaled by a hot iron and needing extensive repairs, she sustained a severe head injury. She has yet to wake up, and they don't know when, or if, she ever will."

It was as if someone had punched Patrick in the gut. His girlfriend was in the ICU, with her parents, whom she'd lied to about everything since she landed in London, and they weren't even sure if she was ever going to wake up.

"I need to see her. Please, Dad, talk to her parents, convince them to let me see her. I need to be there with her."

"I can try, but her parents weren't too happy from what James said. They refused to let him in to see her. I don't know if they'll let you in."

"But she's my girlfriend. Doesn't that count for something?"

Colin shook his head. "Not to them. They don't want anyone who isn't family to see her."

Patrick closed his eyes, tears threatening to spill. "Fuck. Fuck them all."

"Why don't you get some more rest? I'll see what I can do."

Patrick kept his eyes closed. "I need to see her for myself. I need to make sure she's okay. She tried to save me, you know."

"What?" Colin paused at the door.

"She tried to save me. She managed to get out of her ropes and, instead of making a run for it like I told her to, she attacked Fitzgerald and tried to get me out of there. That's why she's hurt. Because she tried to save me. It's all my fault." He sobbed quietly.

Colin moved from the door to the bedside. "It is not your fault, son." Colin took Patrick's hand. "Don't you dare blame yourself for what happened. You don't know what he would have done to her even if she hadn't tried to save you. You could both be dead. She bought you both time, and I'm grateful to her." He sighed. "I came too close to losing my son this week, and I'm so very thankful you're still here with me. I'll convey all of this to Mr. and Mrs. Stevenson as soon as I see them."

"I understand what you're saying, but I still can't help but think it's my fault. I shouldn't have brought her with me. She should be safe back at my flat—"

"And you'd be dead. Look, son, you know I don't enjoy talking in circles. I've said my piece. All I can tell you now is, feeling guilty about the situation isn't going to change anything. You can feel guilty until you give yourself an ulcer, but that's not going to change the fact Evelyn is fighting for her life somewhere in this hospital. What you *can* do is focus on getting better so you can try to help *her* get better."

"How can I help her get better if her fucking parents won't let anyone see her?" Patrick growled.

"Restrictions have never seemed to stop you from getting what you want before, now, have they? I think we can find a way around her parents. But we can't do that if you're still bedridden."

"How much longer until they let me out of here?"

Colin frowned. "A fucking madman tortured you. I don't think you're going to get out of here anytime soon, so I'd get comfortable for the next few days."

"You can't pull any strings and get me out of here sooner?"

"I have no sway over medical personnel. Even if I did, this is one thing we won't negotiate on. You'll be here until the doctors say otherwise. And then you'll go home, relax, and allow James, Mrs. Moore, and myself to take care of you until you're completely healed. Do you understand?"

Patrick rolled his eyes, and even that one little motion seemed to cause his entire body to light up with pain. "Yes, sir."

"Good. Now, I'm going to head down to the intensive care unit and see if I can have a chat with Mr. and Mrs. Stevenson about allowing us to wheel you down to sit with Evelyn for a little bit in the next couple days when the doctors allow you to get out of bed."

Colin leaned over and squeezed Patrick's hand. "I am truly, truly relieved you're okay. Pissed off you didn't drop the case like I asked you to weeks ago, but relieved that not only are you okay, but the bastard who murdered your mother will finally be behind bars."

Patrick turned his hand over, squeezing his dad's in return. "Me, too, Dad. Me, too."

Colin gave Patrick's hand one more squeeze before leaving the room.

As soon as the door closed to the hospital room, Patrick leaned back and closed his eyes again, trying to relax, but all he could see behind his closed lids were visions of Evelyn being hit repeatedly and stabbed with the hot metal poker. He brought his fists up and pressed them against his eyes as hard as he could.

But try as he might, the image of her with a metal rod through her shoulder wouldn't leave him.

Hot tears welled up behind his eyes, and he didn't fight them as they found their way down his cheeks. It was all his fault. He had one job: to protect Evelyn. That was all he had to do. Instead, he led her right into the Fitzgeralds' clutches and allowed her to get tortured by their hands.

The door to his room opened, and he opened his eyes. James walked into the room.

"Hey," he croaked out.

"Hey." James walked over to the chair Colin vacated a few minutes before.

At least Patrick thought it had only been a few minutes. He really had no concept of time right now.

"How're you feeling?" James settled in.

"Like I've been hit by a fucking truck."

"Yeah, but honestly, if an *actual* truck hit you, you'd probably be in much better shape." He smiled.

Patrick smiled and laughed. And then winced. "You're probably right."

James sobered. "Seriously, how are you feeling?"

"Bloody awful. I can't stop seeing Fitzgerald and Evelyn together. Fitzgerald was fucking sadistic. And I was totally helpless. Fucking helpless. I had to watch as he...he groped her and beat her and stabbed her. It's all I can fucking see when I close my eyes. And Colin says her parents won't even let anyone see her who isn't family, but all I want is to see with my own eyes that she's okay. That she's alive." He fought back tears. "It's all my fault."

James sat silently next to his best friend and partner, not interrupting him to tell him it wasn't his fault, which was exactly what Patrick needed, someone to *listen* as he ranted. He was already feeling better being allowed to get everything off his chest, without being corrected and reassured.

"You're right. This whole situation is your fault."

Patrick reeled. "What the fuck?"

James shrugged. "You were the one who grabbed Evie at the airport in the first place, drawing attention to her. You're the one who then led the Fitzgeralds on a chase through Heathrow. And you trusted Harry, which again, put Evelyn on the Fitzgeralds' radar."

"Well, yeah, all those things happened, but—"

"Now, it was my fault they took her the first time," James continued, as if Patrick hadn't tried to interrupt. "I let her leave the flat on her own. But *you* partnered with her for the secret lair hunt, so, of course, it's your fault they captured you."

Patrick stared at his best friend. This wasn't what he wanted. He just wanted to be listened to. Not agreed with. He opened his mouth to protest once more, but James just kept on fucking talking.

"If you want to go back even further, you can even say your fucking crazy vendetta against the Fitzgeralds put this whole thing in motion, so I guess, yes, we can definitely say the fact Evelyn is in this hospital fighting for her life is very much, one hundred percent your fault, and you should spend the rest of your life feeling sorry for yourself and asking for forgiveness."

"You know, mate, this isn't helping. You're making me feel fucking worse."

"Mate, I hate to be the one to break it to you, but as long as you're blaming yourself for everything, you're going to feel like shit. The guilt is going to eat you alive."

"Then what do you suggest? Like you said, everything *is* my fault."

"We can accept that Evelyn would be in this mess, or worse, with or without you."

"What?"

James readjusted himself in his seat, leaning forward, resting his elbows on the bed. "Think about it. She had the bag of evidence. The Fitzgeralds knew what they were looking for, and they weren't going to stop. They thought she knew things she wasn't supposed to know. If you hadn't intervened, they probably would have picked her up in Heathrow and we would have been reading about her body washing up on the banks of the Thames by the end of the week, feeling sorry for the young American girl who got mixed up with the wrong people before moving on and trying to come up with the next step in our march to nail Mickey Fitzgerald to the wall."

Patrick stared at him. A tightness formed in his chest. "You're right," he squeaked. "You're right. If I wasn't there, she would be dead."

"Of course, I'm right. I'm always right," James joked.

Patrick didn't smile. Even though he shouldn't feel guilty, he couldn't help it.

The smile slipped from James's face. "You can't sit here and feel sorry for yourself. You need to accept this happened and move on. Yes, Evelyn is fighting for her life, but she's *alive* because of you. You need to remember you've played a large role in her survival, and you need to focus on that. Stop blaming yourself for things beyond your control and start thinking of the things you've done for her that have kept her alive this whole time."

When James stopped talking, it was like a dam burst inside of Patrick. All the guilt he had been harboring since Evelyn had first been taken to when he woke up here in the hospital just burst out of him. Part of him wanted to blame whatever pain medication he was on for crying again, but he knew the real reason was because he had been holding so much in for so long.

James moved from his spot in the chair and placed himself on the side of the bed, put his arm around his best friend's shoulders, and let him cry until there weren't any more tears left.

"So," Patrick said. "How in the world did you and McCleary know where to find us?"

James had returned to his chair and leaned back, placing his feet on Patrick's bed, crossing them at the ankle. "When you and Evie didn't return when you were supposed to, we retraced your footsteps, so to speak. We found your pocket knife on the ground, so we knew we had to be close. McCleary called in the CIA, and since you had your mobile in your pocket, they could use their super fancy technology and track you down. Led us right to your location."

Patrick shook his head. "We were lucky."

"Damn lucky," James stated.

The two were quiet for a minute.

"Have you been able to see her? I know Colin said she's pretty heavily guarded by her family, but he also said you've been up there."

James took his feet off the side of the bed, sitting up straight. "Yeah, actually. I sneaked in when they were all out eating together and the nurse wasn't looking."

Patrick swallowed hard at the jealous lump that rose in his throat. "How did she look?"

James sighed, leaning forward to place his elbows on his knees. "About as good as you'd expect."

"That doesn't tell me anything."

James sighed again. "Not good, Patrick, not good. When I visited her, she had all kinds of tubes and machines hooked up to her, and she looked so small and pale. I've never seen anything like it. I broke down and cried. I don't know if you should go in there. I don't know if you can handle it."

Patrick shook his head. "I need to see her. I need to be there. I need her to know I haven't deserted her. I'm still here, waiting for her to wake up."

"Mate, I don't know if you realize this, but you're also in the hospital. It's not like you can just waltz to her room and see her. Plus, her room is guarded more tightly than the Crown Jewels. Her parents don't want anyone who, and I quote, 'got her into this situation,' to see her."

Patrick balled up his fist and slammed it on the bed. "Fuck," he shouted.

"Language, my friend. You don't want to be scandalizing any of these sweet nurses, now do you?" James smiled.

Patrick couldn't help but crack a smile before sobering. "It's not fair, you know? She's going to wake up, and she's going to ask for me, you mark my words, and then they're going to *have* to let her see me."

"You're right. You're absolutely right. And until then, you need to focus on getting better because if you want to sneak about and get into her room, you need to not be in a room of your own, hooked up to all of these gadgets."

Patrick nodded. "Hopefully she'll wake up before I get released and they'll allow me to be wheeled down to see her."

He leaned his head back on his pillow, closed his eyes, and fell asleep.

A couple days later, Patrick was sitting up in bed, tying his trainers. They finally cleared him to leave the hospital, with strict orders to go home and continue resting. His ribs were healing nicely, and any vigorous physical activity would set him back.

As the doctor was giving him his discharge instructions, Patrick dutifully nodded along in agreement with everything the doctor said. Go home and lie around in bed and on the couch, sure. Don't drive for at least another week, got it, doc. But the whole time he was listening to the doctor prattle on, he was focused on getting down to the intensive care unit as soon as possible.

He finished tying his trainers and stood. Colin and James were both in the intensive care unit's waiting room, waiting for him. The doctor had given him the option to use a cane, a walker, or to be wheeled in a chair, and Patrick opted for the cane. He was stiff from having lain in bed for a week and a half, and he wasn't sure how far he could walk on his own with his healing ribs and newly inflated lungs. So, he grabbed his cane and winced as he stood fully upright.

Yeah, he'd be going slow. Very. Slow.

He hobbled out of his room and down the hall to the lift. He pushed the button, and when the doors opened, he pushed the button for the third floor and tapped his foot as the lift moved slowly to its destination. After what seemed like an eternity, the doors opened and let him out.

They opened into the waiting room. James and Colin were sitting in the back, whispering to each other. They looked up as he came in, James standing from his chair and moving to help him.

"I wish you would have let us help you make your way here." James took his friend by the arm.

"Well, I needed to see if I could do it on my own. Can't have you two with me all the time. If I have to piss, I'll have to make it to the loo on my own."

"You're not planning on staying here full time, are you, son?" Colin asked as the two young men made it to where he was sitting.

"I was." Patrick hissed as he settled into his chair.

"Are you out of your fucking mind?" James asked. "You'll be going home with me at the end of the day, mate, and I won't hear any arguments from you. You're still healing and there's no way you're going to sleep in these god-awful chairs with broken ribs while you're still healing."

"I'm not leaving. What if she wakes when I'm gone?"

"Then she'll still be awake when I bring you back."

Patrick opened his mouth to protest, but Colin interrupted him. "James is right, son. You'll be going home with either him or myself, and you will rest. One of us will bring you back each morning. But you need to continue to rest and listen to the doctor, even though you're no longer being held hostage, so to speak."

Patrick sighed. "Fine, but you can drop me off and leave. I'm sure you both have work you're needing to catch up on after spending all this time here."

James shook his head. "We have nothing pressing on our plates right now as far as detecting goes. We have a couple cheating spouses, but other than that, the payout we got from Colin's solicitor's office for bringing in Fitzgerald and most of his gang is going to keep us fat and happy for quite a while."

"And I can do any work I have here," Colin replied. "We're not going to let you sit here and wait by yourself. We want to be here for you, Patrick. Let us."

Patrick nodded. "Thank you. Both of you."

"Don't mention it," James said.

Before either of the men could speak up again, a door opened down the hall before closing again. There was a series of footsteps before a middle-aged couple and two young girls came around the corner, heading to the lift and pushing the button. The doors opened, and they stepped in.

As soon as the doors closed, James turned to Patrick. "Now's your chance. That's the Stevensons. They're headed for dinner. You need to hurry if you want the full thirty minutes with Evie."

Patrick took in a deep breath and stood carefully, picking up his cane. "Which room?"

"IC twenty-five. Just down the hall, to the right."

Patrick nodded, taking a deep breath. "Alright. Well, then, here I go."

Slowly, he made his way down the hall and around the corner. He came to the door to Evelyn's room sooner than he thought he would. He paused in front of the tightly closed door before taking a deep breath, looking both ways to make sure no one was watching, and forced his hand to take hold of the handle. He slowly pulled the handle down and pushed the door open. He took two slow steps inside the room before turning to shut the door behind him, just as quietly as he opened it. After taking another deep breath, he turned around.

He wasn't prepared for the sight in front of him, and he nearly collapsed where he was standing when he caught sight of his girlfriend lying on the bed. He could barely see her with everything she had hooked up to her. There were IVs going into her arms, along with blood pressure monitors, heart monitors, catheters, and many other wires coming from her body to machines on either side of the bed. The most glaring thing he noticed was the breathing tube emerging from her throat and the sound of the machine breathing for her.

He walked slowly to the side of her bed and fell into the seat. He looked at her, really looked at her for the first time since he was last with her at the warehouse. She was pale, and her eyes were gently closed, as if she were sleeping. She wasn't broken and bloody like she was the last time he'd seen her, but she looked even smaller and weaker, if possible. Her hair was brushed back, away from her face, and straight down behind her head. Without her fringe on her forehead, she almost didn't look like herself.

Patrick reached out tentatively and brushed her fringe back to where it belonged, making her look a little bit more like herself. However, instead of making him feel better, seeing the woman he was falling in love with, lying in bed, lifeless, was almost too much to handle. He grabbed her hand and, feeling how cold it was, he lost it. He couldn't hold the tears back anymore. Huge sobs erupted out of him.

"I'm so sorry. I'm so, so sorry." He laid his head on the bed next to her and cried.

Soon, Patrick's sobs subsided as he was able to pull himself together. He took a deep breath and sat up. He looked at her and smiled a small smile.

"Hello, love," he breathed, as if he spoke any louder, he'd wake her. "I'm sorry I didn't come and visit you sooner. I was being held hostage in a hospital room of my own. Nothing like this, though. Yours is much louder than mine. You should have a talk with management about that. Get rid of some of this beeping so you can rest easier." He swallowed the lump forming in his throat.

"You're looking much better than the last time we were together, which isn't saying much since you looked bloody awful then. Well, we did it, and I wish you'd wake up so we can go out and celebrate. I owe you a night out on the town to show you London properly. Obviously, we won't need to stage tourist photos for your parents because I'm sure you know they know you've lied to them. But that doesn't mean we still can't go out and have a good time. Show you the sights and eat something a little fancier than fish and chips or curry. Have a proper date." He wiped at a stray tear rolling down his cheek.

"You were really reckless, love. Not that I don't appreciate it. You saved my life, but you really shouldn't have. You're stubborn, like me, and you care too much, and that is your downfall.

If Mickey Fitzgerald wasn't behind bars, I'd hunt him down and beat the fucker to death with my cane for what he did to you.

"You need to wake up soon, Evelyn. Your parents won't let us see you. I had to sneak in here like a bloody criminal to be by your side. And I don't have much time left. So, you need to wake up and tell your parents how you want James and me and even Colin to come and visit you so I can be here with you as you get better. But until then, know I'm here. I'm just outside your door, waiting. I haven't left you. Please don't think that. If I could stay, God, if I could have been here since the beginning, I would have. I want to be here with you. There's nowhere else I'd rather be. I love you. Please get better soon."

He leaned over and placed a kiss on her cheek before slowly standing with the help of his cane. He walked to the door and turned to give one last look at her before turning back to the door. Just as he put his hand on the handle, the door flew open, causing him to lose his balance and take a step back, trying to catch himself before he fell. As he caught his balance and stood, he came eye to eye with a middle-aged man with dark hair and olive skin.

He glared at Patrick. "Who the hell are you?"

"I'm, I'm..." Patrick tried.

"What are you doing in my daughter's room?" the man shouted.

Patrick swallowed and took a deep breath. "I had to see her, Mr. Stevenson. I was worried."

"You're him, aren't you? The man they found in the warehouse with my daughter."

"I am. My name is Patrick Miller. It's a pleasure to make your acquaintance." He extended his hand.

Evelyn's father looked at his offered hand, but didn't take it. "I don't understand why you're here. The police made it sound like you're a random person who happened to be there at the same time as my daughter. And some lawyer came and talked to me about how my daughter risked her life to save yours. And now you're sneaking into my daughter's room because you have to see her. So, tell me, Mr. Miller, what is your connection to my little Evie over there?"

Patrick took a deep breath, trying to decide how much he should really tell her father. He decided to be honest, but minimal. Evelyn could fill in the details when she woke up.

"Well, I actually rescued your daughter from Heathrow when the Fitzgeralds were after her. I've been taking care of her since her first day in London. I'm a private investigator who was working on the Fitzgerald case for my father, that lawyer you met with earlier. Evelyn was staying at my flat, and she insisted while she stayed, she helped with the case. I tried to discourage her, but your daughter is very stubborn. She went out on a reconnaissance mission with me, and they caught us. Your daughter could have stayed where she was and watched while Fitzgerald tortured and eventually killed me, but that's not the kind of woman she is. She figured out how to break free of her ropes, and she tried to save me."

Mr. Stevenson narrowed his eyes. "Why would she risk her life to save a detective she barely knows?"

"Because we're in love," Patrick blurted. "I'm in love with your daughter, and she's in love with me. At least, I'm pretty sure she is."

Mr. Stevenson drew his mouth into a frown. By the look on his face, Patrick was pretty sure he was picturing all the ways he wanted to beat the shit out of him.

"That's why she risked her life to save mine," Patrick rushed to say, "and that's why I snuck in here. I couldn't stand not being able to see her for one more day. My best friend and my father have both been by to beg for you to let me visit while I was admitted to the hospital, but you refused. So, I did what I had to do. I needed to see her again, to try and ease the nightmare I see every time I close my eyes of her being tortured at Fitzgerald's hands."

While he had been talking, Mr. Stevenson had folded his arms across his chest. He grew redder and redder as Patrick kept talking. But Patrick wasn't ready to give up just yet.

"I'm sorry you had to find out this way. I'm sorry we had to meet under these circumstances. I had really hoped to meet you on a trip to visit Evelyn in the States, but it seems Fate had other plans for us. So, I'm asking you to let me come back and sit with her again."

"Out," Mr. Stevenson said quietly.

"Excuse me?" Patrick couldn't quite believe what he was hearing.

"I said, get out," he said a little bit louder. "I don't want to see you anywhere near here again."

"What's going on?" A woman entered the room from behind Mr. Stevenson. She was about Evelyn's height, with long strawberry blonde hair. "Who's this?"

"He's the reason Evelyn's in the hospital. It's his fault our daughter may never wake up."

"What?" The news that there was a chance of Evelyn not waking up hit Patrick like a fist to his stomach. "What do you mean, never wake up?"

"What's he doing here?" The woman, probably Mrs. Stevenson, ignored Patrick's question.

"He claims he and Evelyn were together, that they're in love. He's a private detective whose job it was to capture the man who tortured Evelyn. He dragged her into this whole thing and got her hurt in the process, and then he had the nerve to ask to come back and sit with her until she wakes up."

"That's not what happened. You've got it wrong." It was as if the two people in the room couldn't hear Patrick.

"You need to leave. And you need to take those other two men with you," Mrs. Stevenson said. "I don't want to see any of you here again. If we see you here, we'll call security and have you escorted out. If we see you again after that, we'll call the police and have you arrested for harassment. Is that understood?"

Patrick could only nod.

"Good. I think it would be best for all involved if you forget about our daughter and whatever notions you have that you two are in love. Now, get out."

Mr. and Mrs. Stevenson moved out of the doorway, clearing a path for Patrick to exit.

He gripped his cane tightly and straightened his shoulders before reaching into his back pocket to pull out one of his business cards. He set it on the table nearest him. "That's my number. When she wakes up and asks for me, and she *will* ask for me, call me, yeah?"

He didn't even wait for a reply. He moved slowly past the elder Stevensons, past the younger ones waiting out in the hall, and back out to the waiting room. He didn't even stop to greet James or Colin. He moved directly to the lifts, smashing the button to take him to the car park.

"Patrick?" James shouted, but he didn't turn around.

As soon as the doors to the lift opened, he stepped inside, smashing the floor level he needed with his fist. The doors began to close, but were interrupted by an arm coming in between them.

James and Colin entered the lift with him. They were silent as the doors shut.

"What happened?" James asked.

Patrick didn't say anything.

"Are you upset about seeing her? I know it's a bit hard to look at her with all of those machines, but—"

"Her parents came in. I took too long. I wasn't watching the time and her parents caught me in the room as I was trying to leave."

"Oh," James replied, "and I take it they weren't pleasant."

"We're not allowed to be at the hospital anymore. They said if they see us, they will have us arrested."

"What?! Can they even do that? Is that even possible?"

"Unfortunately, it is," Colin responded. "Did they say why? It's not like we're harassing them by sitting in the waiting room. They've not even glanced our way once since we started holding vigil there a week ago."

The elevator doors opened, and the three men walked out, James and Colin leading the way to the car, with Patrick taking up the rear.

"They blame me. Evelyn is in a critical condition, and they say it is my fault. They said it would be best if I go home and forget about her."

"Did you explain that you two are, you know, together?"

"Yes, and it made things worse. I left my card. They have my number. Evelyn will wake up, regardless of what they believe, and she'll ask for me, and as soon as my mobile rings, I'll be on my way back. I can then rub it in their fucking faces she wanted me there, and I'll make it very bloody clear to her how my absence wasn't my choice."

James and Colin stood back and watched as Patrick stood by his car, trying to catch his breath.

"Now, who's crawling into the backseat? I think it's against doctor's orders for me to climb back there."

CHAPTER 36

EVELYN

For a long time, everything seemed fuzzy and felt heavy at the same time. The surrounding sounds seemed muffled. There were voices, but she couldn't pick out the words or identify the voices. She could hear lots of beeping and whirring of machines, but couldn't quite place where she was. She tried to open her eyes, but it was as if her lids were weighed down.

Eventually, she could pinpoint the voices. Her dad. Her mom. Both of her sisters. And then Patrick. For some reason, when he came to visit her, he had been the clearest voice. She made out some words he said. He was trying to explain what had happened. Trying to take all the blame for what happened to her. She wanted to reassure him it wasn't his fault, that she didn't blame him, but she couldn't get the words out. It was as if something trapped her in her own body. No matter what she did, she couldn't communicate with him. So, she laid there and listened to the soothing sound of his voice. He pressed a kiss to her cheek, and then it was over. The chair shifted as he got up to leave.

Then there was an argument with her parents, and he was gone.

She waited and waited for him to return, but he never did. The only voices left in her room were her parents, her sisters, and her doctors. The doctors kept saying she probably would never wake up and her parents would need to accept it.

No, she screamed in her mind. *I'm here. Why can't you hear me?*

Every day, she tried and tried to wake herself up, and then one day, in the middle of the afternoon, surrounded by her entire family, she did.

"Evelyn?" her mom asked as she blinked her eyes open in the bright hospital room.

She tried to speak, but couldn't. There was something down her throat.

She turned her head. Her mom was sitting next to her bed with a relieved expression.

Evelyn turned her head again and her dad and sisters were all around her.

She scanned the room again, confused. Where was Patrick? Why wasn't he here? She lifted an arm, and that one movement took almost more effort than she could handle. But she did it, and she made a gesture with her hand as if she wanted to write. Her middle sister, Elizabeth, seemed to understand right away, and rushed to grab a pen and pad of paper for her. She placed the pen in Evelyn's hand, holding the pad for her to write.

Evelyn struggled. She was trying to do too much for just having woken up. Finally, she finished the one word she wanted to write. Her arm dropped like a lead weight back to the mattress.

Elizabeth turned the pad around and read it aloud. "Patrick?"

Everyone exchanged glances.

"He's not here, dear," her mom replied. "We sent him away."

Evelyn lifted her arm with the pen again, and Elizabeth brought the pad back. She could write what she wanted more quickly now.

Elizabeth read it. "Why?"

"Because only family should be here. Because it's his fault you're in here to begin with. We didn't want to watch you fight for your life with the man responsible for your condition sitting right there," her mom explained.

Evelyn shook her head, her eyes filling with tears. She gestured at the tube in her throat.

"Tony, dear, go get the doctor. Tell them she's awake."

Her dad nodded and left the room.

The four women who remained sat in silence. It didn't take long before Dad re-entered the room, a team of doctors following.

Evelyn tried to keep up as they all talked, but her head still was fuzzy, and all she wanted to do was go back to sleep.

The doctors finally determined she should be okay breathing on her own, and before she knew it, she was coughing up the breathing tube and taking a deep breath.

The doctors and her parents exchanged a few more words, and the doctors exited, leaving the family alone again.

"How long?" Evelyn rasped, finding it both difficult and exhausting to talk.

Michelle brought her a cup of water and held it for her as she sipped from the straw. Her throat immediately relaxed as the cold water slipped down.

"A week," her mom replied. "A very, very long week."

"How did you find out?"

"The embassy called. As soon as the CIA found you and they brought you to the hospital, they contacted the embassy, who contacted us, and they flew us out right away. We've been here ever since," her dad explained.

"What we don't understand is why you *lied* to us about why you were here," her mom stated.

"Sue," her dad started. "She just woke up. Give her some time."

"No, I need to know. I need to know why she told us she missed her flight and was spending some time sightseeing in London before getting re-booked on her way to Greece when she was really here acting as if she were Nancy Drew or in an Agatha Christie novel or something. Putting her life in danger. Or how about why she's been living with two strange men instead of at a hotel, and one of whom had the gall to sneak into the room while we were away and claim the two of them are in a relationship?"

"Mom," Evelyn started.

"Why did you lie to us, Evelyn? What would have happened if you didn't get hurt? Were you going to continue to uphold the lie?"

Evelyn closed her eyes. "That was the plan, yes."

Her mom gasped.

Evelyn spoke up before her mother could get in another word. "Do you want to know why I lied? Because I didn't want you to worry."

She started coughing. Michelle rushed to pour her a cup of water. She brought it over and helped Evelyn take a sip.

"She has a point, Mom," Elizabeth pointed out. "You and dad were already really worried about her going on her trip to begin with."

"'Don't talk to strangers or we'll be seeing you on an episode of *Dateline*,'" Michelle mimicked her mom's voice.

"'Don't look strange men in the eye or you'll be *Taken*, and I'm not Liam Neeson, so I won't be able to rescue you,'" Elizabeth said, lowering her voice to mimic her father.

"Was I supposed to call you and tell you a high-ranking London crime family wanted me?" Evelyn continued, her voice raspy. "But don't worry, two handsome private detectives rescued me and now I'm living in their flat. I'll call you when I'm heading home."

Michelle helped her take another sip of water.

"I'm pretty sure you would have taken the news very well."

"We would have understood. We would have tried to contact the CIA. We would have contacted the embassy. You should have trusted us to help you!"

"I'm an adult, Mom. I can take care of myself. The situation was under control. I had it under control."

"Obviously you didn't or else you wouldn't have been lying in the hospital for a week fighting for your life!"

Evelyn closed her eyes as tears sprang to them immediately. "I'm sorry," she whispered.

Her mom immediately dropped her bravado and fell into comforting mode. "Oh, sweetie. I'm sorry. A week of watching you struggle for your life, and I just built all of that up. You have nothing to be sorry for. I'm sure if you hadn't gotten hurt, you would have told us, and we would laugh over all of your misadventures."

Evelyn reached up and wiped a stray tear from her cheek. "I have quite a few stories to tell, but those can wait. I need to see Patrick."

"Honey," her mom started.

"No, Mom, listen. I need to see him and make sure he's okay and make sure he knows me being here isn't his fault."

"I'm sorry, but I'm going to have to disagree with you on that. Of course, it's his fault! He dragged you into all of this. He put you in the situation to get hurt," her dad bellowed.

Evelyn shook her head. "No, he didn't. I did."

She didn't continue for a long time. The urge to cry was very strong, and holding it back made her throat ache. But the thought of crying made her even more exhausted than she already was.

"Maybe we should just let this go for now and let her sleep," Elizabeth suggested. "She just woke up, and all you're doing is upsetting her."

"We're just trying to make sense of what happened," their dad defended.

"Right now? This could have waited until Evie was a little better. Able to talk more and defend herself," Michelle pointed out.

"We would have waited, but how could we when she immediately brought up the man who put her here?" their mom whisper yelled, gesturing wildly at the bed Evelyn was currently lying in.

"I'm the one who ran into the woman in the airport and swapped bags." Evelyn spoke as loudly as her throat would allow. "I was the one who didn't listen to him and tried to leave. I'm the one who insisted on being a part of the investigation. I'm the one who tried to distract Fitzgerald in order to save Patrick, causing Fitzgerald to lash out at me. It's my fault I'm in this bed. Not his, and you need to stop blaming him."

"Fine, it's your fault. You're in control of your own actions. But we're not calling him in here. You're not going to see him. You need your rest. You need to focus on healing so we can get you home," her mom said.

"But—"

"No buts. You're resting without a strange British man at your side, and that's final."

Evelyn closed her eyes and leaned back against the pillow, knowing it was fruitless to argue with her mother.

"Are you hungry?" her mother asked.

"A little. I'm mostly thirsty."

"The food here is decent. Why don't I go down and pick something up for you from the cafeteria? And then, if you get hungry, it'll be here for you to snack on."

"That sounds okay."

Her mother smiled. "Good. I'll be right back."

"I'll go with you," her dad stated, and the two of them left.

They left Evelyn alone in her hospital room with her sisters. Her best friends.

"All those emails and not one mention you were living with a hot Brit?" Elizabeth moved to the chair beside her bed.

"You were holding out on us, Evie. You let us go on and on about celebrities and movies, and not once did you tell us you were living in a James Bond movie." Michelle took the other chair.

"I'm sorry," she said weakly. "Next time, I'll make sure to keep you in the loop."

"God, I hope there isn't a next time. This was some scary stuff, Evie."

"I'm sorry, Lizzy."

"You don't need to apologize. Just know the parents are upset mostly because it's an emotion they can express their extreme fear through. Shelley and I are adults, and they haven't let us leave this hospital to go sightseeing. It's here or the hotel. That's it."

"Are you trying to make me feel guilty? Because I'm already feeling that in troves."

"No, what she's trying to do, and failing spectacularly at, is trying to illustrate that Mom and Dad's sudden protective streak is coming from a place of love," Michelle replied.

"I know that. I knew going into this whole mess they'd be angry. But they weren't supposed to find out about it until they were like ninety and on their deathbeds. When they wouldn't be able to react so forcefully."

"So, tell us about that British hunk we found crying over your bed a few days ago." Elizabeth leaned forward, putting her elbows on her knees.

"Yes, dish!" said Michelle.

"Okay. Well, his name is Patrick, and he's a private investigator."

"Yes, yes, we know all of this. Get to the good stuff." Elizabeth made a motion with her hands to try and move the story along.

Evelyn laughed, which caused her to cough.

Michelle immediately handed her a cup of water. She took a sip.

After a pause to make sure she wouldn't start coughing again, Evelyn started listing everything she loved about Patrick. "He knows how to drive me crazy and push all my buttons. I don't think I've ever fought with anyone like I've fought with him."

"Not even us?" Elizabeth asked, grinning.

Evelyn shook her head. "After like the first day, it became a sort of game to rile each other up. He's incredibly stubborn."

"No wonder you two get along," Michelle joked.

"I can picture him at home with his best friend, James, pouting about being sidelined." Evelyn paused and swallowed. Her throat was so raw from the breathing tube. She took another sip of water.

"He stepped in front of a gun for me, and he's done nothing but try to protect me this entire time." She tried to ignore the gasps her sisters made at the mention of the gun, but couldn't. It was pretty fucking scary to look back on. To see the danger they were in.

"He's gentle and caring, and I love him." Her voice cracked, a combination of emotion and from being on the breathing tube. "It's not fair that Mom and Dad won't let me call him because, right now, he's the only person I want to see in the entire world, and I can't," she finished, her voice not much louder than a whisper.

"We can fix that."

"What do you mean?"

"He left his card. We can call him for you. And then we can distract Mom and Dad so you can see him. Once you're better, you'll be able to see him as much as you want. You're an adult. They can't stop you," Elizabeth replied.

"You'd do all of that for me?"

"Of course. You're our big sister, our best friend, and this is something straight out of a love story. And some day, when you're sitting down with your children, you can tell them that Aunties Liz and Shell totally made your future happen."

Evelyn laughed. "Deal. Although, I think we're getting way ahead of ourselves here. We're not quite at the discussing children part of our relationship yet. We've barely defined it, and I haven't told him I love him."

"Oh, I don't think we're getting ahead of ourselves. The look on your face when you talk about him says it all. You're destined for a beautiful future," Michelle stated.

"You watch too many rom-coms."

The door to the room opened, and their parents entered, carrying a tray full of every single one of her favorite foods and beverages.

"We didn't know what you might want, so we got you a bit of everything we thought you might like." Her dad set the tray in front of her.

"Thank you."

"You're welcome, Evie."

As her parents fussed around her, making sure she was comfortable, Evelyn peeked around her mom's body and watched as Michelle grabbed Patrick's card off the side table and snuck out of the room.

CHAPTER 37

PATRICK

Rehabilitation and relaxation were two things Patrick didn't do well. After three days sitting in his flat with nothing but the internet and James to keep him company, he was getting a major case of cabin fever. He was getting restless. He needed to go for a walk or take some reconnaissance photos of cheating spouses, something. But James wouldn't let him out. Either Colin or James were constantly around to make sure he followed the doctor's orders and did nothing too strenuous.

So, there he sat. Either in his bed or on the couch, and he read. He was so bored, he actually read Evelyn's thesis at one point, which he found increasingly fascinating. He couldn't wait to talk to her about it and have her explain a few things she wrote about he didn't quite understand.

At the thought of Evelyn, he glanced at his phone again. The damn thing had only rung once since he'd left Evelyn's room a few days ago. And it was some lady asking for some help because she was certain her husband was fucking the nanny on the side and needed proof. He immediately handed the call off to James, who set up a time and date for him to stalk the cheating husband. The phone had been silent since.

He reached for his cane, leaning against the table beside his bed, and scooted himself so he could stand. He needed to take a lap around the flat. Get some new scenery for a bit and stop staring at his bloody phone. He swung his legs over the side of his bed and stood. He'd taken two steps toward the door of his room when his phone rang. He paused before turning around and moving quicker than he probably should have, as a sharp pain shot through his ribs. He rushed over to his phone to answer it before he missed the call.

He pressed the button. "Hello?".

"Hello? Is this Patrick?" the voice of a woman with an American accent came through the phone.

"This is Patrick."

"This is Michelle Stevenson, Evelyn's sister. She's awake, and she's asking for you."

Patrick couldn't believe his ears. "She's awake?"

"Yes."

"And she asked for me?"

"Yes, but my parents refused to call you. We wanted to make sure you know so you can come down here. Once you get here, we'll distract my parents so you can see Evelyn."

"Okay, yeah, thank you. I'll get someone to drive me there right away."

"You're welcome. It's really quite romantic, don't you think? You were the first person she asked for when she woke up. I really hope you feel half as much for her as she does for you."

"She did?" Patrick couldn't hold back his smile. "You tell her I'll be there as soon as I can, yeah?"

"I will. Shit, my parents are looking for me. See you soon." There was a click, and the line went dead.

Patrick stared at the phone, taking a moment to try to absorb what Evelyn's sister had just said. She was awake.

"Woohoo!" he shouted, throwing his hands above his head, unable to hold in the intense feelings flowing through him at the news.

James threw open his door and stuck his head in. "What's going on?"

"She's awake."

"What?"

"Didn't you hear me, you bloody idiot? She's awake!"

"How do you know? Did her parents call you?"

Patrick shook his head. "Her sister."

James let out a laugh and his own cheer. "This is great news! What are we waiting for? I'd think you'd already be in the car waiting for me."

"Well, I would be, but you're blocking the doorway."

Patrick had the biggest grin on his face since before his kidnapping.

"Now, if you're going to stand there, make yourself fucking useful and help me down to the car. We need to stop somewhere and get Evelyn the biggest fucking teddy bear in all of London. Think it will fit in the Coop?"

James laughed and shook his head. "We may have to get the second largest teddy bear in all of London in order for it to fit in the car, but I think we can make do."

Patrick grabbed the cane leaning against the night table and grimaced as he straightened, his ribs still making it hard to move around. But he wasn't going to let that get him down. She was awake.

And she asked for him.

CHAPTER 38

EVELYN

Evelyn was lying on her bed in a thankfully empty room. Her sisters had begged their parents to take them somewhere to sightsee for a couple of hours. Michelle had whispered to Evelyn that she had managed to make a call to Patrick. The plan was in motion.

So, now the family was off to go look at the guards in front of Buckingham Palace and see Big Ben. Evelyn had recommended an enjoyable walk along the Southbank Promenade, as well. She sounded so local when she said it. And once everyone had left, she realized how nice it was to be in a mostly quiet room, with just the sounds of machines rather than the constant chatter which had been buzzing around her since she'd awoken. Between her parents fussing over her every time she flinched or said she was thirsty to the nurses coming in every thirty minutes to check on her, she was glad to be alone.

Although, she hoped Patrick came by soon.

She tried to roll over, but every time she moved, the damn machine sounded alarms and the nurses came rushing in to make sure she was okay. So, she laid still. On her back. Enjoying the silence. She was just closing her eyes as footsteps came from outside her door.

"If you're a nurse, please keep walking," she whispered to herself.

The door opened slowly, and one set of footsteps came in the room before quietly shutting the door behind them. And then nothing. She opened her eyes and slowly turned her head.

"Oh my God," she whispered, tears immediately springing to her eyes.

"I didn't wake you, did I? I was trying to be quiet," Patrick whispered back.

"I wasn't asleep, I was just resting my eyes."

She watched him slowly walk to the side of her bed, noting the cane he used before settling in the chair closest to her bed.

"Your sister, Michelle, called and told me you woke up. So, I had James drive me down here right away."

"James is here? Where is he?"

"In the waiting room. He wanted to give me a chance to see you alone first." He placed a hand on her cheek.

She brought her hand up and covered his.

"How are you feeling, love? The last time I was allowed in, your parents implied you may never wake up. I've been so scared for you."

"I hurt everywhere. I'm exhausted, which makes no sense since I was basically sleeping for a week. And even though I've only been awake for a few hours, I'm already tired of this hospital. All I want to do is go back to your flat and curl up in your bed and sleep for a month."

"Well, you need to hurry up and get better, and we can make that happen. I'm on strict relaxation orders from the doctors. We can curl up in bed together and make James wait on us hand and foot until we're allowed to do things on our own. Or until he catches on that he doesn't have to be our personal slave anymore."

She laughed, and then grimaced. "Ouch. Don't make me laugh."

He smiled. "I'll try not to, but it's so tempting. It drives home the point you're going to be okay when I see you laughing."

"Are you okay? How long were you in the hospital?"

"A few days. I'm fine. I woke up after two days, and the rest was the doctors making sure my lung re-inflated properly and my ribs were healing. My injuries were nothing compared to yours."

"But you're using a cane." She gestured at the offending object.

"Oh, that's only because trying to walk with broken ribs fucking hurts. I can't stand up straight, so I use the cane to support myself so I can walk and breathe at the same time. It's bloody awful. I've been spending a lot of time in bed and on the couch."

"Oh, man, again? How are you managing? Does James want to kill you yet?" she teased.

"Ha, ha. I'll have you know I'm going bloody insane. I'm running out of things to keep me occupied, so you better get released from this place soon so you can keep me company. I was so bored, I read your thesis the other day."

"You didn't!"

"I did! I didn't understand seventy-five percent of what you wrote, but I found it immensely interesting. You'll have to explain what most of it means."

"It's not finished."

"Doesn't matter. I enjoyed it all the same."

"Well, when I get out of here, I'll have to explain it to you, and you'll have to read the rest of it when I get it finished. Which will hopefully happen before my parents whisk me back home."

He looked at his lap.

"What's wrong? You had to know that, with my parents involved, I wasn't going to get to stay here as long as we originally talked about."

He shook his head. "It's not that. It's that I hope your parents are aware of the legal implications of your involvement with the case."

"Legal implications?"

"You're a witness in the case. Not just a witness, but what Colin keeps referring to as a 'star witness.' He and the rest of the solicitors at his firm are adamant you not leave the country. You'll need to stay here until the end of the trial. They don't want to take the chance you won't come back and testify. Especially since they're bringing Fitzgerald up on international charges."

"Oh."

"What? You're sounding a little bit disappointed."

"I'm not disappointed. Believe me, I'm happy to have whatever time I can here with you and James and the chance to explore, but my parents may not agree."

"Ah, no one's talked to them about the case."

"Well, now, I don't know that per se, but I do know they haven't mentioned anything about the case to me since I woke up. It may be because they don't want to stress me out. I mean, I just woke up from a coma a few hours ago."

"Oh, yeah, the coma thing. That may explain why you're not up to date on current events."

She laughed, grimacing again at the pain. "I told you to stop making me laugh."

"Can't help it, love. Reminds me you're alive."

The two of them sobered.

"I'm so sorry, Evelyn."

"You don't need to be sorry."

"Yes, I do. I was supposed to protect you, and I did a piss-poor job at it. A really piss-poor job. I mean, I couldn't have failed more spectacularly at my one job than I did."

She gave him a weak smile. "You didn't fail. I would have been dead long ago if it weren't for you. You could have left me in the airport on that first day to fend for myself. But you didn't. Ever since then, you've done amazing at trying to help me and keep me alive. I've been the one making things super difficult for you. I haven't stayed in one place. I've ventured out on my own, which got me kidnapped the first time. You essentially took a bullet for me. I don't think you failed, Patrick. I think you did the best you could under the circumstances. And the circumstances weren't the best. The odds were stacked mightily high against us."

He shook his head. "I can't believe you're stuck in a hospital bed hooked up to dozens of machines and you're still fucking optimistic."

She shrugged. "Can't help it. It's in my nature."

He leaned over, placing a soft kiss on her lips. "I'm glad you're okay," he whispered.

"I'm glad you're okay, too," she whispered back. "I was so worried about you. Watching Fitzgerald do what he was doing, I just I had to stop him, you know? I was so worried that if I didn't, he'd kill you, right there, in front of me."

"I appreciate it, love, I do. I just wish you'd stayed put. James and McCleary and the CIA came in not much longer after you came to my rescue. If you had just waited it out—"

"You could still be dead. We didn't know James and McCleary were coming. We didn't even know they knew where we were. I couldn't gamble with your life. Yes, hindsight is twenty-twenty and all that, but you have to remember, in that moment, when it was us versus Fitzgerald, we didn't know we were going to have backup. We didn't know rescue was imminent, and so I did what I had to do to make sure some psycho didn't murder the man I love right in front of me."

"By placing your own life in danger!" Patrick almost shouted. "Do you know how many times I've replayed that scene from the warehouse since that day? Every time I close my eyes, I see Fitzgerald stabbing you with that fucking metal poker. Over and over and over again. You can't even imagine how I've felt since I snuck in to see you and your parents told me you may never wake up. To have the last image of your girlfriend alive be of a man fucking stabbing her, that's brutal."

"I'm sorry!" she said as forcefully as she dared. "I'm sorry. I really am. I'm sorry for putting myself in a situation that worried both you and my family. At that moment, I wasn't thinking about myself. I didn't think about what Fitzgerald would do to me. I could see you hanging from a rope, bloody and beaten, and I did what my instincts told me to do. I'm so sorry," she sobbed. Each sob sent a sharp pain through her chest.

"Hey." He took her hand. "Hey, don't cry, love. Please don't cry. I get why you did what you did. I do. I really do. It's just hard, you know? Remembering the last week. But that's past us, yeah? You're awake, I'm getting better, and you'll be getting better. We'll be back at my flat before we know it, recuperating together, and we'll be able to look back on this whole thing with whatever the opposite of fondness is."

She nodded, bringing her free hand up to wipe the tears from her face. "You're right. You're absolutely right. We need to focus on getting better, making sure Colin and his partners have an airtight case against Fitzgerald and everyone else they arrested, so they can stay behind bars for a very long time."

"That's the spirit, love!" He smiled. "Let's lock those fuckers up for a very, very long time. From what Colin was saying the other day, they have a pretty airtight case already, as long as you're sticking around and willing to testify."

"Oh, I'm willing. I'm very willing."

"Good. Because they're building their entire case around you. The CIA is bringing him up on some major charges. Kidnapping, assault, attempted murder of an American national, and Megan's murder. McCleary is bringing him in on some of the lesser local charges. Either way, the fucker is going away."

"What happened with the police who were being paid to look the other way?"

"They're suspended without pay, pending an investigation. Scotland Yard is pissed. They're scrambling to fill the borough's office. James and I even got calls to convince us to rejoin the force."

"Yeah? And you said?"

"Piss off. What do you think we said? I'm bloody injured, and James is my nursemaid, and he's trying to keep our business afloat while I'm laid up. Poor bloke has had to go on two whole stakeouts on his own in the last week."

"Oh man, two whole stakeouts in one week. He sounds pretty overworked. You better give him a vacation."

"Love, when this whole thing is over, I think we should all go on holiday somewhere warm and sunny, and with alcohol. Lots of alcohol."

"Sounds marvelous."

"So, it's a date, then? When the trial is over, and we're all healed, the three of us on holiday, funded by the fee from a bunch of rich solicitors?"

"It's a date."

Epilogue

EVELYN

ONE YEAR LATER

The airport was busy. People were rushing to check into their flights, store their luggage, get through security, and get on their flights. Besides all the people milling about, there were the people standing in the lobby, trying to say goodbye to their loved ones before boarding their flights.

"I don't know what I'm going to do without you." Patrick wrapped his arms tighter around Evelyn, who had her arms wrapped around his neck, her head pressed into his chest.

The trial had ended a few days earlier. It was the trial of the century. Every television network aired it as it happened. Evelyn, Patrick, and James spent several days each on the stand being questioned and cross-examined repeatedly. When it was all done, the jury didn't even take a full day to deliberate before coming back with a guilty verdict for every single member of the Fitzgerald family on trial. Fitzgerald, of course, had the most charges brought up against him. They sentenced him to whole-life order, which was a term Evelyn grew familiar with as the trial progressed. He yelled he would get revenge against the trio as they dragged him out of the court. They tried to shrug it off, but inevitably decided it would probably be a good idea to be vigilant for a while, always looking over their shoulders.

"I'm only going home for a week. Then, I'll be meeting you and James in Tahiti. I think you'll be fine."

"It's going to be weird not having you here all the time. I don't know why you need to go back home, anyway."

"You know why. I need to pack and start shipping things over. And besides, this will give you and James an opportunity to pack all of your things. The new flat is available as soon as we get back from vacation."

"I still don't know why we need to move. I thought our flat was very adequate."

"It's too small for the three of us, and you know it."

"True. Your bear takes up half the living room. I don't know why we bought you that fucking bear."

"Because you love me. That thing kept me company for the long days I was alone in that hospital room after my family went back home, and you and James had to work."

"Yeah, that's a good bear."

She laughed. "You're so fickle. I better see that bear right where I left him when we get back."

"Don't worry. I won't hurt your bear. Are you excited about seeing your parents? I mean, it's not like you haven't seen them. You guy's Skype every other night, but *really* see them?"

"Yeah, I am. I can't wait to get back to Iowa and eat at my favorite restaurants and see some of my friends. Defend my thesis, get my degree, you know, the little things."

"I wish I were going with you. To support you, you know. Help you out."

"I do, too, but you know this is the right plan. My parents and sisters have already started sorting through my things, so it'll be easier for me to pick what's important enough to ship over and what to pack or what to give away. Shit. You're right, I wish you were coming. I think I've overestimated what I can accomplish in a week."

"Hey." He leaned down, placing a kiss on her forehead. "You'll be fine. You've got this. You have plenty of help there. And then we'll be in Tahiti, with sands and beaches and alcohol. Lots of alcohol."

"Hmmm," she murmured. "That sounds absolutely marvelous. Okay, I think I can get through this week now, knowing what's waiting for me at the end of it."

The clock in the airport rang twice.

Patrick sighed. "You better get going if you're going to make it through security and to your flight on time."

She held him, tears springing to her eyes. "Why is this so hard? I don't want to say goodbye to you."

He held her tight. "I don't want to say goodbye, either. But it's not forever, yeah? We'll see each other in a week for our holiday, and then you're back here and we can start planning for the rest of our lives together."

She smiled through her tears, lifting her left hand from his shoulder, holding it up where she could see it. The ring on her third finger caught the light and gleamed.

"You're right. This isn't goodbye. We'll be back together before we know it, and we have our whole lives ahead of us."

She pulled back before pressing her lips to his. "I love you," she whispered.

"I love you, too."

One more kiss, and they parted.

Evelyn headed toward the security gate, turning back to take one more look at her fiancé and her future.

CHECK OUT THE REST OF THE
LONDON DETECTIVE AGENCY SERIES NOW!

CHECK OUT THESE OTHER GREAT
ROWAN PROSE PUBLISHING TITLES!

Stephanie R. Caffrey is a debut romantic suspense author who lives with her family in the Midwest. When she's not working on her books, she's a substitute teacher, and loves to write fanfiction. She is a proud marginalized voice in the Mexican-American community. Besides writing, she enjoys sewing, knitting, and cross stitching.

www.srcaffrey.com